WICKED LOVELY

melissa marr

HARPERTEEN

An Imprint of HarperCollins*Publishers*

HarperTeen is an imprint of HarperCollins Publishers.

Wicked Lovely
Copyright © 2007 by Melissa Marr
All rights reserved. Printed in the United States of America. No
part of this book may be used or reproduced in any manner
whatsoever without written permission except in the case of
brief quotations embodied in critical articles and reviews. For
information address HarperCollins Children's Books, a division
of HarperCollins Publishers, 1350 Avenue of the Americas,
New York, NY 10019.
www.harperteen.com

Library of Congress Cataloging-in-Publication Data
is available.
ISBN: 978-0-06-121465-3 (trade bdg.)
ISBN: 978-0-06-121466-0 (lib. bdg.)

Typography by Christopher Stengel
5 6 7 8 9 10
❖
First Edition

For Loch, Dylan, and Asia,
who believed in me even when I didn't,
and
the memories of John Marr Sr. and Marjorie Marr,
whose presences linger and give me strength
when I would falter

ACKNOWLEDGMENTS

I've been lucky enough to have some pretty wonderful people keeping me steady along the path: my lovely and fierce agent, Rachel Vater; my insightful and passionate editors, Anne Hoppe and Nick Lake (as well as the whole amazing Harper team, including Camilla, Alison, and Tasha); my readers—Anne Gill and Randy Simpson; my dear friend, Kelly Kincy; and my mentors and friends—Michael Grimwood and Tony Harrison. I am humbled by the faith and enthusiasm you've shared with me along this journey.

And to those who have inspired and encouraged me throughout my life—John and Vanessa Marr, for teaching me about believing, about courage, about the things beyond our sight; Dylan and Asia, for reminding me every day that the impossible *can* come true; and Loch, for showing me that true bliss is possible on this side of the veil. Without you, there'd be nothing.

PROLOGUE

The Summer King knelt before her. "Is this what you freely choose, to risk winter's chill?"

She watched him—the boy she'd fallen in love with these past weeks. She'd never dreamed he was something other than human, but now his skin glowed as if flames flickered just under the surface, so strange and beautiful she couldn't look away. "It's what I want."

"You understand that if you are not the one, you'll carry the Winter Queen's chill until the next mortal risks this? And you'll warn her not to trust me?" He paused, glancing at her with pain in his eyes.

She nodded.

"If she refuses me, you will tell the next girl and the next"—he moved closer—"and not until one accepts, will you be free of the cold."

"I do understand." She smiled as reassuringly as she could, and then she walked over to the hawthorn bush. The leaves brushed against her arms as she bent down and reached under it.

Her finger wrapped around the Winter Queen's staff. It was a plain thing, worn as if countless hands had clenched the wood. It was those hands, those other girls who'd stood where she now did, she didn't want to think about.

She stood, hopeful and afraid.

Behind her, he moved closer. The rustling of trees grew almost deafening. The brightness from his skin, his hair, intensified. Her shadow fell on the ground in front of her.

He whispered, "Please. Let her be the one. . . ."

She held the Winter Queen's staff—and hoped. For a moment she even believed, but then ice pierced her, filled her like shards of glass in her veins.

She screamed his name: "Keenan!"

She stumbled toward him, but he walked away, no longer glowing, no longer looking at her.

Then she was alone—with only a wolf for companion-ship—waiting to tell the next girl what a folly it was to love him, to trust him.

CHAPTER 1

SEERS, or Men of the SECOND SIGHT, . . . have very terrifying Encounters with [the FAIRIES, they call *Sleagh Maith*, or the Good People].

—*The Secret Commonwealth* by Robert Kirk
and Andrew Lang (1893)

"Four-ball, side pocket." Aislinn pushed the cue forward with a short, quick thrust; the ball dropped into the pocket with a satisfying clack.

Her playing partner, Denny, motioned toward a harder shot, a bank shot.

She rolled her eyes. "What? You in a hurry?"

He pointed with the cue.

"Right." *Focus and control, that's what it's all about.* She sank the two.

He nodded once, as close as he got to praise.

Aislinn circled the table, paused, and chalked the cue. Around her the cracks of balls colliding, low laughter, even the endless stream of country and blues from the jukebox kept her grounded in the real world: the human world, the *safe* world. It wasn't the only world, no matter how much Aislinn wanted it to be. But it hid the other world—the ugly one—for brief moments.

"Three, corner pocket." She sighted down the cue. It was a good shot.

Focus. Control.

Then she felt it: warm air on her skin. A faery, its too-hot breath on her neck, sniffed her hair. His pointed chin pressed against her skin. All the focus in the world didn't make Pointy-Face's attention tolerable.

She scratched: the only ball that dropped was the cue ball.

Denny took the ball in hand. "What was that?"

"Weak-assed?" She forced a smile, looking at Denny, at the table, anywhere but at the horde coming in the door. Even when she looked away, she heard them: laughing and squealing, gnashing teeth and beating wings, a cacophony she couldn't escape. They were out in droves now, freer somehow as evening fell, invading her space, ending any chance of the peace she'd sought.

Denny didn't stare at her, didn't ask hard questions. He just motioned for her to step away from the table and called out, "Gracie, play something for Ash."

At the jukebox Grace keyed in one of the few not-country-or-blues songs: Limp Bizkit's "Break Stuff."

As the oddly comforting lyrics in that gravelly voice took off, building to the inevitable stomach-tightening rage, Aislinn smiled. *If I could let go like that, let the years of aggression spill out onto the fey . . .* She slid her hand over the smooth wood of the cue, watching Pointy-Face gyrate beside Grace. *I'd start with him. Right here, right now.* She bit her lip. Of course, everyone would think she was utterly mad if she started swinging her cue at invisible bodies, everyone but the fey.

Before the song was over, Denny had cleared the table.

"Nice." Aislinn walked over to the wall rack and slid the cue back into an empty spot. Behind her, Pointy-Face giggled—high and shrill—and tore out a couple strands of her hair.

"Rack 'em again?" But Denny's tone said what he didn't: that he knew the answer before he asked. He didn't know why, but he could read the signs.

Pointy-Face slid the strands of her hair over his face.

Aislinn cleared her throat. "Rain check?"

"Sure." Denny began disassembling his cue. The regulars never commented on her odd mood swings or unexplainable habits.

She walked away from the table, murmuring good-byes as she went, consciously not staring at the faeries. They moved balls out of line, bumped into people—anything to cause trouble—but they hadn't stepped in her path tonight, not yet. At the table nearest the door, she paused. "I'm out of here."

One of the guys straightened up from a pretty combination shot. He rubbed his goatee, stroking the gray-shot hair. "Cinderella time?"

"You know how it is—got to get home before the shoe falls off." She lifted her foot, clad in a battered tennis shoe. "No sense tempting any princes."

He snorted and turned back to the table.

A doe-eyed faery eased across the room; bone-thin with too many joints, she was vulgar and gorgeous all at once. Her eyes were far too large for her face, giving her a startled look. Combined with an emaciated body, those eyes made her seem vulnerable, innocent. She wasn't.

None of them are.

The woman at the table beside Aislinn flicked a long ash into an already overflowing ashtray. "See you next weekend."

Aislinn nodded, too tense to answer.

In a blurringly quick move, Doe-Eyes flicked a thin blue tongue out at a cloven-hoofed faery. The faery stepped back, but a trail of blood already dripped down his hollowed cheeks. Doe-Eyes giggled.

Aislinn bit her lip, hard, and lifted a hand in a last half wave to Denny. *Focus.* She fought to keep her steps even, calm: everything she wasn't feeling inside.

She stepped outside, lips firmly shut against dangerous words. She wanted to speak, to tell the fey to leave so she didn't have to, but she couldn't. *Ever.* If she did, they'd know her secret: they'd know she could see them.

The only way to survive was to keep that secret; Grams taught her that rule before she could even write her name: *Keep your head down and your mouth closed.* It felt wrong to have to hide, but if she even hinted at such a rebellious idea, Grams would have her in lockdown—homeschooled, no pool halls, no parties, no freedom, no Seth. She'd spent enough time in that situation during middle school.

Never again.

So—rage in check—Aislinn headed downtown, toward the relative safety of iron bars and steel doors. Whether in its base form or altered into the purer form of steel, iron was poisonous to fey and thus gloriously comforting to her. Despite the faeries that walked her streets, Huntsdale was home. She'd visited Pittsburgh, walked around D.C., explored Atlanta. They were nice enough, but they were too thriving, too alive, too filled with parks and trees. Huntsdale wasn't thriving. It hadn't been for years. That meant the fey didn't thrive here either.

Revelry rang from most of the alcoves and alleys she passed, but it wasn't ever as bad as the thronging choke of faeries that cavorted on the Mall in D.C. or at the Botanical Gardens in Pittsburgh. She tried to comfort herself with that thought as she walked. There were less fey here—less people, too.

Less is good.

The streets weren't empty: people went about their business, shopping, walking, laughing. It was easier for them: they didn't see the blue faery who had cornered several

winged fey behind a dirty window; they never saw the
faeries with lions' manes racing across power lines, tumbling over one another, landing on a towering woman with
angled teeth.

To be so blind . . . It was a wish Aislinn had held in secret
her whole life. But wishing didn't change what *was*. And
even if she could somehow stop seeing the fey, a person
can't un-know the truth.

She tucked her hands in her pockets and kept walking,
past the mother with her obviously exhausted children, past
shop windows with frost creeping over them, past the
frozen gray sludge all along the street. She shivered. The
seemingly endless winter had already begun.

She'd passed the corner of Harper and Third—*almost
there*—when *they* stepped out of an alley: the same two
faeries who'd followed her almost every day the past two
weeks. The girl had long white hair, streaming out like
spirals of smoke. Her lips were blue—not lipstick blue,
but corpse blue. She wore a faded brown leather skirt
stitched with thick cords. Beside her was a huge white
wolf that she'd alternately lean on or ride. When the other
faery touched her, steam rose from her skin. She bared her
teeth at him, shoved him, slapped him: he did nothing
but smile.

And he was devastating when he did. He glowed faintly
all the time, as if hot coals burned inside him. His collar-
length hair shimmered like strands of copper that would
slice her skin if Aislinn were to slide her fingers through

it—not that she would. Even if he were truly human, he wouldn't be her type—tan and too beautiful to touch, walking with a swagger that said he knew exactly how attractive he was. He moved as if he were in charge of everyone and everything, seeming taller for it. But he wasn't really that tall—not as tall as the bone-girls by the river or the strange tree-bark men that roamed the city. He was almost average in size, only a head taller than she was.

Whenever he came near, she could smell wildflowers, could hear the rustle of willow branches, as if she were sitting by a pond on one of those rare summer days: a taste of midsummer in the start of the frigid fall. And she wanted to keep that taste, bask in it, roll in it until the warmth soaked into her very skin. It terrified her, the almost irresistible urge to get closer to him, to get closer to any of the fey. *He* terrified her.

Aislinn walked a little faster, not running, but faster. *Don't run.* If she ran, they'd chase: faeries always gave chase.

She ducked inside The Comix Connexion. She felt safer among the rows of unpainted wooden bins that lined the shop. *My space.*

Every night she'd slipped away from them, hiding until they passed, waiting until they were out of sight. Sometimes it took a few tries, but so far it had worked.

She waited inside Comix, hoping they hadn't seen.

Then he walked in—wearing a glamour, hiding that glow, passing for human—visible to everyone.

That's new. And new wasn't good, not where the fey were

concerned. Faeries walked past her—past everyone—daily, invisible and impossible to hear unless they willed it. The really strong ones, those that could venture further into the city, could weave a glamour—faery manipulation—to hide in plain sight as humans. They frightened her more than the others.

This faery was even worse: he had donned a glamour between one step and the next, becoming suddenly visible, as if revealing himself didn't matter at all.

He stopped at the counter and talked to Eddy—leaning close to be heard over the music that blared from the speakers in the corners.

Eddy glanced her way, and then back at the faery. He said her name. She saw it, even though she couldn't hear it. *No.*

The faery started walking toward her, smiling, looking for all the world like one of her wealthier classmates.

She turned away and picked up an old issue of *Nightmares and Fairy Tales*. She clutched it, hoping her hands weren't shaking.

"Aislinn, right?" Faery-boy was beside her, his arm against hers, far too close. He glanced down at the comic, smiling wryly. "Is that any good?"

She stepped back and slowly looked him over. If he was trying to pass for a human she'd want to talk to, he'd failed. From the hems of his faded jeans to his heavy wool coat, he was too uptown. He'd dulled his copper hair to sandy-blond, hidden that strange rustle of summer, but even in his human glamour, he was too pretty to be real.

"Not interested." She slid the comic back in place and walked down the next aisle, trying to keep the fear at bay, and failing.

He followed, steady and too close.

She didn't think he'd hurt her, not here, not in public. For all their flaws, the fey seemed to be better behaved when they wore human faces. Maybe it was fear of the steel bars in human jails. It didn't really matter why: what mattered was that it was a rule they seemed to follow.

But when Aislinn glanced at him, she still wanted to run. He was like one of the big cats in the zoo—stalking its prey from across a ravine.

Deadgirl waited at the front of the shop, invisible, seated on her wolf's back. She had a pensive look on her face, eyes shimmering like an oil slick—strange glints of color in a black puddle.

Don't stare at invisible faeries, Rule #3. Aislinn glanced back down at the bin in front of her calmly, as if she'd been doing nothing more than gazing around the store.

"I'm meeting some people for coffee." Faery-boy moved closer. "You want to come?"

"No." She stepped sideways, putting more distance between them. She swallowed, but it didn't help how dry her mouth was, how terrified and tempted she felt.

He followed. "Some other night."

It wasn't a question, not really. Aislinn shook her head. "Actually, no."

"She already immune to your charms, Keenan?" Deadgirl called out. Her voice was lilting, but there was a harsh edge under the words. "Smart girl."

Aislinn didn't reply: Deadgirl wasn't visible. *Don't answer invisible faeries, Rule #2.*

He didn't answer her, either, didn't even glance her way. "Can I text you? E-mail? Something?"

"No." Her voice was rough. Her mouth was dry. She swallowed. Her tongue stuck to the roof of her mouth, making a soft clicking noise when she tried to speak. "I'm not interested at all."

But she was.

She hated herself for it, but the closer he stood to her, the more she wanted to say *yes, yes, please yes* to whatever he wanted. She wouldn't, couldn't.

He pulled a piece of paper from his pocket and scrawled something on it. "Here's mine. When you change your mind. . ."

"I won't." She took it—trying not to let her fingers too near his skin, afraid the contact would somehow make it worse—and shoved it in her pocket. *Passive resistance,* that was what Grams would counsel. *Just get through it and get away.*

Eddy was watching her; Deadgirl was watching her.

Faery-boy leaned closer and whispered, "I'd really like to get to know you. . . ." He sniffed her like he really was some sort of animal, no different than the less-human-looking ones. "Really."

And that would be Rule #1: Don't ever attract faeries' attention. Aislinn almost tripped trying to get away—from him and from her own inexplicable urge to give in. She did stumble in the doorway when Deadgirl whispered, "Run while you can."

Keenan watched Aislinn leave. She didn't really run, but she wanted to. He could feel it, her fear, like the thrumming heart of a startled animal. Mortals didn't usually run from him, especially girls: only one had ever done so in all the years he'd played this game.

This one, though, she was afraid. Her already-pale skin blanched when he reached out to her, making her look like a wraith framed by her straight blue-black hair. *Delicate.* It made her seem more vulnerable, easier to approach. Or maybe that was just because she was so slight. He imagined he could tuck her head under his chin and fit her whole body in the spare fold of his coat. *Perfect.* She'd need some guidance on attire—replace the common clothes she seemed to prefer, add a few bits of jewelry—but that was inevitable these days. At least she had long hair.

She'd be a refreshing challenge, too, in strange control of her emotions. Most of the girls he'd picked were so fiery, so volatile. Once he'd thought that was a good indicator— Summer Queen, fiery passion. It had made sense.

Donia interrupted his thoughts: "I don't think she likes you."

"So?"

Donia pursed her blue lips—the only spot of color in her cold, white face.

If he studied her, he could find proof of the changes in her—the blond hair faded to the white of a snow squall, the pallor that made her lips seem so blue—but she was still as beautiful as she had been when she'd taken over as the Winter Girl. *Beautiful, but not mine, not like Aislinn will be.*

"Keenan," Donia snapped, a cloud of frigid air slipping out with her voice. "She doesn't like you."

"She will." He stepped outside and shook off the glamour. Then he said the words that'd sealed so many mortal girls' fates. "I've dreamed about her. She's the one."

And with that Aislinn's mortality began to fade. Unless she became the Winter Girl, she was his now—for better or for worse.

CHAPTER 2

[The Sleagh Maith, or the Good People, are] terrifyed by
nothing earthly so much as by cold Iron.
                      —*The Secret Commonwealth* by Robert Kirk
                                and Andrew Lang (1893)

As freaked as she was by the faery approaching her, Aislinn
couldn't go home. If everything seemed calm, Grams didn't
put many restrictions on her, but if Grams suspected trouble, that leniency would vanish. Aislinn wasn't about to risk
that, not if she had a choice, so she needed to keep her
panic in check.

And she was panicked, more than she'd been in years—
enough that she'd actually run for a block, attracting faery
followers. Several gave chase at first, until one of the lupine
faeries snarled at the others and they'd dropped off—all but
one female. She loped alongside Aislinn on all fours as they
ran up Third Avenue. The wolf-girl's crystalline fur chimed
with an eerily appealing melody, as if it would lull the lis-
tener to trust.

Aislinn slowed, hoping to discourage her, wanting to stop that chiming song. It didn't work.

She concentrated on the sound of her feet hitting the pavement, the cars that drove by, a stereo with too much bass, anything but that chiming song. As she rounded the corner onto Crofter, the red neon sign for the Crow's Nest reflected on the faery's fur, emphasizing holly-red eyes. Like the rest of downtown Huntsdale, the building that housed the grungy club showed how far the city had fallen. Facades that were presumably once attractive now bore telltale signs of age and decay. Scrubby weeds sprouted from cracked sidewalks and half-abandoned lots. Outside the club, near the deserted railroad yard, the people she passed were as likely as not looking to score—seeking something, anything, to numb their minds. It wasn't an option she could indulge in, but she didn't begrudge them their chemical refuge.

A few girls she recognized waved, but didn't motion for her to stop. Aislinn inclined her head in greeting as she slowed to a normal walking speed.

Almost there.

Then one of Seth's friends, Glenn, stepped in her path. He had so many bars in his face, she'd need to touch them to count them all.

Behind her, the wolf-girl paced, circling closer until the pungent scent of her fur was chokingly heady.

"Tell Seth his speakers came in," Glenn started.

The wolf-girl, still on all fours, nudged Aislinn with her head.

Aislinn stumbled, clutching Glenn's arm for balance.

He reached out when she tried to step back. "You okay?"

"I guess I just ran too fast"—she forced a smile and tried to look like she was winded from her run—"trying to keep warm, you know?"

"Right." The look he gave her was a familiar one: unbelieving.

As she started to walk past him, to reach the shortcut to Seth's, the door to the Crow's Nest opened, letting out discordant music. The thump of the drums beat faster even than her racing heart.

Glenn cleared his throat. "Seth's not good with you going through there"—he gestured toward the shadowy alley alongside the building—"alone. He'd be upset, you know, if you got messed up."

She couldn't tell him the truth: the scary things weren't the guys smoking in the alley, but the lupine fey growling at her feet. "It's early."

Glenn crossed his arms over his chest and shook his head.

"Right." Aislinn stepped away from the mouth of the alley, away from the shortcut to the safety of Seth's steel walls.

Glenn watched until she turned back to the street.

The wolf-girl snapped at the air behind Aislinn's ankles until she gave in to her fear and took off jogging the rest of the way to the railroad yard.

At the edge of Seth's lot, Aislinn stopped to compose herself. Seth was pretty together, but he still freaked out sometimes when she was upset.

The wolf-girl howled as Aislinn walked the last couple yards up to the train, but it didn't bother Aislinn as much, not here.

Seth's train was beautiful on so many levels. *How could I be upset here?* The outside was decorated in murals that ran the gamut from anime to abstract; beautiful and unexpected, they faded into one another like a collage that begged the viewer to make sense of the images, to find an order behind the colorful pastiche. In one of the few warmer months, she'd sat with Seth in his odd garden studying the art and realized that the beauty wasn't in the order, but in the unplanned harmony.

Like being with Seth.

It wasn't just paintings that decorated the garden: sprouting like unnatural trees along the perimeter was a series of metalwork sculptures Seth had made over the past couple years. Between those sculptures—and in some cases twining around them—were flowering plants and shrubs. Despite the ravages of the lengthy winter months, the plants thrived under Seth's watchful care.

Heartbeat calm now, Aislinn lifted her hand to knock.

Before she could, the door swung open, and Seth stood in the doorway, grinning. The streetlights made him look a bit intimidating, illuminating the bars in his eyebrows and the ring in his lower lip. His blue-black hair fell over his face when he moved, like tiny arrows pointing to pronounced cheekbones. "Starting to think you were going to bail on me."

"Didn't know you were expecting me," she said in what she hoped was a casual voice.

He gets sexier every day.

"Not expecting, but hoping. Always hoping." He rubbed his arms, mostly bare under the sleeves of a black T-shirt. He wasn't bulky, but his arms—and the rest of him—had obvious definition. He lifted one eyebrow and asked, "You going to come in or stand there?"

"Anybody else in the house?"

"Just me and Boomer."

His teakettle whistled, and he went back inside, calling out as he went, "Picked up a sub earlier. Want half?"

"Just tea."

Aislinn already felt better; being around him made her feel more confident. Seth was the epitome of calm. When his parents had left on some mission thing and given him every-thing they owned, he didn't go on a binge. Aside from buying the train cars and converting them into a trailer of sorts, he'd kept it pretty normal—hung out, partied some. He talked about college, art school, but he wasn't in any rush.

She stepped around the piles of books on the floor: Chaucer and Nietzsche sat beside *The Prose Edda;* the *Kama Sutra* tilted against *A World History of Architecture* and a Clare Dunkle novel. Seth read everything.

"Just move Boomer. He's sluggish tonight." He gestured toward the boa napping on one of the ergonomic chairs in the front of the train—his common room. One green and one bright orange, the chairs curved backward like the letter C. They had no arms, so you could sit with your legs up if you wanted. Beside each of them were plain wood tables with books and papers stacked on them.

Carefully she scooped up the coiled boa and moved him from the chair onto the sofa on the other side of the narrow room.

Seth came over with two china saucers. A matching cup with blue flowers sat on each of them, two-thirds full of tea. "High Mountain oolong. Just came in this morning."

She took one—sloshing a bit over the edge—and tasted. "Good."

He sat down across from her, holding his cup in one hand, the saucer in the other, and managing to look strangely dignified—despite his black nail polish. "So, anyone out at the Crow's Nest?"

"Glenn stopped me. Your speakers came in."

"Good you didn't go inside. They got raided last night." He scowled briefly. "Glenn didn't tell you?"

"No, but he knew I wasn't staying." She tucked her feet up, pleased when Seth's scowl faded. "So who'd they get?"

She sipped her tea and settled in for the latest rumors. Half the time she could just curl up and listen while he talked to the people who filled his house most nights. Then she could pretend—for a short time, at least—that the world was as it seemed to be, no more, no less. Seth gave her that: a private space to believe in the illusion of normalcy.

It wasn't why she'd started visiting him when they met a

couple years ago; *that* was purely a result of learning he lived in a house of steel walls. It was, however, one of the reasons she'd recently started having the wildly stupid thoughts about him, thoughts about giving in to his flirting, but Seth didn't date. He had a reputation as a great one-night stand, but she wasn't interested in that. Well, she *was* interested, but not if it meant losing either his friendship or access to his steel-walled haven.

"You okay?"

She'd been staring. *Again.* "Sure. Just, I don't know, tired I guess."

"You want to talk about it?"

"About what?" She sipped the tea and hoped that he'd drop it, almost as much as she hoped he wouldn't.

How good would it feel to tell someone? To just talk about it? Grams didn't talk about the fey if she could avoid it. She was old, seeming more tired by the day, too tired to question what Aislinn did when she was out, too tired to ask questions about where she went after dark.

Aislinn dared another smile, carefully calm, at Seth. *I could tell him.* But she couldn't, not really; it was the one rule Grams had insisted they never break.

Would he believe me?

Somewhere in the depths of the second train car, music played—another of his mixes with everything from Godsmack to the Dresden Dolls, Sugarcult to Rachmaninoff, and other stuff she couldn't actually identify.

It was peaceful—until Seth stopped mid-story and set his

tea on the table beside him. "*Please* tell me what's going on?"

Her hand shook, spilling tea on the floor. He didn't usually push her; it wasn't his way. "What do you mean? There's nothing—"

He interrupted, "Come on, Ash. You look worried lately. You're here a lot more often, and unless it's something about us"—he stared at her with an unreadable expression—"is it?"

Avoiding eye contact, she said, "We're fine."

She went to the kitchen and grabbed a rag to mop up the tea.

"What then? Are you in some sort of trouble?" He reached for her as she walked past.

"I'm fine." She dodged his outstretched hand and went to sop up the tea, staring at the floor, trying to ignore the fact that he was watching her. "So, umm, where is everyone?"

"I told everyone I needed a few days. I wanted a chance to see you alone. Talk and stuff." With a sigh, he reached down and pulled the rag away from her. He tossed it toward the kitchen, where it landed on the table with a splat. "Talk to me."

She stood up, but he caught her hand before she could walk away again.

He pulled her closer. "I'm here. I'll be here. Whatever it is."

"It's nothing. Really." She stood there, one hand in his, the other hanging uselessly at her side. "I just need to be somewhere safe with good company."

"Did someone hurt you?" He sounded weirder then, tense.

"No." She bit her lip; she hadn't thought he would ask

so many questions, counted on it, in fact.

"Someone want to?" He pulled her down into his lap, tucking her head under his chin, holding her securely.

She didn't resist. He'd held her every year when she came back from visiting her mom's grave, had held her when Grams had gotten sick last year. His holding her wasn't strange; the questions were.

"I don't know." She felt stupid for it, but she started crying, big dumb tears she couldn't stop. "I don't know what they want."

Seth stroked her hair, running his hand down the length of it and on to her back. "But you do know who they are?"

"Sort of." She nodded, sniffling. *Bet that's attractive.* She tried to pull away.

"So, that's a good place to start." He wrapped one arm tighter around her and leaned over to pick a notebook and pen up off the floor. Propping the notebook on her knee, he held the pen poised over it. With a reassuring smile, he prompted, "Tell me. We'll figure it out. Talk to some people. Check out the police blotter."

"Police blotter?"

"Sure. Find out more about them." He gave her a reassuring look. "Ask Rabbit down at the tat shop. He hears everything. We find out who they are. Then we take care of it."

"There's not going to be anything in the blotter. Not on these two." Aislinn smiled at the idea of faeries' crimes being reported in the blotter. They'd need a whole section of the daily paper just for faery crimes, especially in the safe neighborhoods: the upscale homes were in greener areas, outside the safety of steel frames and bridges.

"So we use other routes." He pushed her hair away from her face, wiping a tear off her cheek in the process. "Seriously, I'm a research god. Give me a clue, and I'll find something we can use. Blackmail, deal, whatever. Maybe they're wanted for something. If not, maybe they're breaking a law. Harassment or something. That's a crime, right? If not, there's people Rabbit knows."

Aislinn disentangled herself from his arms and went over to the sofa. Boomer barely stirred when she sat down next to him. *Too cold.* She shivered. *It's always too cold.* She stroked his skin while she thought. *Seth hasn't ever told anyone about Mom or anything. He can be careful.*

Seth sat back and crossed his ankles, waiting.

She stared at the worn vintage T he had on—damp from her tears now; the peeling white letters proclaimed: PIXIES. *Maybe it's a sign.* She'd thought about it so often, imagined telling him.

He looked expectantly at her.

She wiped her cheeks again. "Okay."

When she didn't say anything else, he crooked one glittering eyebrow and prompted her again, "Ash?"

"Right." She swallowed and said, as calmly as she could, "Faeries. Faeries are stalking me."

"Faeries?"

"Faeries." She pulled her legs up to sit cross-legged on the sofa. Boomer lifted his head to look at her, his tongue flicking out, and slid farther onto her lap.

Seth picked up his tea and took a drink.

She'd never told anyone before. It was one of Grams' unbreakable rules: *Never know who's listening. Never know when* They *are hiding nearby.*

Aislinn's heart thudded. She could feel herself getting nauseous. *What did I do?* But she wanted him to know, wanted someone to talk to.

Aislinn took several calming breaths and added, "Two of them. They've been following me for a couple of weeks."

Carefully, as if he were moving in slow motion, Seth leaned forward, sitting on the edge of his chair, almost close enough to touch. "You messing with me?"

"No." She bit her lip and waited.

Boomer slithered closer, dragging the front of his body up over her chest. Absently she stroked his head.

Seth poked at the ring in his lip, a stalling gesture, the way some people lick their lips in tense conversations. "Like little winged people?"

"No. Like our size and terrifying." She tried to smile, but it didn't work. Her chest hurt, like someone had kicked her. She was breaking the rules she'd lived by, her mother had lived by, her Grams, everyone in her family for so long.

"How do you know they're faeries?"

"Never mind." She looked away. "Just forget—"

"Don't do that." His voice had a bite of frustration in it. "Talk to me."

"And say what?"

He stared at her as he answered, "Say you'll trust me. Say you'll let me in for real, finally."

She didn't answer, didn't know what to say. Sure, she'd kept things from him, but she kept things from everyone. That was just the way it was.

He sighed. Then he put on his glasses and held the pen poised over the notebook. "Right. Tell me what you know. What do they look like?"

"You won't be able to see them."

He paused again. "Why?"

She didn't look away this time. "They're invisible."

Seth didn't answer.

For a moment they just sat there, quietly staring at each other. Her hand stilled on Boomer as she waited, but the boa didn't move away.

Finally Seth started writing. Then he looked up. "What else?"

"Why? Why are you doing this?"

Seth shrugged, but his voice wasn't nonchalant when he answered, "Because I want you to trust me? Because I want you to stop looking so haunted? Because I care about you?"

"Say you do go research. What if they . . . I don't know, hurt you? Attack you?" She knew how awful they could be even if he didn't—*couldn't*—get it.

"For going to the library?" He crooked his eyebrow again.

She was still trying to get her head together, to find a line between begging him to really believe her and telling him she wasn't serious. She pushed Boomer off her onto the sofa cushion and stood up.

"You see them hurt anyone?"

"Yes," she started, but she stopped herself. She paced over to the window. Three faeries lingered outside, not doing anything, but undeniably there. Two of them were almost human-looking, but the third was as far from human as they got—too big and covered in dark tufts of fur, like a bear that walked upright. She looked away and shuddered. "Not these two but . . . I don't know. Faeries grope people, trip them, pinch them. Stupid stuff usually. Sometimes it's worse, though. A lot worse. You don't want to get involved."

"I *do* want to. Trust me, Ash. Please?" Half smiling then, he added, "And I don't mind being groped. Perks for helping."

"You should. Faeries are . . ." She shook her head again. He was *joking* about it. "You can't see what they look like."

Without meaning to, she pictured Keenan. Blushing, she stammered, "Most of them are pretty horrible."

"Not all of them, though?" Seth asked quietly, not smiling anymore.

"Most of them"—she looked back at the three faeries outside, unwilling to look at Seth when she admitted it—"but no, not all of them."

CHAPTER 3

[Faeries] could make themselves seen or not seen at will. And when they took people they took the body and soul together.
—*The Fairy Faith in Celtic Countries*
by W. Y. Evans-Wentz (1911)

Aislinn closed her eyes as she finished describing the faeries who'd been stalking her. "They're court fey; I know that much. They move in the circle of a king or queen, have enough influence to act without consequences. They're too strong, too arrogant to be anything else." She thought about their disdain, their disregard for the fey watching them. These were the most dangerous sort of faeries: ones with power.

She shivered and added, "I just don't know what they want. There's this whole other world no one else sees. But I do. . . . I watch them, but they've never noticed me—not any more than they do anyone else."

"So you see others that aren't following you?"

It was such a simple question, such an obvious one. She

looked at him and laughed, not because it was funny, but because it was so awful. Tears ran down her face.

He just waited, calm, unflappable, until she stopped laughing. "I guess that was a yes?"

"Yes." She wiped her cheeks. "They're real, Seth. It's not that I see things. There are faeries, creatures, almost everywhere. Awful things. Beautiful ones. Some that are both at once. Sometimes they're horrible to each other, doing really"—she shuddered at the images she didn't want to share with him—"*bad* things, sick things."

He waited.

"This one, this Keenan, he *approached* me, made himself look like a human and tried to get me to go with him." She looked away, trying to summon the calm she relied on when the things she saw got too weird. It wasn't working.

"So what about this court thing? Could you talk to their king or whatever?" Seth turned the page.

Aislinn listened to the soft whisper of paper falling, loud in the room despite the music, despite the impossibility of hearing such a soft sound. *Since when can I hear a sheet of paper falling?*

She thought about Keenan, thought about how to explain that sense of strength he exuded. He'd seemed immune to the iron downtown—a terrifying possibility; at the very least, he'd been strong enough to hold a glamour around it. Deadgirl had seemed weakened by it, but it hadn't repelled her either. "No. Grams says court fey are the cruelest ones. I don't think I could face anything stronger even if I could reveal myself, and I can't. They can't find out that I can see them. Grams says they'll kill or blind us if they find out we see them."

"Suppose they're something else, Ash?" Seth was moving now, standing in front of her. "What if there's another explanation for what you saw?"

She folded her hand into a loose fist as she stared at him, feeling her fingernails dig ever so slightly into the palm of her hand. "I'd love to believe there's another answer. I've seen them since I was born. Grams sees them. It's real. *They're* real."

She couldn't look at him; instead she stared down at Boomer, who had twisted his entire length into a tight coil in her lap. She trailed her finger down the side of his head gently.

Seth cupped her chin and tilted her head back so she was looking at him. "There's got to be something we can do."

"Can we talk about it tomorrow? I need . . ." She shook her head. "I just can't deal with any more tonight."

Seth reached down and lifted Boomer. The boa didn't uncoil as Seth carried him to his terrarium and gently lowered him to the heat rock.

She didn't say anything else as Seth latched the lid to keep Boomer from wandering off. Given half a chance, Boomer found a way to slither outside if he was left home alone, and in most months the temperature out there could be fatal for him.

"Come on, I'll walk you home," Seth said.

"You don't need to."

He crooked his eyebrow and held out his hand.

"But you can." She took his hand.

Seth led her through the streets, as unaware of the fey as everyone else they passed, but just having his arm around her made it seem less awful.

They walked silently for almost a block. Then he asked, "You want to stop at Rianne's?"

"Why?" Aislinn walked a little faster as the wolf-girl who'd given chase earlier started circling predatorily.

"Her party? The one *you* told me about?" Seth grinned, acting like they were okay, like the whole faery conversation hadn't happened.

"God, no. That's the last thing I need." She shivered at the thought. She'd taken Seth to a couple parties with the Bishop O.C. crowd; by the second one it was pretty clear that the mixing of the two worlds was typically a bad plan.

"You need my jacket?" Seth pulled her closer, attentive as always to the slightest detail.

She shook her head no, but leaned closer to him, enjoying the excuse to be held by him.

He didn't object, but he didn't let his hands brush anywhere they shouldn't, either. He might flirt, but he never made a move that was anything other than just-friends.

"Stop at Pins and Needles with me?" he asked.

The tat shop wasn't out of the way, and she wasn't in any hurry to be away from Seth. She nodded, and then asked,

"Did you finally pick something to get?"

"Not yet, but Glenn said the new guy started this week. I thought I'd see what his work looks like, what styles, you know."

She laughed. "Right, wouldn't want to get the wrong style."

Mock scowling, he tweaked a strand of her hair. "We could find one we both like. Get a matched pair."

"Sure, I'll do that—right after you meet Grams and convince her to sign a consent form."

"So, no ink for you then. Ever."

"She's nice." The argument was an old one, but she hadn't given up yet—or made any progress.

"Nope. Not going to risk it." He kissed her forehead. "As long as she doesn't meet me she can't look at me, and say, 'Stay away from my girl.'"

"Nothing wrong with how you look."

"Yeah?" He smiled gently. "Would she think that?"

Aislinn thought so, but she hadn't been able to convince Seth of it.

They continued in silence until they reached the shop. The front of the tat shop was almost all windows, making it seem less intimidating to any curious ink seekers, but unlike the tattoo parlors she'd seen when they went up to Pittsburgh, this was not a glossy shop. Pins and Needles retained some of the grit of the art, not catering to the trendy crowd—not that Huntsdale had much of a trendy crowd.

The cowbell on the door clanged when they walked in.

Rabbit, the owner, peeked out of one of the rooms, waved, and disappeared.

Seth went to a long coffee table against the wall that had portfolios piled on top of it. He found the new one and sat down with it. "You want to look with me?"

"Nope." Aislinn went up to the glass case where bars, rings, and studs were laid out. That's what she wanted. She only had a single hole in each ear, but every time they came in, she considered getting a piercing. Nothing in her face, though, not this year: Bishop O'Connell High School had strict rules about facial piercings.

One of the two piercers stood up behind the cabinet. "You ready for a labret yet?"

"Not till I graduate."

He shrugged and went back to cleaning the glass.

The bell clanged again. Leslie, a friend from school, walked in with a heavily inked guy, far from the sort she dated. He was beautiful: close-cropped hair, perfect features, blue-black eyes. He was also fey.

Aislinn froze, watching him, feeling the world tilt under her. *Too many faeries wearing human faces tonight. Too many strong fey.*

But this faery barely looked her way as he went to the back room, trailing his hands over one of the steel-framed jewelry cabinets he passed.

She couldn't look away, not yet. Most faeries didn't walk downtown; they didn't touch iron bars; and they sure as hell didn't walk around able to hold a glamour while touching poisonous metal. There were rules. She'd lived by those rules. There were a few exceptions—the rare strong fey—but not this many, not at the same time, and not in her safe spaces.

"Ash?" Leslie reached her hand out. "Hey. You all right?"

Aislinn shook her head. *Nothing is right anymore. Nothing.*

"I'm good." She looked toward the room where the faery waited. "Who's your friend?"

"Tasty, isn't he?" Leslie made a noise somewhere between a moan and a sigh. "I just met him outside."

Seth put the book down and crossed the room.

"You ready to go?" He slid a steadying arm around Aislinn's waist. "I can—"

"In a sec." She glanced at the faery with Rabbit; their voices were barely more than a whisper. Forcing her paranoia aside, she turned her attention to Leslie. "You're not taking him to Ri's, are you?"

"Irial? What, you don't think he'd be a hit?"

"He's certainly different than your usual"—she bit her lip and tried to act like everything was normal—"vic— . . . I mean, partners."

Leslie shot him a longing look. "Unfortunately he doesn't seem interested."

Aislinn held in the sigh of relief that Leslie wasn't going to try to pursue the faery. Life was already complicated enough.

"I wanted to see if you're coming to the party." Leslie grinned—somewhat viciously—at Seth. "Both of you."

"No." Seth didn't elaborate. He tolerated Leslie, but tolerate was the best he could do. Most of the girls who went to Bishop O.C. weren't people he willingly hung with.

"Something better going on?" Leslie asked in a conspiratorial voice.

"Always. I only go to those fiascos if she insists." Seth gestured toward Aislinn. "You ready?"

"Five minutes," Aislinn murmured, and then felt guilty immediately: it wasn't like they were on a date or anything.

She didn't want to make Seth wait, but she didn't want to leave a friend alone with a faery strong enough to touch iron. She certainly wasn't leaving a friend alone with one wearing a human guise that would make even the shyest girls pant. And Leslie definitely wasn't shy.

Aislinn glanced back at Seth. "If you want to head out, I can go with Leslie. . . ."

"No." He gave her a briefly irritated look before he wandered away to look at the flash on the walls.

"So what *are* you doing?" Leslie asked.

"What?" Aislinn looked back at Leslie, who was grinning. "Oh, nothing really. He's just walking me home."

"Hmm." Leslie tapped her fingernails on the glass case, oblivious to the piercer's glares as she did so.

Aislinn knocked Leslie's hand off the case. "What?"

"And that's better than a party?" Leslie linked an arm around Aislinn and whispered, "When are you going to give the poor thing a break, Ash? It's sad, really, how you string him along."

"I don't . . . we're friends. He'd say something if he"—she

lowered her voice and glanced back at Seth—"you know."

"He's talking, girl. You're just too thick to hear it."

"He's just flirty. Even if he meant it, I don't want a one-nighter, especially with him."

Leslie shook her head and sighed melodramatically. "You need to live a little, girl. There's nothing wrong with a little quick love *if* they're good. I hear he's good."

Aislinn didn't want to think about that, about him with other girls. She knew Seth went out; even if she didn't see the girls, she was sure they were there. Better to be just friends than one of his throwaway girls. She didn't want to talk about Seth, so she asked Leslie, "Who's going tonight?"

Trying to keep unpleasant thoughts at bay, Aislinn half listened to Leslie go on about the party. Rianne's cousin had invited some of the guys from his frat.

Glad we're skipping it. Seth would hate that crowd.

When Leslie's brother walked in, Seth came back over and put his arm around Aislinn's shoulder, almost territorially, while they talked.

Leslie mouthed, "Deaf."

Aislinn leaned on Seth, ignoring Leslie, her brother's comments about scoring some X, the faery in the back room, all of it. When Seth was beside her, she could keep it together. Why would she be stupid enough to risk what they had, to risk him, for a fling?

Chapter 4

"When you will be King of Summer she will be your queen. Of this your mother, Queen Beira, has full knowledge, and it is her wish to keep you away from [her], so that her own reign may be prolonged."

—*Wonder Tales from Scottish Myth and Legend*
by Donald Alexander Mackenzie (1917)

On the outskirts of Huntsdale in a gorgeous Victorian estate that no realtor could sell—or remember to show—Keenan hesitated, hand lifted. He paused, watching silent figures in the thorn-heavy garden move as fluidly as the shadows that danced under the icy trees. The frost never melted in this yard, never would, but the mortals passing on the street saw only the shadows. They looked away, if they dared look at all. No one—mortal or fey—stepped on Beira's frigid lawn without her consent. It was anything but inviting.

Behind him, cars drove by on the street, tires grinding

the frozen slush into a dirty gray mess, but the sound was muted by the almost tangible chill that rested like a pall over Beira's home. It hurt to breathe.

Welcome home.

Of course, it'd never felt like home, but then again, Beira had never felt like a mother. Inside her domain the air itself made him ache, sapped the little strength he had. He tried to resist it, but until he came into his full power, she could send him to his knees. And she did—every single visit.

Maybe Aislinn will be the one. Maybe she'll make it different.

Keenan braced himself and knocked.

Beira flung open the door. In her free hand she held a tray of steaming chocolate cookies aloft. She leaned forward and kissed the air near his face. "Cookies, darling?"

She looked as she had for the past half century or so when he stopped in for these damnable meetings: a mockery of a mortal epitome of motherhood, she was clad in a modest floral dress, frilly apron, and single strand of pearls. Her hair was twisted up in what she called a "chignon."

She waggled the tray a little. "They're fresh. Just for you."

"No." Ignoring her, he walked into the room.

She'd redecorated again—some modern nightmare, complete with a sleek silver table; stiff, awkwardly shaped black chairs; and framed black-and-white prints of murders, hangings, and a few torture scenes. The walls alternated between stark white and flat black with large geometric patterns in the opposite color. Selected images on the hanging prints—a dress, lips, bleeding wounds—were hand painted red. Those splashes of luridness were the only true color in the room. It fit her far better than the costume she insisted on wearing when he visited.

From behind the wet bar, a badly bruised wood-sprite asked, "Drink, sir?"

"Keenan, sweetheart, tell the girl what you want. I need to check on the roast." Beira paused, still holding the tray of cookies. "You are staying for dinner, aren't you, dear?"

"Do I have a choice?" He ignored the sprite to walk over to a print on the far wall. In it a woman with cherry-red lips stared out from the platform of a gallows. Behind her were craggy dunes that seemed to go on endlessly. He glanced over at Beira. "One of yours?"

"In the desert? Darling, really." Blushing, she looked down, giving him a coquettish smile and toying with her pearls. "Even with the lovely chill I've had growing these past few centuries, *that* place is still off limits. For now. But it's sweet of you to ask."

Keenan turned back to the print. The girl stared out at him, seeming desperate. He wondered if she had truly died there or was merely a model for a photographer.

"Well . . . you get comfortable. I'll be back in a jiff. Then you can tell me all about your new girl. You know I *do* look forward to these little visits." Then, humming a lullaby from his childhood—something about frozen fingers—Beira left to check on the roast.

He knew that if he followed her, there'd be a bevy of unhappy wood-sprites bustling about her restaurant-sized

kitchen. Beira's cloyingly sweet act didn't include actual cooking, just the image of the sort of mother who would cook.

"Drink, sir?" The sprite carried over two trays—one with
milk, tea, hot cocoa, and a variety of prepackaged nutri-
tional drinks; the other had carrot sticks, celery, apples, and
other equally mundane foods. "Your mother is most insistent you have a healthy snack." The sprite glanced in the
direction of the kitchen. "It's not wise to anger the mistress."

He took a cup of tea and an apple. "You think?"

Growing up in the Winter Court had made him far too
familiar with what happened to those who angered—or
even irritated—the Winter Queen. But he would do his
best to anger her; that's what he'd come to do, after all.

"Almost ready," Beira announced as she returned. She sat
on one of the awful chairs and patted the one nearest her.
"Come. Tell me everything."

Keenan sat in the chair across from her, keeping his distance as long as he could.

"She's difficult, resisted my initial approach." He
paused, thinking of the fear in Aislinn's eyes. It wasn't the
response he usually elicited from mortal girls. "She didn't
trust me at all."

"I see." Beira nodded, crossed her ankles, and leaned
forward—the picture of an attentive parent. "And did . . .
you know, the *last* girlfriend approve of her?"

Without looking away from him, Beira motioned to the
sprite, who promptly brought her a glass of something clear

to drink. As Beira wrapped her hand around the stem of the glass, frost crept over it until the outside of the glass was entirely coated in a thin white layer.

"Donia agreed to her."

Beira tapped her fingernails on the side of her glass. "Lovely, and how is Dawn?"

Keenan ground his teeth: Beira knew Donia's name. After over half a century as Winter Girl, Donia'd been around enough that his mother's feigned memory slip bordered on comical. "*Donia* is as she's been for decades, Mother. She's angry with me. She's tired. She's everything you've made her."

Beira lifted her other manicured hand to examine it idly. "What I made her? Oh, do tell."

"It's your staff, your binding, your treachery that started this game. You knew what would happen to the mortals when they took your chill. Mortals aren't made for—"

"Aah, sweetling, but *you* asked her to do it. *You* chose her, and she chose you." Beira sat back in her chair, smug now that he was angry. She held open her hand, and the staff in question drifted into her grip, a reminder of the power she wielded. "She could've joined your little coterie of Summer Girls, but she thought it was worth the risk. She thought you were worth risking the pain she's in now." She *tsk*ed at him. "Sad, really. She was such a pretty girl, so full of life."

"She still is."

"Is she, now?" Beira lowered her voice to a stage whisper,

"I hear she's getting weaker and weaker"—she paused and feigned a pout—"just *sick* with it. It'd be a shame if she fades."

"Donia's fine." He heard the edge in his voice, hated that she could anger him so easily. The idea of Donia becoming a shade—dying, but trapped and silent for eternity—was one that never failed to rouse his temper. Fey death was always a tragedy, for there was no afterlife for the fey. *It's why she mentions it.* How his father had ever put up with Beira long enough for her to conceive was beyond him. The woman was infuriating.

Beira made a purring noise, almost a growl, deep in her throat. "Let's not argue, dear. I'm sure Diane will be fine until the new girl can be convinced you're worth such a sacrifice. Why with being so ill, she might not even work against you this time. Maybe she'll encourage the new lovely to accept you instead of telling her all those awful tales of your wicked intentions?"

"Donia will do her part; I'll do mine. Nothing changes, not till I find the Summer Queen." Keenan stood up and stepped forward until he was looking down at Beira. He couldn't afford to let her browbeat him, no matter that she still held all the power, no matter that she'd sooner kill him than help him. Kings didn't grovel; kings commanded. His power might be bound—no more than a warm breath against her glacial cold—but he was still the Summer King. He still stood against her, and he couldn't let her ignore that.

Might as well get it over with.

"You know I'll find her, Mother. One of these girls will take the staff in hand, and your cold won't fill her."

Beira sat down her glass and looked up at him. "Really?"

I hate this part. Keenan leaned down and put a hand on either side of her chair. "One day I'll have the full strength of the King of Summer, just as Father did. Your reign will end. No more growing cold. No more unchecked power." He lowered his voice, hoping to hide the trembling. "Then we'll see who's truly stronger."

She sat there for a moment, silent and still. Then she put one cold hand on his chest and stood, pushing him ever so slightly. Ice formed in a web growing outward from her hand, crawling over him until he ached so fiercely that he couldn't have moved if the Wild Hunt itself were bearing down on him.

"What a charming speech. It gets more entertaining every time—like one those TV shows." She kissed both of his cheeks, leaving behind a frostbitten trace of her lips, letting her cold seep under his skin, reminding him that she— *not me, not yet*—had all the power. "That's one of the lovely things about our little arrangement—if I had to deal with a *real* king, I'd miss our games."

Keenan didn't answer—couldn't. If he were gone, would another fill his place?

Nature abhors a vacuum.

Would a new king, an unbound king, come into power? She'd taunted him with that—*If you want to protect them, end it. Let a real king reign.* But would another king ascend with full power if he failed? He had no way of knowing. He swayed on his feet, hating her, hating the whole situation.

Then Beira leaned in and whispered, so her icy breath blew against his lips, "I'm sure you'll find your little queen. Perhaps you already have. Maybe it was Siobhan or that Eliza from a few centuries back. Now she was a sweet girl, Eliza. Would've made a lovely queen, don't you think?"

Keenan shivered, his body starting to shut down from the cold. He tried to push the cold back, push it out.

I am the Summer King. She cannot do this.

He swallowed, concentrating on staying upright.

"Imagine, all this time, all these centuries, if she were right there in the bevy of girls too weak to risk it. Too timid to pick up the staff and find out."

Several fox-maidens came into the room. "His room is ready, mistress."

"The poor dear is tired. And he was so unpleasant to his mummy." She sighed, as if it had truly wounded her.

With one finger under his chin, she tilted his head back. "To bed without dinner again. One of these times, you'll be able to stay awake"—she kissed him on the chin—"maybe."

Then everything went dark as the fox-maidens carried him off to the room Beira kept for him.

CHAPTER 5

These Subterraneans have Controversies, Doubts, Disputes,
Feuds, and Siding of Parties.

—*The Secret Commonwealth* by Robert Kirk
and Andrew Lang (1893)

Donia knew Beira approached when the wind shifted,
bringing a wave of biting cold over the cottage.

As if it would be anyone else.

No one visited, despite the location of Donia's cottage—
outside the iron-laden city, in one of the few wooded areas
in reach of Huntsdale. When Keenan had chosen
Huntsdale, they'd all followed him and settled into their
homes to wait. When she picked the cottage, she thought—
hoped—the fey could have their revelries among those trees,
but they didn't. They wouldn't. No one got too close to her,
as if Keenan still had a claim. Not even the representatives
of the other fey courts came near her: only the heads of the
Summer and Winter Courts dared approach.

Donia opened her door and stepped back. *No sense pretending I don't know she's here.*

Beira blew through the doorway, posing like some old vampy actress on the threshold. After air kissing and artificial pleasantries, she stretched out on the sofa, crossing her ankles, dangling her dainty feet off the edge. The femme fatale image was ruined only by the crude staff she held lightly in her hand. "I was just thinking about you, darling."

"I'm sure." The staff wasn't any danger to her—*not now*—but Donia walked away. She leaned against the stone wall by the hearth. Warmth seeped into her skin, not enough to assuage the cold that slithered over her, but better than sitting near the source of that awful chill.

The cold never bothered Beira; she was *of* it and could thus control it. Donia carried it inside her, but not in comfort, not without yearning for warmth. Beira didn't seek warmth; she reveled in the cold, wearing it like a cloud of icy perfume—especially when it made others suffer.

"My baby stopped in this evening," Beira said in her usual deceptively casual voice.

"I figured he would." Donia tried to keep her voice even, but despite decades of practice the edge of concern slipped out. She folded her arms over her chest, embarrassed that she still worried about Keenan.

Beira smiled at Donia's reaction and let the pause grow uncomfortably long. Then, still smiling, she stretched out her free hand as if a glass would materialize in it. It didn't. With a long-suffering sigh, she looked around. "Still no servants?"

"No."

"Really, sweets. You simply must get a few. The wood-sprites are an obedient sort. Can't stand a brownie, though." She made an unpleasant face. "Terribly independent lot. I could lend you a few of my sprites, just to help out."

"And spy on me?"

"Well, of course, but that's really a minor detail." She fluttered her hand airily. "The place is . . . squalid, truly. It's worse than the last one. That other little city . . . or was that another of my son's discarded lovers? It's so hard to remember."

Donia didn't take the bait. "It's clean."

"But still so *blah*. No style." Beira trailed her fingers over the sandstone carvings on the rough-hewn table by the sofa. "These aren't from your time."

She picked up a bear fetish—its right paw raised, miniature claws exposed. "This was Liseli's work, right?"

Donia nodded, though an answer wasn't necessary. Beira knew exactly whose it was. It irritated Beira that Liseli still visited Donia—and Keenan. She hadn't done so in a few years, but she would again. Since she'd been freed from the burden of carrying Beira's cold, she wandered the world—often choosing desert regions where there was no chance of seeing Beira or her ilk. Every few years she showed up to remind Donia that the cold wouldn't last forever, no matter how many times it seemed as if it would.

"And those awful ragged pants you insist on wearing?"

"Rika's. We're the same size."

Rika hadn't visited in more than two decades, but she

was a strange girl: more at ease with carrying the cold than with the idea of being Keenan's queen. They were different, every one of them. All that the Winter Girls had in common was a strength of will. *Better that than sharing traits with the vapid Summer Girls, who followed Keenan like children.*

Beira waited expectantly as Donia tried not to show her impatience.

Giving in, Donia asked, "Do you have a reason for visiting?"

"I have a reason for everything." Beira came to stand beside her; she rested her hand on the small of Donia's back.

Donia didn't bother asking Beira to move her hand; doing so would only encourage her to put it there more often in the future. "Are you going to tell me what it is?"

"*Tsk, tsk*, you're worse than my son. Not as temperamental, though." Beira moved closer, sliding her hand around Donia's waist, digging her fingers into Donia's hip. "You'd be so much prettier if you dressed better. Maybe do something more flattering with your hair."

Donia stepped away, ostensibly to prop open the back door, letting the growing cold out. She wished she were as "temperamental" as Keenan—but that was the nature of the Summer King. He was as volatile as summer storms, moody and unpredictable, as likely to laugh as he was to rage. But it wasn't *his* power that flooded her; it was Beira's cold power that had filled Donia when she'd lifted the staff so long ago. If it hadn't, if she'd been immune to the Winter

Queen's chill, she would've joined Keenan, had eternity with him. But the chill that rested inside the Winter Queen's staff had filled her—consumed her until she was little more than a breathing extension of the Winter Queen's staff. Donia still wasn't sure whom she resented more: Keenan, for convincing her he loved her, or Beira, for killing that dream. If he'd truly loved her enough, wouldn't she be the one? Wouldn't she be his queen?

Donia stepped outside. The trees were reaching toward the gray sky, gnarled limbs seeking the last bit of sun. Somewhere in the distance she heard the huffing of the deer that wandered through the small nature preserve that abutted her yard. *Familiar sights. Comforting sounds.* It should've been idyllic, but it wasn't. Nothing was peaceful when the game began.

In the shadows she saw a score of Keenan's lackeys. Rowan-men, fox-faeries, and other court soldiers—even those that looked almost mortal were still somehow strange to her after decades of their presence. They were always there, watching her, carrying word of her every move back to *him.* No matter that she told him innumerable times that she wanted them gone. No matter that she felt trapped by their watching and waiting.

"It's the order of things, Don. The Winter Girl is my responsibility. It's always been so." He tried to take her hand, to wrap those now-painful fingers around hers.

She walked away. "Not anymore. I mean it,

Keenan. Get rid of them, or I will."

He hadn't stayed to see her weep, but she knew
he'd heard. Everyone *had.*

He didn't listen, though. He'd been too used to Rika's coop-
eration, too used to everyone kowtowing to him. So Donia
had frozen a number of the guards during the first decade.
If they came too close to her, she let a thick rime cover them
until they couldn't move. Most had recovered, but not all.

Keenan merely sent more. He didn't even complain. No
matter how awful she was to him, he insisted on sending
more of his guards to keep watch over her. And she kept lash-
ing out, freezing them until eventually he told the next round
of guards to stand in the safety of the furthest trees or perch
in the boughs of the yew and oak. It was progress of a sort.

Beira stepped up to stand shoulder to shoulder with her.
"They still watch. Obedient little pawns he sends to watch
over you."

"They saw you arrive. Keenan will know." She didn't
look at Beira, staring instead at a young rowan-man who
never kept his distance as well as the others.

He winked. In the past decades he'd rarely left his post
outside her house. The others rotated in and out, staying
constant in number, but not in face. The rowan-man was
different. Although they never spoke more than a handful
of words, she almost regarded him as a friend.

"Undoubtedly. But not *now"*—Beira laughed, an awful
sound like ravens squabbling over carrion—"poor dear's out
cold."

Pretending she wasn't worried never worked; showing concern never worked, so Donia looked toward the thicket, trying to change the topic before she asked how badly it had gone for Keenan. "And where are your lackeys tonight?"

Beira made a "come here" motion in the direction of the copse of trees.

They came then: a trio of enormous shaggy black goats rounded the corner with three of Beira's faithful hags astride them. Though they were withered things—looking like the mere husks of women—the hags were eerily strong, able to rend the limbs from even the eldest mountain trolls. They terrified Donia as they cackled like mad hens and paraded around the yard—as if they dared Keenan's waiting guards to come closer.

Donia stepped up to the porch rail, away from Beira, closer to the wretched women who served the Winter Queen. "Looking lovely, Agatha."

Agatha spat at her.

It was foolish to taunt them, but Donia did it every time they came around. She had to prove, to herself and to them, that she wasn't intimidated. "You do realize that it's not *you* who keep the guards at bay?"

Of course, it wasn't her threat either that made the guards keep their distance. If Keenan said they should approach, they would. Her desires be damned. Their injuries and deaths be damned. Keenan's will was all that mattered to them.

The hags scowled at her, but they didn't answer. Like Keenan's guards, Beira's lackeys kept their distance from her. No one wanted to anger Beira, except Keenan.

Talk about dysfunctional families. Both Keenan and Beira protected her, as if the other one were a worse threat.

When the hags refused to say anything, Donia turned back to Beira. "I'm tired. What do you want?"

For a moment Donia thought she'd been too blunt, that Beira would lash out at her. The Winter Queen was usually as calculating as Keenan was capricious, but her temper was a truly horrifying thing when she did release it.

Beira only smiled, a characteristically frightening smile, but less dangerous than anger. "There are those who'd see Keenan happy, those who want him to find the girl who'll share the throne with him. I do not."

She let the full weight of her chill roll off of her; it slammed into Donia, leaving her feeling like she was being absorbed into the heart of a glacier. If she were still mortal, it would kill her.

Beira lifted Donia's almost-limp hand and wrapped it around the staff, under her own frigid hand. It didn't react, didn't change anything, but the mere touch of it brought back the memories of those first few years when the pain was still raw.

While Donia was struggling to breathe, Beira continued, "Keep this one from taking the staff, and I'll withdraw my cold from you—free you. He can't offer you that freedom. I can. Or"—Beira traced a fingernail down the center of

Donia's chest in a perverse mockery of a caress—"if you'd rather, we can see how much cold I can push through you before it uses you up."

Donia might be able to direct the chill, but she couldn't contain it. The cold poured out, answering Beira's touch, making quite clear who had the power.

In a ragged voice Donia said, "I know my place. I convince her not to trust him. I agreed to that when I took up the staff."

"Don't fail. Lie. Cheat. Whatever. Don't let her touch the staff." Beira flattened her palm on Donia's chest, fingers slightly curled, nails scraping skin through Donia's blouse.

"What?" Donia stumbled forward, trying to flee Beira without angering her further, trying to make her thoughts focus.

There were rules. Everyone knew them. They sucked for Keenan, but they were there. What Beira suggested was far outside the rules.

Beira let go of the staff and wrapped her arm around Donia, holding her up, and whispered, "If you fail me, it's well within my power to take away this body of yours. He can't stop me. You can't stop me. You'll be a shade, wandering, colder than even *you* can imagine. Think about it." Then she let go.

Donia swayed on her feet, upright only because of the staff she was still clutching. She dropped the staff, sick at the touch of it in her hands, remembering the pain the first time she'd touched it, the despair each time the newest

mortal didn't take it from her. Donia gripped the porch rail-
ing and tried to hold herself upright. It didn't work.

"Tootles." Beira gave Keenan's guards a finger wave and
disappeared into the darkness with her hags.

When Keenan woke, Beira sat in a rocker by the bed—a
basket of scraps at her feet, a needle in her hand.

"Quilting?" He coughed, cleared his throat. It was raw
from the ice he'd swallowed when she'd frozen him. "Isn't
that a bit over the top, even for you?"

She held up the patches she'd sewn together. "Do you
think so? I'm rather good at it."

He pushed himself upright. Thick furs—some still
bloody—were piled over him. "It's a far sight better than
your real hobbies."

She waved a hand in a gesture of dismissal, letting go of
the needle. It still darted in and out of the cloth. "She's not
the one, the new girl."

"She could be." He thought of Aislinn's obvious control
of her emotions. "She's the one I dream of. . . ."

A fox-maiden brought in a tray of hot drinks and steaming soup. She left them on the low table alongside his bed.

"So were the other ones, dear." Beira sighed and settled
back in her chair. "You know I don't want to fight with you.
If I'd known what would happen . . . You were conceived
that very day. How could I know this would happen when
I killed him? I didn't even know you *were* yet."

That didn't explain why she'd bound his powers, why

she'd used their common blood to have the Dark Court curse him. She never offered explanations for *that*, only for the origin of his mantle, not for the way she'd bound him.

Keenan took a steaming cup of chocolate. The warmth felt wonderful in his hands, even better on his throat. "Just tell me who she is," he said.

When Beira didn't respond, Keenan continued, "We can compromise. Divide the year, divide the regions, like it used to be with Father." He finished the cup and picked up another, just to feel the heat in his hands.

She laughed then, setting a tiny snow squall spiraling around the room. "Give up everything? Wither like a hag? For what?"

"Me? Because it's right? Because . . ." He swung his feet to the floor, wincing when they sank into a small snowdrift. Sometimes the old traditions were the worst, lines they'd exchanged like a script for centuries. "I have to ask. You know that."

Beira took the needle back in hand, jabbing it into the cloth. "I do. Your father always asked too. Followed every rule right down to the line. He was like that"—she scowled and picked up another patch from the basket—"so predictable."

"The mortals starve more every year. The cold . . . crops wither. People die." Keenan drew a deep breath and coughed again. The air in the room was frigid. Now that he was weakened, the longer he stayed in her presence, the longer it'd be until he recovered. "They need more sun. They need a proper Summer King again."

"That's really not my concern." She dropped her quilt-ing in the basket and turned to leave. She paused at the door. "You know the rules."

"Right. The rules . . ." Rules made in her favor, rules he'd been trapped by for centuries. "Yeah, I know the rules."

CHAPTER 6

The sight of a soutane [priest's cassock], or the sound of a
bell, puts [the faeries] to flight.

—*The Fairy Mythology* by Thomas Keightley (1870)

On Monday Aislinn woke before the alarm went off. After
a quick shower, she dressed in her uniform and went to the
kitchen. Grams was at the stove, fixing eggs and bacon.

Leaning over to give her a peck on the cheek, Aislinn
asked, "Special occasion?"

"Brat." Grams swatted at her. "I just thought I'd cook
you a good breakfast."

"Are you feeling okay?" Aislinn put a hand on Grams'
forehead.

Grams smiled wanly. "You seem tired lately. Thought
you could use something other than yogurt."

Aislinn poured a small cup of coffee from the half-full
carafe and added a couple generous spoonfuls of sugar
before she came to stand beside Grams.

"SATs are coming up soon, didn't do as well as I wanted on the last English essay"—Aislinn rolled her eyes as Grams shot her a disbelieving frown—"well, I didn't. I'm not saying I did *badly*, just that I could've done better."

Grams scooped the eggs onto the waiting plates and went to the tiny table with them. "So it's a school thing?"

"Mostly." Aislinn sat down and picked up her fork. She pushed the eggs around, staring at the plate.

"What else?" Grams asked in that worried tone. Her hand tensed on her coffee mug.

And Aislinn couldn't tell her. She couldn't say that court faeries were following her, that one of them had donned a glamour to talk to her, that it took everything she had not to reach out toward him when he stood beside her. So she mentioned the only other person that made her feel so tempted. "Umm, there's this guy. . . ."

Grams' grip on the cup relaxed a little.

Aislinn added, "He's wonderful, everything I want, but he's just a friend."

"Do you like him?"

Aislinn nodded.

"Then he's an idiot. You're smart and pretty, and if he turned you down—"

Aislinn interrupted, "I didn't actually ask him out."

"Well, there's your problem." Grams nodded with a self-satisfied look. "Ask him out. Stop worrying. When I was a girl, we didn't have the sort of freedom you do, but . . ." And Grams was off, talking about one of her favorite subjects—the progress in women's rights.

Aislinn ate her breakfast, nodding in the right places and asking questions to keep Grams talking until it was time to leave for school. Far better to let Grams think that boys and school were the source of her worries. Grams had faced enough worries in her life: Grandpa had died when she was still a young mother, and she'd had to raise a daughter and then a granddaughter with the Sight on her own. And if Grams found out how strange the fey were acting . . . well, any chance of Aislinn keeping her freedom would be quickly quashed.

By the time Carla knocked on the door to walk to school, Aislinn and Grams were both smiling.

Then Aislinn opened the door and saw three faeries standing in the hallway behind Carla. They kept their distance from the door—no doubt uncomfortable because of the wrought-iron curlicues that covered the outside of the door. Grams had needed special permission to install the new door, but it was well worth it.

"Wow," Carla quipped when Aislinn's smile faltered. "Not trying to ruin your mood."

"Not you. It's just"—she tried to rein in the force of her scowl—"Monday, you know?"

Carla looked to be sure Grams wasn't in earshot and asked in a soft voice, "You want to ditch?"

"And get further behind in Calc?" Aislinn snorted. She grabbed her bag and waved to Grams before stepping into the hallway.

Carla shrugged. "I'll tutor you if you want. There's a sale down at the electronics shop. . . ."

"Not today. Come on." Aislinn ran down the stairs, past several more faeries. They didn't usually come into the apartment building. It was one of the safer areas, no greenery in sight, steel security bars on the windows—not a bad neighborhood, but far from the dangerous trees and shrubs in the suburbs.

As they walked the few blocks to school, Aislinn's good mood vanished entirely. Faeries crouched in the alcoves, walked behind them, murmured as they passed. It was beyond disconcerting.

And like an echo as she walked, she remembered Deadgirl's comment: "Run while you can." Aislinn didn't think she could actually run, but if she knew what she was running from, it might at least ease the panic that she couldn't seem to end.

Then one of the lupine faeries sniffed her, crystalline fur clattering like tiny glass chimes as he moved, and Aislinn trembled. Maybe knowing wouldn't be enough to ease the panic.

As Aislinn went through her day, she pushed the morning's worries to the back of her mind. It wasn't like she could tell Father James she wasn't paying attention because faeries were following her. The Church might caution against the dangers of the occult, but finding a modern priest who believed in anything supernatural—other than God himself—was about as likely as finding one who'd suggest women should be able to be priests too.

Actually, she thought with a wry smile as she headed toward her last-period English class, there might be some priests out there more likely to suggest female equality, just not at Bishop O.C.

"Did you finish the reading?" Leslie asked as she yanked her bag out of her locker and slammed it shut.

"Yeah." Aislinn rolled her eyes. "Othello was an ass."

Leslie winked and said, "They all are, sweetie. They all are."

"How was the party?" Aislinn asked as they slipped into the room.

"Same as always, but"—Leslie leaned across the aisle— "Dominic's parents are away *all week*. Fun to be had, trips to take, guys to make . . ."

"Not my scene."

"Come on, Ash." Leslie checked to be sure no one who shouldn't hear stood nearby—glancing up and down the aisle furtively—before she added, "Ri's *friend* at the music shop got her that extra package she ordered, too."

Sometimes Aislinn wished she could smoke a little, drink a little, but she couldn't. Once in a while she indulged if she planned to crash on Seth's sofa, but she couldn't risk walking through Huntsdale with her defenses down.

"I don't think so," she said more firmly.

"You could come along. You don't need to party, just hang with us. It's not like I get lit. Just a little relaxed." Leslie tried again. "Some of Dom's cousins are going to be there."

"Thought they were all asses?" Aislinn asked with a smirk.

"Sure, but his cousins are asses with hot, hot bods. If you aren't going to do anything about Seth"—Leslie gave her a lascivious grin—"a girl's got needs, right? Just think about it."

Sister Mary Louise came in, saving Aislinn from declining again.

With her usual flourish, Sister Mary Louise paced across the front of the room, eying them from behind her patently unattractive glasses. "Well, what can you tell me?"

It was one of the many reasons the class was Aislinn's favorite: Sister Mary Louise didn't simply launch into a lecture. She got them talking, and then she slipped in her points, revealing every bit as much information, but with more style than any of the other teachers.

Before anyone else could speak, Leslie announced, "If Othello had trusted Des, it would've all gone differently."

Sister Mary Louise rewarded her with an encouraging smile and then turned to Jeff, who objected to most of Leslie's comments. "Do you agree?"

The class quickly turned into a debate with Aislinn and Leslie on one side and Jeff's lone male voice on the other side. A few other people joined in periodically, but it was mostly her and Leslie against Jeff.

Afterward Aislinn left Leslie at her locker and joined the crowd surging to the door. In all, her mood was a good one.

Ending the day with her favorite class wasn't quite as good as starting with it—instead of starting with the torture that was Calculus—but it was a close second.

Then Aislinn stepped outside the main door. The fear she'd stifled that morning came flooding back: outside, seated on the back of the wolf, was Deadgirl—looking every bit as terrifying as the other faery, Keenan, had at Comix.

CHAPTER 7

The fairies, beside being revengeful, are also very arrogant,
and allow no interference with their old-established rights.

—*Ancient Legends, Mystic Charms, and Superstitions of
Ireland* by Lady Francesca Speranza Wilde (1887)

"Hello?" Leslie snapped her fingers in front of Aislinn's face,
her silver nail polish catching Aislinn's attention. "Are you
coming or not?"

"What?"

"To Dom's." Leslie sighed, a familiar look of irritation
on her face.

Beside them, Carla smothered a laugh.

Leslie exhaled noisily, blowing her too-long bangs away
from her face. "You weren't listening to a word I said, were
you?"

"Hold up," Rianne yelled as she ran down the steps. Like
Leslie, Rianne already had her blazer off, but she also had
the top two buttons of her blouse undone. It was all show,

but it was a show that led to lectures from more than a few of the faculty at Bishop O.C.

From the side of the building, Father Edwin called, "You're still on school property, ladies."

"Not now." Rianne stepped off the curb into the street and blew a kiss to him. "See you tomorrow, Father."

Father Edwin tugged his Roman collar, his version of clearing his throat. "Try to stay out of trouble."

"Yes, Father," Leslie said obediently. Then she lowered her voice. "So are you coming, Ash?" She didn't pause, walking toward the corner, expecting everyone to follow her.

Aislinn shook her head. "I'm meeting Seth at the library."

"Now, *he's* yummy." Rianne gave an exaggerated sigh. "You holding out on us? Les said that's why you bailed the other night."

Across the street, listening to everything they said, was Deadgirl. She followed them, her wolf loping down the street, keeping pace with them.

"We're friends." Aislinn blushed, feeling more embarrassed than usual with the faery eavesdropping.

Aislinn stopped, bent down, and pulled off her shoe as if there were something in it. She glanced back: Deadgirl and her wolf lingered in the shadows of the alley across the street. Humans walked past—oblivious as always—talking, laughing, completely unaware of the unnaturally large wolf and its feral rider.

"Bet you could be *more*." Rianne linked her arm through Aislinn's and urged her forward. "Don't you think, Les?"

Leslie smiled, slowly and deliberately. "From what I hear, he's got enough experience to be a prime candidate for the job. Trust me: for your first, you want someone with finesse."

In a throaty voice, Rianne said, "And I hear Seth's got *finesse.*"

Carla and Leslie laughed; Aislinn shook her head.

"Sheila said that when she was in Father E.'s office, she saw the new student who's coming this week, some orphan," Carla said as they stood at the crosswalk. "Said he's definitely a hi-cal dessert."

"Orphan? She really said *orphan*?" Leslie rolled her eyes.

Glad the conversation had drifted away from her, Aislinn only half listened, more concerned with her faery stalker than new students. The faery stayed precisely even with them as they walked. From the way the faeries that passed treated Deadgirl, she was special. None of them approached her. Some bowed their heads as she passed. She, however, didn't acknowledge any of them.

At the corner of Edgehill and Vine, where they usually split ways, Carla asked again, "You sure? You could bring him."

"What?" Aislinn shook her head. "No. Seth's helping me study, umm, for government. I'll call you later." The light changed, and she started across the street, calling back, "Have fun."

Deadgirl didn't follow.

Maybe she went away.

"Hey, Ash?" Leslie called, once they were far enough

apart that she had to yell, far enough that everyone would hear. "You do know there's no test in there this month."

Rianne shook her finger. "Naughty, naughty."

The people walking by didn't pay any attention, but Aislinn's face still burned. "Whatever."

Aislinn cut across the park toward the library, thinking about Seth, about Deadgirl following her. She wasn't paying much attention to her surroundings until someone—a *human* someone—grabbed her arm and pulled her against his chest, holding her securely immobile.

"Well, if it isn't a nice little Catholic girl . . . Nice skirt."

He tugged her pleated skirt, and the other two guys with him laughed. "Whatcha doing, baby?"

Aislinn tried to kick him, but her foot made little impact on his leg. "Stop it."

"Stop it," his friends mocked. "Oh no, stop it."

Where is everyone? The park wasn't usually deserted this early. No people, no faeries, no one at all was in sight.

She opened her mouth to scream, and he clamped his other hand over her jaw, his index finger between her half-open lips.

She bit down. It tasted like old cigarettes.

"Bitch." But he didn't remove his hand. He squeezed tighter until the inside of her cheek was pushed so tightly against her teeth that it bled.

The guy to her right laughed. "Guess she likes it a little rough, huh?"

Aislinn felt tears in her eyes. The arm around her was bruisingly tight. The hand over her mouth squeezed again, and she could taste fresh blood in her mouth. She tried to think, to remember what she knew about self-defense.

Use whatever you can. Scream. Go limp. She did, letting her weight droop.

He just shifted his hold.

Then she heard a growl.

Beside her was Deadgirl's wolf, teeth bared. He looked like a big dog, but Aislinn knew what he was. Plainly visible to everyone and looking deceptively human, Deadgirl stood holding the wolf's leash, letting him close enough to the three losers that it wouldn't take much of a lunge to draw blood.

Her voice was frighteningly calm. "Remove your hands."

The two guys who weren't holding Aislinn backed away, but the one holding her said, "Not your business, blondie. Keep walking."

The faery waited for a moment, and then she shrugged and let go of the leash. "So be it. Sasha, arm."

The wolf—Sasha—ripped a gash in the guy's wrist.

He shrieked and let go of Aislinn, clasping his bleeding arm. She dropped to the ground.

Without another word they ran, all three of them. The wolf sprinted behind them, nipping at their legs as they went.

Deadgirl crouched down. Her expression was unreadable

as she asked, "Are you able to stand?"

"Why did you . . ." Aislinn flinched away as Deadgirl reached out toward her chin. "Thank you."

Deadgirl winced at the words.

"I don't know what happened." Aislinn stared in the direction they'd run. Huntsdale wasn't a bad city, maybe a bit rough in the late hours; maybe the lack of jobs and excess of bars made it wise to skip too many shortcuts through dark alleys late at night. Still, any sort of attack in the park . . . it was beyond odd. She caught the faery's gaze and whispered, "Why?"

At first Deadgirl didn't answer, then—avoiding the question—she reached her hand out slowly. "I'm sorry I wasn't here sooner."

"Why were . . ." Aislinn stopped, bit her lip, and stood.

"I'm Donia."

"Ash." She offered a shaky smile.

"Come then, Ash." Donia started toward the library, staying beside her, not touching, but too close for comfort.

Aislinn stopped in front of one of the columns that stood on either side of the door. "Shouldn't you go find your, umm, dog?"

"No. Sasha will come back." Donia offered what would be a comforting smile were she a human. Then she motioned toward the door. "Come."

Aislinn opened the ornate wooden door, starting to calm down. The door to the library, like the columns, was at odds with the nondescript architecture that dominated Huntsdale.

It was as if some city father had decided that they needed one beacon of beauty among the otherwise dingy structures.

She felt like laughing, not in amusement, but at the growing sense that the rules she'd lived by were suddenly off. It wasn't faeries that attacked her, but humans. *Rule #1: Don't ever attract faeries' attention.* She had, though, and if she hadn't, what would've happened outside?

Aislinn's feet felt heavy; her stomach lurched.

"Do you need to sit?" Donia was gentle, steering Aislinn toward the hallway where the restrooms were. "It's frightening, what they did."

"I feel foolish," Aislinn whispered. "Nothing happened, not really."

"Sometimes the threat of a thing is awful enough. . . ." Donia shrugged. "Go wash your face. You'll feel better."

Alone inside the tiny bathroom, Aislinn washed the blood from her face and felt her side. She'd have a bruise where his fingers had dug into her skin. Her already-dry lip had split. All things considered, it wasn't bad. *It could have been, though.*

Aislinn washed her face again and straightened her hair. She tugged off her uniform, balling it up and shoving it into her bag, and slipped into a well-worn pair of jeans and a long tunic-cut blouse she'd found at the thrift store. Then she stepped back into the seemingly empty hallway, letting the bathroom door close softly behind her.

Donia stood, invisible now, talking to one of the bone-girls. Like the rest of the bone-girls, this one was ghastly white and so thin that each of her bones could be seen under her almost-translucent skin. The fact that she was mobile seemed to break some basic law. *Surely things that looked so frail should have trouble moving?* But the bone-girls glided over the ground without any visible effort. Despite their cadaverous mien, they were eerily beautiful to watch.

It was Donia who was terrible to behold: her white hair whipped around as if a storm surrounded her, and only her. Tiny icicles clattered to the ground beside her. "Find them. Find out why they attacked the girl. If anyone compelled them to do so, I want to know. Aislinn is not to be harmed."

The bone-girl's voice was a dry whisper, as if the words had to rush over something rough before they found form. "Should I tell Keenan?"

Donia didn't answer, but her eyes darkened to the same oil-black sheen they had in Comix.

The bone-girl stepped back, hands held up in supplication. And Donia stepped around the corner, away from the bone-girl, and out of sight.

Momentarily, though, she came back around that same corner—plainly visible to humans now—and smiled at Aislinn. "All better?"

Aislinn's voice wasn't much louder than the bone-girl's had been when she answered, "Sure. I'm fine."

She wasn't fine, though; she was confused about so many things. They—Keenan and Donia—had some reason for following her, but she couldn't ask. *Are they just bored, toying with me to pass the time?* There were lots of old stories like that, but Donia seemed livid about the guys outside, seemed to believe someone could have sent those guys to hurt her. *Why? What's going on?*

"I was just reading while I waited. I wanted to see if you have someone to walk you home before I leave." Donia tilted her head, smiling. Her whole posture seemed friendly, safe. She walked back toward the rows of tables. "Ash? Are you . . . well?"

"Yeah." Aislinn followed Donia around the corner to a table with an open book and a ragged bag.

"Is there someone you can call?"

"Yeah. I'm good."

Donia nodded. She stuffed her book into her leather bag.

The door opened, and a mother with a couple kids came in.

Behind them was a group of faeries, invisible to the other patrons. All six were beautiful—moving like models, wearing clothes that looked like they'd been tailored for their willowy bodies. If it weren't for the flowering vines slithering across their skin, they'd look human. The vines, though, were like living tattoos, moving of their own volition, crawling on the girls' bodies.

One of the girls spun across the floor, in some old-fashioned dance. The others giggled and bowed to one another before following her.

Then the first one saw Donia. She murmured something to the others, and they stopped. Even the undulating vines stilled.

Several moments passed.

Donia didn't say a word; neither did Aislinn. *Since we're both pretending not to see them, what could we say?*

Finally Aislinn said, "If you hadn't been there . . ."

"What?" The expression on Donia's face was pained as she looked away from the faeries.

"Outside. If you hadn't been there . . ."

"But I was." She smiled, but there was a drawn look on her face, making her seem anxious, eager to leave.

"Right. I need to find my . . . someone." Aislinn motioned toward the stairs that led to the library basement. "Get something, but I wanted to say thanks for everything."

Donia shot a brief glare at the faeries, who were giggling again. "Just be sure to keep your someone with you when you leave. Will you do that?"

"Sure."

"Good. I'll catch you around sometime. Under better circumstances, I'm sure." Then Donia smiled. The faery was beautiful—stunning—the way a storm is when you wake up and see lightning streak across the sky.

And probably just as dangerous.

CHAPTER 8

A Cornish woman who chanced to find herself the guardian of an elf-child was given certain water with which to wash its face . . . and the woman ventured to try it upon herself, and in doing so splashed a little into one eye. This gave her the fairy sight.

—*Legends and Romances of Brittany*
by Lewis Spence (1917)

Aislinn stood motionless, gazing in the direction of the vanishing faery. In that brief moment Donia had been so devastatingly lovely that Aislinn had felt near tears.

Seth came up behind her. She knew it was him before he slipped his arms around her, but she wasn't sure *how* she knew. She just did. There were a lot of things like that lately, knowing stuff without any reason why. It was kind of creepy.

He whispered, "Who's she?"

"What?" It was hard to whisper back to him when he stood behind her; he was almost a foot taller than she was.

"Her. The one you were talking to." He inclined his head in the direction Donia had gone.

She wasn't sure how to answer. But when she turned, Seth saw her face, and he no longer seemed to care about his unanswered question.

"What happened?" He stared at her swollen lip, reached out as if he'd touch it.

"Tell you everything at home?" She hugged him. She didn't want to think about it, not now. She just wanted to leave, go to Seth's, where she could feel safer.

"Let me grab my notes." Then he walked away, right past the group of faeries headed toward Aislinn.

One of the faery girls circled behind her. *She's the new one.*

A second one stroked a hand over Aislinn's hair. *Pretty thing.*

Another shrugged. *I suppose.*

Aislinn tried to keep her face blank. *Focus.* She concentrated on the rustling of the leaves against the girls' clothes, not the strange sugary-sweet scent that seemed to pervade the air around them, not the too-hot brush of their skin as they inspected her with their hands. It wasn't comfortable—at all—but after the fiasco outside, their touch seemed somehow less awful. The violence of the three guys . . . She shuddered.

The faeries chattered back and forth, louder now that Donia had left and, presumably, no one in the library could hear them.

The Winter Girl seems to be making progress.

This one's a no-touch now.

Who cares? I'm not fond of girls. *Now her friend . . . He's touchable. Tasty.*

They giggled.

Maybe she'll share once she joins us.

If she's the one, she won't have a choice, will she? Her friend will be free game.

As Seth walked back toward her, his bag slung over his shoulder, Aislinn held out both hands where he could see them, like she was holding her arms open for another hug.

He gave her a questioning look.

Who says we need to wait? One of the faeries stroked his cheek; another pinched him.

Seth's eyes widened.

Aislinn's heart thumped. *He felt it.* She'd never had to try to speak so the faeries didn't understand her, not with anyone but Grams, not with anyone who couldn't see them. Hoping the faeries were as daft as they looked, she slid her arm around his waist and tugged him toward the door, away from lascivious faeries. "Ready to go home?"

"Definitely." He sped up a little, and draped an arm over her shoulders.

The Summer King might have some competition.

You want to tell him that? "Oh, Keenan, love . . . her toy is yummy."

Don't be mean. The king's good fun.

They all giggled again.

How much fun will he be with her *around? You know how he gets.*

*I'll volunteer to distract the mortal, so Keenan can woo her.
Mmm, me too. Look at all those rings on his face. Wonder
if he has a tongue ring?*

Once they were safely within the metal framework of
Seth's train, Aislinn let out a breath. The walk over had
been like some medieval gauntlet with faeries watching
and easing closer to them. They hadn't touched her, not
once, but Seth would have more than a few unexplained
bruises the next morning. She was glad he couldn't see
them.

She hugged him, just a quick embrace before stepping
away. "I'm sorry."

"For what?" He uncoiled Boomer from the teakettle and
lowered him into the terrarium.

"For *them*." She hopped up on a counter.

Seth flicked on the switch for the power strip, turning
on the warming rock and heat lamps for Boomer. "Tea?"

"Sure . . . Did you feel them?"

"Maybe." He paused, swished water around in the
teakettle. "At the library there was something. . . . Tell me
about before, first—about that." He gestured toward her
bruised face.

So she told him. She told him about the guys outside the
library, about Donia's rescue and fury afterward when she
talked to the bone-girl. She let her words tumble out, not
holding back anything.

For several tense moments he stood there. His voice was

strained when he asked, "You okay?"

"Yeah. Nothing happened, not really. Just scared me. I'm good." And she was.

Seth, however, looked like he was struggling to stay calm. His jaw was clamped tightly shut; his features were tense. He'd turned away from her while he tried to relax, but she knew him too well for it to work.

"Seriously, I'm fine," she assured him. "My face hurts where he grabbed me, but it wasn't a big deal."

Once when she was younger she'd seen a group of faeries drag a delicate-looking faery into a copse of trees in the park. The faery had screamed, awful shrieking sounds that echoed in Aislinn's nightmares for months. Being grabbed and held against her will for a few short minutes wasn't anywhere near what could happen.

"Donia saved me before it could turn into something *bad*," she told him again.

"I don't know what I'd do if something happened to you. . . ." He broke off, an unfamiliar panic in his eyes.

"It didn't, though." She wished she could erase his worry, so she changed the subject, "Now, about *your* faery encounters . . ."

He nodded, accepting her implicit need to change the topic. "How about we both write down what happened?"

"Why?"

"So I know it's not my imagination or your suggestions." He seemed unsure, and she couldn't blame him. She couldn't avoid the fey; he could. He had a choice, something she'd never had with them.

She took the pen and pad he offered and wrote: *Pinched ass, library. Patted cheek, library. Licked neck, corner of Willow Ave. Poked, prodded, and tripped, Sixth Street, Joe's Deli, crosswalk by Keelie's house, under bridge.* She looked up. Seth was staring at her growing list.

He flipped his paper over so she could see it: *Pinched at the library. Shoved (?) outside the deli. Stumbled under bridge?*

She let him take her—still unfinished—list.

"So faeries, huh?" He smiled, but not like he was happy. "How come I felt it?"

"Maybe because you're aware of the possibility now? I don't know." She took a deep breath. Knowing she should tell him to get away before they focused on him too much was one thing; going back to being alone in this was something totally different. He deserved it, though, the chance to get away from the awfulness of the faeries while he could. "You know you can still tell me to go away, pretend none of this happened. I'd understand."

He poked his tongue at the silver ring in his bottom lip. "Why would I do that?"

"Because they're *touching* you." She blew out her breath in a huff and scooted further back on the counter. "You know it now. You felt them."

"It's worth it." He picked up the teakettle, but he didn't fill it. He just looked at her. "Thought they did stuff like that anyhow."

"Yeah, but you felt it more . . . and they were all staring

at you. Something's changed now that those two are following me." She didn't try to hide the worry or the fear in her
voice. If he was going to know about them, he deserved the
truth of how afraid she really was.

He filled the teakettle and came over to stand in front
of her.

She wrapped her arms around him.

"I'm sorry I wasn't there earlier," he whispered, holding
her tightly to him.

She didn't say anything. She didn't know what *to* say. If
she told him about the things she'd seen over the years, it
would make him worry more. If she let herself think about
what could have happened, she might freak out. She didn't
want to think about it, about what could've happened,
about why they grabbed her.

Finally she pulled back a little and told Seth about the
faeries at the library who'd been circling her and talking
about him. Then she asked, "So what do you think?"

He wrapped a long strand of her hair around his finger
and stared at her. "About tongue rings?"

"About the faeries' comments," she corrected, blushing.
She slid forward like she was going to hop off the counter.
"They seem to know what's going on. Maybe you could see
if there's anything about groups of Rianne-like faeries? You
know, ones that are overly shallow and, umm, Seth . . ."

"Mmm?" Instead of moving back to give her room, Seth
had stepped forward, pushing slightly against her knees.

"You need to move if I'm going to get down from here."

She sounded breathless, not at all like herself, and it felt good—much better than the worries she had been trying to avoid, much better than thinking about the bad thing she'd avoided, or the faery that saved her, or them noticing Seth.

Seth ignored her comment, staying perfectly still.

She didn't move or push him back. She could've. Instead she asked again, "What do you think?"

He lifted one eyebrow, staring at her as he did. "Can never have too many piercings."

She opened her knees, putting one on either side of his ribs, thinking thoughts she shouldn't—*couldn't*—about him. "That's . . ."

"What?" He didn't move any farther, didn't close the distance between them. He might tease, flirt, but he didn't pursue her. It was her choice. In a world where so many choices weren't hers, it was a wonderful feeling.

"That's not what I meant." She blushed again and felt foolish for flirting back. She shouldn't let it get weird. A one-nighter would mess up their friendship. She was just riding some post-danger rush.

She scooted backward. "Promise you'll tell me if anything happens when I'm not there."

He stepped away then, giving her room.

She slid down. Her legs felt wobbly. "I don't like the faeries paying so much attention to you."

He poured them each a cup of tea and opened a tin of shortbread cookies. Then he put on his glasses and pulled out a stack of photocopies and books.

She picked up her tea and followed him to the sofa, glad
to be back on comfortable ground.

His knee bumped against her leg as he sorted out his
papers.

Well, not entirely glad.

"One way to protect yourself is iron or steel, which you
already knew." He gestured at his walls. "I like knowing I
sleep somewhere safe, but I am going to stop by Pins and
Needles. Just to get steel rings to replace the titanium ones.
Unless"—he paused and turned to stare at her—"you think
the tongue thing's a good idea. Seriously, I could do that."

He watched her, an expectant look on his face now, like
he was waiting for her to say something.

She didn't, couldn't. She blushed even brighter than
before. *He's still teasing to distract me.* It had worked. *Too
well.* She bit down on her lip and looked away.

"Right. Well, supposedly 'sacred symbols' work too—a
cross, especially an iron one, holy water." He set that page
aside and picked up a book with passages marked by
brightly colored sticky notes. He thumbed through them,
summarizing. "Spread churchyard dirt in front of them.
Bread and salt are also good 'protections,' but I'm not sure
what you're to do with them. Spread them like the dirt?
Throw them?"

Aislinn got up to pace.

He glanced up at her, and then turned back to the
marked passages. "Turn your clothes inside out to hide
from them. It makes you look like someone else to

them. . . . Plants and herbs that work as counter-charms: four-leafed clover, Saint John's-wort, red verbena—they all help you see through a glamour."

He put that book aside and ate a cookie, staring past her, at nothing, waiting.

Aislinn flopped back down on the sofa, farther away from him than she'd normally sit. "I don't know. I can't see walking around with my clothes inside out all the time, and I don't know about throwing bread at them. What am I supposed to do? Carry bagels and toast everywhere?"

"Salt's easier." He laid the pages on one of the side tables and got up. He pulled open a drawer on the plastic cupboards stacked in the corner. After rummaging around for a minute, he held up a handful of packets of salt. "Here. Extras from all the takeout. Stuff these in your pockets." He tossed some to her and put a few in his pocket, too. "Just in case."

"Does it say how much salt and what to do with it?"

"Sprinkle it on them? Toss it at them? I don't know. I didn't see anything in this book, but I'll follow up on that one, too. I ordered some books from interlibrary loan." He came back to the table and scrawled a note on one of the pages. "Now what about the herbs? I can pick some up. Any ideas on which ones?"

"I can already see them, Seth," she said impatiently. She caught herself—took a deep breath—and grabbed a cookie from the tin beside her. "Why would I need herbs?"

"I might be more help if I can see them too. . . ." He

wrote another note: *Look for more recipes. Paste? Tea? How use herbs for sight? Chamomile tea for Ash.*

"Chamomile?"

"Helps you relax." He leaned over and stroked her hair soothingly, pausing to let his hand rest on the back of her neck. "You're snapping at me."

"Sorry." She frowned. "I thought I was keeping it together, but today . . . If Donia hadn't been there . . . But that's the thing. She *shouldn't* have been there. I've seen them my whole life, but they never paid attention to me. Now it's like they've all stopped whatever they were doing before to watch me. It's never been like this."

He stood there, twirling one of the studs in his ear, staring at her. Then he grabbed the book and sat down in the chair across from her. "Wearing daisies is supposed to keep kids safe from faery kidnapping. I don't know if the daisies work once you aren't a kid."

He dropped that one and flipped open the last book. "Carry a staff of rowan wood. If they chase you, leap over running water, especially if it's flowing south."

"There's one river here, and I don't see me jumping over it unless I sprout springs in my feet. None of this helps much." She hated how whiny she sounded. "What do I do with a staff? Hit them? And wouldn't they know I saw them if I did these things?"

Seth took his glasses back off and sat them on top of a stack of books on the floor. He rubbed his eyes. "I'm trying, Ash. It's only the first day I looked. We'll find out more."

"What if I don't have time? The rules are changing, and I don't know why. I need to do something *now*." She shivered, remembering the strange stillness of the faeries when she passed them. It was frightening.

"Like what?" He still sounded calm. The more anxious she got, the calmer he sounded.

"Find them. Talk to the two that started it—Keenan and Donia." She put her hand over her mouth and took several breaths.

Calm down. It didn't help much.

He leaned back in his chair, rocking it so it teetered on the back legs. "You sure that's a good idea? Especially after those guys—"

She interrupted, "Faeries, court faeries, are *following* me. What they could do is a whole lot worse. They want something, and I don't like being the only one who doesn't know what it is." She stopped, thinking about what the faeries at the library had said. "The faeries—when they weren't lusting on you—called Keenan the 'Summer King.'"

His chair thunked down, back on all four legs. "He's a king?"

"Maybe."

He looked worried then—a flash of something like panic crossed his face—but he nodded. "I'll see what I can find out about that title tomorrow. I'd planned to check online while I wait on the other books."

"Sounds good." She smiled, trying to keep her own panic in check, not wanting to think about the possibility that not just court fey but a faery *king* was following her.

Seth watched her the way you watch a person standing on a ledge, not sure if they're going to go over or not. He didn't ask her to think further on that dangerous possibility, didn't ask her to talk about it. Instead he asked, "Are you staying to eat?"

"No." She got up, rinsed her cup, and took another deep breath. Tucking her hands into her pockets so he wouldn't see them shaking, she turned and—before she could back down—told him, "I think I'm going to see what's out there walking tonight. Maybe one of them will say something like the ones at the library. Come with me?"

"Just a sec." Seth opened an old steamer trunk labeled TEXTBOOKS and pulled out several cigar boxes of jewelry. Inside were leather bracelets with big metal rings, delicate cameos, and velvety jewelers' boxes. As he rummaged through the cigar boxes, he sat several pieces to the side, including one of the leather wristbands.

He dug around a little longer and pulled out a can of pepper spray. "For humans, but maybe it works on faeries, too. I don't know."

"Seth, I . . ."

"Just stuff it in your pocket with the salt." He grinned. Then he held up a necklace and bracelet of thick chain links, very much his style. "Steel. It's supposed to burn them, or maybe just weaken them."

"I know, but . . ."

"Look, it makes sense to use whatever you can, right?"

When she nodded, he came over and motioned for her to turn around. He brushed her hair to the side, piling it over her shoulder. "Hold that."

Silently she did. It felt weird, too close after the earlier tension, but she stood there while Seth draped a necklace around her throat.

Maybe he's right. She could use whatever help she could get. The idea of looking for faeries went against every rule she'd ever learned, but she was going to do it, to try it. It was better than waiting. *I need to try something. Do something.*

Even now she could see more faeries outside the window: one was perched on top of a hedge that couldn't possibly hold him up, but did.

Seth hooked the heavy chain around her throat, let it fall against her skin. Then he kissed the back of her neck and walked past her to the door. "Let's go."

CHAPTER 9

The "fair folk" were most skilled in music, and . . . of the great enchantments and allurements to stay with them was their music.

—*Notes on the Folk-Lore of the North-East of Scotland*
by Walter Gregor (1881)

As she tried to make sense of the earlier events—*Why would mortals attack Ash? Was it mere chance?*—Donia walked. She passed the vagrants leaning against the faded redbrick buildings, the group of young men with their too-loud comments on her "assets," the unconcealed exchange of cash for crack between two skinny guys.

In all Donia's decades, Beira had never broken the rules. No one knew *why*, but there was plenty of speculation. Centuries past, Beira had meted out especially cruel punishments when a group of winter fey had tampered with the game. *No one interferes.* But the odds of the park being clear of all fey . . . it couldn't be random. Either

Beira willed it or allowed it.

As Donia walked, she let the glamour fade away, becoming once more invisible to the mortals. Unfortunately she couldn't hide from the fey as easily.

She fought to keep her voice even, but it never seemed to work with Keenan, today even less so than usual. "What do you want?"

"Happiness. Beira to grow a conscience. Forgiveness." He leaned in to kiss her cheek.

She moved out of reach, stepping into a puddle. "Can't help you."

"Not even on the forgiveness?" Absently he blew a gentle breeze toward a couple of shivering crackheads, not changing his stride as he did so.

She kept her silence, debating how much she could omit without lying.

He was as impatient as always, though, questioning her before she could get her thoughts sorted. "Did you see her?"

"Yes."

"Talk to her?" He held out a hand to carry her bag, always solicitous, even now with his eyes glimmering over thoughts of *her*, of Aislinn.

Donia clutched the strap of her bag, then felt foolish for being petty, and held it out.

Sasha ran toward her at full speed, bounding over the debris. His tail was held high when he came to a stop beside her.

"Good boy." She bent to ruffle his fur—and check for any

blood on his muzzle—before continuing down the street.

Across the street several of Keenan's guardsmen kept a discreet distance, winding their way around the people, leaning into the crumbling facades of the buildings in this part of the city, and somehow still managing to keep the edges of their long coats from dragging through any of the filth on the ground.

With a shake of her head, she looked back at Keenan.

And he smiled at her.

For an instant she forgot everything—his betrayal, her suspicions about Beira, the aching cold. *He's as beautiful as he was when we met. I look pale and awful, but he's still gorgeous.* She tore her gaze away and walked faster.

He stayed beside her adjusting his stride to match hers. "Donia? Did you?"

"I spoke with her." She thought again about what had almost happened, what could have happened if she hadn't been there. She didn't tell him. "The girl's kind, good. . . . Totally too good for you."

"So were you." He kissed her cheek, singed it with his lips. "You still are."

"Bastard." She shoved him, ignoring the burning in her palm from touching him.

He put a hand on his shoulder, melting the ice that formed where she'd pushed too hard. It crackled under his touch. "Only because Beira murdered my father."

⤜⊰⊱⤛

Keenan kept pace with Donia until they reached the mouth of a barricaded alley. She said nothing, offered him nothing in the way of even the barest civility. Even after all these years, it still hurt to see the disdain on her face.

Finally he stepped in front of her, blocking her path. "You saw Beira."

She didn't answer him, but it wasn't a question.

"What did she want?" he prompted.

She stepped around him, going farther toward the railroad yard. "Nothing I can't handle."

She was hiding something. He could see the tightening in her hands, hear her breathing catch just a little.

He followed. "Seems odd for her just to stop by to visit. I didn't think you enjoyed being around her."

"It's not much worse than seeing you, but somehow I endure that." She stopped and leaned against one of the fire-blackened buildings outside the railroad yard, closing her eyes, breathing deeply. Sasha stretched out at her feet.

Since she'd been mortal once, being that close to iron wasn't as hard for her as it was for most fey, but it still hurt her. If it hurt Sasha, she wouldn't come, but the wolf was immune to it.

The guards were keeping their distance, but even being near that much iron had to be painful for them. Keenan motioned for them to pull back farther.

"Donia?" He reached out to take her hand, but didn't. His touch would hurt her more than the iron did. Instead he splayed his arms out on the wall on either side of her, palms covering part of the graffiti on the wall, making a prison of sorts with his arms. "Why do you come down here?"

"To remind myself of what I lost." She opened her eyes, holding his gaze. "To remind myself not to trust any of you."

She was utterly impossible.

He grimaced at her accusing look, at the decades-long argument. "I didn't lie to you."

"You didn't tell me the truth, either." She closed her eyes again.

Neither of them spoke for several minutes. Her cold breath mingled with his equally warm breath in the small space between them, rising like steam above them.

"Go away, Keenan. I don't like you any more today than I did yesterday, or the day before that, or the—"

He interrupted, "But I still *like* you. That's the beauty of this, isn't it? I still miss you. Every single time we do this, Don." He lowered his voice to try and hide how close it was to raw. "I miss you."

She didn't even open her eyes to look at him.

Any love she might have felt died decades ago. If things were different . . . but they aren't. He shook his head. Donia wasn't *her.* She was one of the girls he'd never have. He needed to think about how to get close to Aislinn, not about the one he'd lost and loved.

He sighed. "Are you going to tell me what Beira wanted?"

Donia did look at him then, leaning her face close enough that he felt her words on his lips. "Beira wants the same thing you do: me to do her bidding."

He took several steps back. "Damn it, Donia, I don't want—"

"Stop. Just stop." She pushed away from the building. "She wants me to convince Aislinn not to trust you. Just a little pep talk in case I forgot my job."

She was hiding something: Beira wouldn't visit her for that alone. Evan, the rowan-man who watched over Donia, had said she was terrified when Beira left.

Terrified. But she didn't trust him enough to tell him why. *And why should she?* He started to follow her, to try again.

"Please." Her voice wavered. "Not today. Just leave me alone today."

Then she walked away, closer to the railroad yard, as close as she could stand to go without collapsing. And there was nothing he could do to stop her, to help her. So he watched her until she ducked behind a wall and he couldn't see her anymore.

By nightfall Donia was composed again, but being down at the railroad yard had made her tired, so she'd stopped to rest by the fountain on Willow, a block over from Aislinn's house. She'd sent Sasha out to run, unwilling to ask the wolf to stay still when he wanted to roam.

The harsh streetlights reflected on the surface of the

fountain, casting plum shadows in the courtyard. An old man with a well-loved sax played for the people who passed. Donia stretched her legs out on the bench, relishing the shadows, listening to the sax-man, and thinking.

In talking to the fey earlier, Donia had only learned that no one wanted to talk. Neither Beira's winter fey nor Irial's dark fey—who worked closely with the Winter Court— would admit to involvement. The solitary fey would only say they weren't comfortable in the park. The lack of answers was answer enough: by consent or directive, Beira had interfered.

She thinks this girl is different.

The sax-man played another mournful song. Donia shifted again, stretching out further, enjoying her solitude, cherishing the brief illusion of belonging with humanity. She'd never be that again—human. She didn't belong to their world, never again would. It still ached when she thought of what she'd given up for Keenan. Once the next girl lifted the staff, she would become just another faery— no allegiance to any of the courts, no responsibility, no place at all where she *belonged.*

She still wanted that, belonging. Once she'd thought she belonged with Keenan. When she met him—before she knew what he was—he'd taken her to hear his friends' band. He'd even bought her a dress—a short little number with strands of beads hanging everywhere, swaying when she danced. And did they dance!

The band was unlike anything she'd ever heard before—

three tall, thin men made love with the songs they wrenched
from their horns, while a woman with a sexy torch voice
crooned to the crowd, promising everything with her words
and her body. There were others, a heavyset man with fingers that stroked the piano keys like he was caressing it.
When they played, gods, it was like they funneled pure emotions into the instruments. Nothing had ever felt as good as
listening to them play—nothing except moving across the
floor in Keenan's arms. Nothing ever would.

Shaking off the longing, she closed her eyes, listening to
the sax-man in front of her. His song was flat compared to
the faery band in her memories, but blessedly mortal. There
was no trickery in his song, no lie woven into the notes. It
was flawed, and somehow lovelier for it.

She laughed aloud at the absurdity of it all: she could
hear the most perfect music any day—fey with voices of
unmatchable purity—but a half-talented old man playing
for change in the park pleased her more.

From beside her, she heard Aislinn's voice, wary and
thin, as the girl approached. "Donia?"

"Umm?"

She was wary, far more than Donia had ever been when
the Winter Girl and Summer King had played her. *She'll
need something to even the odds, especially if she* is *the one he's
been seeking.*

"We were walking by and saw you. Sasha's not here, so I
thought . . ." Aislinn's voice trailed off. "Did he come back?"

"Sasha is fine. Sit with me." Donia kept her eyes closed,

but turned her head to smile in Aislinn's direction. Aislinn's mortal didn't speak, but Donia heard his steady heartbeat as he stood protectively by her side.

Aislinn started, "We weren't—"

"Stay. Relax with me. We could both use it."

And it was true. After Keenan whispered his hollow words, his protests and reminders of what they'd once had, what she couldn't have, she was always out of sorts. If it'd been true winter, he'd be unable to bother her, but spring through fall he was out and about, tormenting her with his very presence. Never mind that he'd tempted her with empty promises; forget the fact that he'd stolen her mortality. Until another girl was willing to believe in him, she was trapped—watching him make them fall in love with him, knowing that the girls who chose not to risk the cold shared his bed. And they'd all refused the risk—choosing instead to be Summer Girls, refusing to lift the staff. *I love—loved— him enough to risk the cold; they didn't.* Yet they had him.

"Ash?" The mortal—Seth—motioned to a group of equally pierced people who'd called out to him.

"I'll be right here," Aislinn murmured to him with a weak smile. She folded her arms tightly over her chest.

"When you're ready . . ." He looked like he'd rather stay beside Aislinn, but she motioned him off—watching him as he passed the fountain.

Inside it young kelpies were playing. Like most of the water fey, they cared little for the other faeries in the park. They were still disquieting to Donia in a way that most of the fey no longer were, preying on mortals when given the slightest chance, drinking down their last breaths, somehow making death a sexual thing. Not even Irial's Dark Court disturbed her the way the water fey did.

Of course, Seth—like most mortals—didn't glance at them, but as he passed them they stilled, watching him with that eerie hunger they had. They could see the passion in him, feel it somehow, or they wouldn't watch him so.

Aislinn watched him too. Her breathing sped up; her cheeks flushed. Her willingness to be separated from him seemed to be a show for his benefit. She didn't speak, didn't relax.

Only a few minutes had passed when she announced, "I can't stay here."

"Still feeling weird about the attack?"

Donia felt pretty unsettled about it too, but for quite different reasons. If Beira knew Donia suspected her of violating the rules, if Keenan knew that Donia suspected that this mortal was the missing Summer Queen . . . *caught between them yet again.* Nothing was simple anymore. It hadn't been in so very long.

Beside her, Aislinn shuddered. She stared at the fountain, or perhaps past it where her mortal stood. "I guess it freaked me out a little. Seems unreal, you know? And the sort of things that come out at night . . ."

Donia sat up. "Things?"

It was an odd word to chose, an odd tone in her voice as Aislinn stared toward the kelpies.

Can she see them? How very unexpected that would be. There were stories of sighted mortals, but Donia'd never met one.

With a strange half-mocking tone, Aislinn said, "It's not just guys like those today. Even the pretty ones can be awful. Don't trust them just because they're pretty."

Donia laughed, coldly, sounding every bit Beira's creature in that moment. "Where were you when I needed that advice? I've already gone out with the biggest mistake a girl can make."

"Be sure to point him out if you see him around." Aislinn stood up and slung her bag over her shoulder.

And with that, Seth was already returning, attentive to Aislinn's every move.

Donia smiled at them, wishing someone waited for her like that—the way Keenan once had.

"Thanks again for the save." Aislinn nodded then and walked off, headed straight toward the cadaverous Scrimshaw Sisters, who were gliding over the ground with their usual macabre beauty.

She'll swerve if she can see them.

She didn't. She kept walking forward until one of the Scrimshaw Sisters drifted out of her path at the last possible second.

Mortals don't see the fey. Donia smiled wryly: if they did, Keenan would never have convinced any of them to trust him.

Chapter 10

Sometimes they contrived to induce, by their fair and winning ways, unwary men and women to go with them.

—*Notes on the Folk-Lore of the North-East of Scotland*
by Walter Gregor (1881)

By the time she was far enough away from the fountain to
feel comfortable stopping, Aislinn thought she was going to
be sick. She leaned into Seth, knowing he'd wrap his arms
around her again.

His lips were against her ear when he asked, "More than
meets the eye?"

"Yeah."

Seth held on to her, but he didn't say anything else.

"What would I do without you?" She closed her eyes,
not wanting to see the vine-girls—or any of the other
faeries—who stood watching them.

"You'll never need to find that out." He kept an arm
around her shoulders as they started walking, past the place

where the guys had grabbed her, past the omnipresent faeries with their crackled skin.

Being more assertive sounded good in theory, but she'd need to learn to relax a lot more if she was going to be able to talk to faeries. Donia might have rescued her once, but that didn't change what she was.

When they got to her building, Seth slipped money into her hand. "Take a taxi tomorrow."

She didn't like accepting money from him, but she couldn't ask Grams for it without making her suspicious. She tucked it into her pocket. "You want to come up?"

He lifted both eyebrows. "Pass."

Aislinn went up the stairs, hoping Grams was asleep. Right now, avoiding those too-observant eyes seemed like a good plan. She went inside and tried to walk past the living room.

"You missed dinner again." Grams didn't take her eyes off the news. "Bad things out there, Aislinn."

"I know." She paused in the doorway to the living room, but she didn't go in.

Grams sat in her bright purple lounger, feet propped up on the stone and steel coffee table. Her reading glasses hung by a chain around her neck. She might not be as young as she was in Aislinn's childhood memories, but she still looked as fierce as she had then, still thin and healthier than many women her age. Even when she spent the day at home, she was dressed for the possibility of "callers"—her long gray hair coiled up into a simple bun or contained in an intricate plait, dressing gown traded in for a sedate skirt and blouse.

Grams wasn't staid or sedate, though: she was uncommonly forward-thinking, and entirely too clever when she paid attention. "Something happen?"

It felt like a normal question, and if anyone heard, it'd sound like it too. *Always careful, that's the key to surviving among them.* Still, Grams' strong voice had more than a thread of worry in it.

"I'm fine, Grams. Just tired." Aislinn went in, leaned down, and kissed her. *I need to tell her, just not yet.* She already worried too much.

"You're wearing new steel." Grams eyed the necklace Seth had given Aislinn.

Aislinn stood there—wavering. *How much do I say?* Grams wouldn't understand, or approve, of Aislinn taking an active approach to finding out what they wanted. Hide and look away: that was Grams' credo.

"Aislinn?" Grams turned up the volume on the news and grabbed a piece of paper. She wrote: *Have They done something? Are you hurt?* and held out the paper.

"No."

With a stern look, Grams pointed at the paper.

Sighing, Aislinn took the paper and pen. Using the coffee table as a desk, she wrote: *Two of them are following me.*

Grams sucked in her breath, quietly gasping. She snatched the paper. *I'll call the school, fill out papers to home-school, and . . .*

"No. Please," Aislinn whispered. She put her hand over Grams' hand. She took the pen and wrote, *I'm not sure what they want, but I don't want to hide.* Then she said, "Please? Let me try it this way. I'll be careful."

At first Grams stared at Aislinn, as if there were answers hidden under the skin that she could see if only she looked carefully.

Aislinn willed herself to look as reassuring as possible.

Finally Grams wrote, *Stay away from them as much as you can. Remember the rules.*

Aislinn nodded. She didn't often try to hide things from Grams, but she wasn't going to admit that she'd tried to follow them or tell her about Seth's research.

Grams had always insisted that avoidance was the best and only plan. Aislinn no longer thought that was a good answer—if she was honest, she'd never thought it was.

She simply said, "I'm being careful. I know what's out there."

Grams frowned and gripped Aislinn's wrist briefly. "Keep your cell phone in your pocket. I want to be able to reach you."

"Yes, Grams."

"And keep me updated on your schedule in case—" Her voice broke. She wrote, *We'll try your way for a few days. Wait them out. No mistakes.* Then she starting tearing the paper into tiny pieces. "Go on. Get something to eat. You need to keep your wits about you."

"Sure," Aislinn murmured as she gave Grams a quick squeeze.

Wait them out? Aislinn wasn't sure that was possible. If

Grams knew they were court fey, Aislinn would be on lock-down. She'd bought herself a little time, but it wouldn't last. *I need answers now.* Hiding wasn't the answer. Neither was running.

She wanted a normal life—college, a relationship, simple things. She didn't want all of her decisions to be based on the whims of faeries. Grams had lived that way, and she wasn't happy. Aislinn's mother hadn't even had a chance to find out if she could have a normal life. Aislinn didn't want to take either of their paths. But she didn't know how to make it any different, either.

Faeries—*court faeries*—didn't stalk a person for no reason. Unless she found out what they wanted, found out how to undo whatever had caught their attention, she doubted they'd be going away anytime soon. And if they didn't go away, Aislinn's freedom would. That wasn't an option she liked. *At all.*

After grabbing a quick bite, Aislinn retreated to her room and closed the door. It wasn't a sanctuary. It didn't reflect her personality like Seth's house or Rianne's too-girly bed-room. It was just a room, a place to sleep.

Seth's feels more like home. Seth feels like home.

There were some things that mattered to her in her room, things that made her feel connected—a poetry book that was her mother's, black-and-white prints of photos from an exhibit in Pittsburgh. Grams had surprised her that day—authorized ditching school and taken her to the

Carnegie Museum. It was great.

Beside those prints were some of hers that Grams had blown up for her birthday one year. One shot of the railroad yard still made her smile. She'd started taking photos to see if faeries would show up on film: since she saw them when she looked through the lens, would they show on film? They didn't, but she enjoyed the process of taking photos enough that she was glad she'd tried the experiment.

It wasn't much, though, the proof of her personality in the room. *It's only glimpses.* Life felt like that sometimes— like everything she revealed or did had to be preplanned. *Focus. Control.*

She turned out the lights, crawled into bed, and pulled out her cell.

Seth answered on the first ring. "Miss me already?"

"Maybe." She closed her eyes and stretched.

"Everything okay?" He sounded tense, but she didn't ask why. She didn't want to talk about anything bad, any worries.

"Tell me a story," she whispered. He always made the bad things seem less awful.

"What kind of story?"

"One that'll make me have good dreams."

He laughed then, low and sexy. "Better give me a rating for that dream."

"Surprise me." She bit her lip. *I know better.* She really needed to stop flirting with him before she crossed a line she couldn't back away from.

He didn't say anything for a minute, but she could hear him breathing.

"Seth?"

"I'm here." His voice was soft, hesitant. "Once upon a time, there was a girl. . . ."

"Not a princess."

"No. Definitely not. She was too smart to be a princess. Tough, too."

"Yeah?"

"Oh yeah. Stronger than anyone realized."

"Does she live happily ever after?"

"Shouldn't there be something in the middle?"

"I like to read the ending first." She waited, curled up in her bed, to hear his assurances, to believe—for a minute at least—that everything could be okay. "So did she?"

He didn't hesitate. "Yes."

Neither of them said anything for a few minutes. She heard the sounds of traffic, of his breathing. She'd fallen asleep like that before—just holding the phone while he walked home, feeling that connection to him.

Finally he said, "Did I mention how sexy she was?"

She laughed.

"She was so unbelievably beautiful that—" He paused and she heard the unmistakable screech as he opened his door. "And this is the part where the rating changes."

"You're at home?" She could hear him moving around, door closing, keys clanking on the counter, his jacket dropping—probably on the table. "I'll let you go then."

"What if I don't want you to?" he asked.

She heard the music as he walked toward his room, some sort of jazz. Her heart sped up, thinking of him getting stretched out on his bed too, but her voice only sounded a little off when she said, "Good night, Seth."

"So you're running again, then?" One of his boots thudded on the floor.

"I'm not running."

The other boot hit the floor. "Really?"

"Really. It's just—" She stopped; she didn't have anything that would finish that sentence and be honest.

"Maybe you should slow down, so I can catch you." He paused, waiting. He seemed to do that more and more lately, make statements that invited her to admit something dangerous to their friendship. When she didn't answer he added, "Sweet dreams, Ash."

After they hung up, Aislinn held the phone in her hand, still thinking about Seth. *It would be a bad idea. A really, really bad idea . . .* She smiled. *He thinks I'm smart* and *sexy.*

She was still smiling when she fell asleep.

CHAPTER 11

[The Sidhe] are shape-changers; they can grow small or grow large, they can take what shape they choose; . . . they are as many as the blades of grass. They are everywhere.

—*Visions and Beliefs in the West of Ireland* by Lady Augusta Gregory (1920)

When Aislinn walked up the steps to Bishop O.C. the next morning, she saw them: fey things lingering outside the door, watching everyone, and seeming strangely serious.

Inside more faeries clustered at the doorway to the principal's office. *WTF?* They usually avoided the school— whether from the rows of steel lockers or the abundance of religious artifacts, she didn't know. *Both, maybe.*

By the time she reached her locker, the presence of faeries overwhelmed her. They weren't to come here. There were rules: this was supposed to be a safe space.

"Miss Foy?"

She turned. Standing beside Father Myers was the one

faery she was supremely unprepared to face.

"Keenan," she whispered.

"You know one another?" Father Myers nodded, beam-ing now. "Good. Good."

He turned to the two other—equally visible—faeries standing beside him. If she glanced at them quickly, they looked like they weren't much older than her, but the taller of the two had a strange solemnity that made Aislinn sus-pect that he was *old*. He had unusually long hair for such a serious demeanor; under his glamour it glittered like thick silver cords. A smallish black sun tattoo was visible on the side of his throat, exposed by his tightly plaited hair. The second faery had almost shorn wood-brown hair, and a face that would be somehow forgettable but for the long scar that ran from his temple to the corner of his mouth.

Father Myers assured the faeries, "Aislinn's an honor stu-dent, and her schedule is the same as your nephew's. She'll help him get caught up."

She stood there, trying not to bolt, refusing to look at Keenan—even though he watched her expectantly—while several more faeries walked up behind Father Myers.

One of the ones whose skin looked like bark—crackled and grayish—caught Keenan's gaze. He gestured at the others who were fanned out at the entrance and said, "All clear."

"Miss Foy? Aislinn?" Father Myers cleared his throat.

She looked away from the retinue of faeries that had invaded Bishop O'Connell. "I'm sorry, Father. What?"

"Can you show Keenan to Calculus?"

Keenan waited, a battered leather bag over his shoulder, looking at her attentively. His "uncles" and Father Myers watched her.

She had no choice. She forced her fear away and said, "Sure."

Wait them out? Not likely. Every rule she'd lived with, that'd kept her safe, they were *all* failing her.

By midday, Aislinn's control of her temper was steadily being worn away by Keenan's false humanity. He followed her, talking, acting like he was safe, like he was real.

He isn't.

She shoved her books into her locker, scraping her knuckles in the process. Keenan stayed beside her, an unwanted shadow she couldn't shake.

They watched each other, and she wondered again if it would hurt to touch his metallic hair. The copper strands glistened under his glamour, compelling her attention despite her best efforts.

Rianne stopped and leaned hard against the row of closed lockers. The clang made people pause to stare.

"I heard he was edible, but"—Rianne put a hand on her chest as if she was having trouble breathing and looked at Keenan—slowly and appraisingly—"damn. Definite finesse."

"I wouldn't know." Aislinn blushed. *And I'm not going to, either.* Whatever the weird compulsion to touch him was, she was stronger than any instinct. *Just focus.*

Leslie and Carla joined them as Rianne pushed off the wall of lockers. She stepped closer to Keenan and examined him as if he were a slab of meat on a plate. "Bet you could."

Carla patted his arm. "She's harmless."

Aislinn grabbed her books for the afternoon classes. Her friends shouldn't be talking to him; he shouldn't be in her space. And he definitely shouldn't radiate that inviting heat, making her think of lazy days, of closing her eyes, of relaxing . . . *Control. Focus.* She could do this. She *had* to.

She sorted her things, so what she'd need to take home was on top of the stack in the locker. When the day ended, she'd be ready to make a quick getaway.

With a forced smile, she shooed her friends away. "I'll catch up. Save me a seat."

"We'll save two. You can't let that"—Rianne waved her hand at Keenan—"morsel wander around unsupervised."

"One seat, Ri, just *one.*"

None of them turned around. Rianne waved her hand over her shoulder, dismissively.

After a steadying breath, Aislinn turned to Keenan. "I'm sure you can figure out lunch without help. So, umm, go make friends or whatever."

And she walked away.

He sped up to stay beside her as they entered the cafeteria. "May I join you?"

"No."

He stepped in front of her. "Please?"

"No." She dropped her bag into a chair next to Rianne's

things. Ignoring him—and the stares they were attracting—she opened her bag.

He hadn't moved.

With a shaky gesture, she pointed. "The line's over there."

He looked at the throng slowly progressing to the vats of
food. "Can I get you something?"

"A little space?"

A flare of anger flashed over his too-beautiful face, but
he said nothing. He just walked away.

She wanted to believe she'd get rid of him by her refusal
to be drawn in by his attention. *I can hope.* Because if not, she
didn't know what she would do. He was compelling, pulling
her attention away from all that she knew as wise and good.

At the far side of the cafeteria, Rianne had left her spot
in line and was talking to him. They both looked over at
her: Rianne smiling conspiratorially, Keenan looking
pleased.

Great. Aislinn unpacked part of her lunch, pulling out a
yogurt and spoon. *Stalker-faery has a new ally.*

While she was alone, Aislinn made a quick phone call to
request the cabbie she and Seth had met at the tat shop a
few months ago. The cabbie had told them how to get dis-
patch to send him specifically and assured them that he'd be
on time or get a friend to be there if they requested him. So
far he'd been as good as his word.

She kept her voice as low as she could in hopes that
Keenan's guards wouldn't hear.

One of them was already moving closer to her.

Too late. She hid her brief smile—any success against them was a pleasure—as she disconnected.

She stirred her yogurt and wondered yet again why Keenan had singled her out. She knew it wasn't about the Sight; she'd lived by the rules, done everything right.

So why me?

All day girls had tried to talk to him, offered to show him around. He was polite but adamant that he needed *Aislinn* to show him around, not them.

Pretty girls, cheerleaders, geek girls, everyone was lusting on him. It felt good to be the one they all looked at with envy for a change. *It'd feel better if he were a normal guy, like Seth.*

Along with half the students at school, Keenan's faeries watched them, unabashed as the fey always were. They seemed tired, shifting in and out of the school in small groups. Although the metal-laden building must be painful for them, they stood alert and observant, keeping Keenan in their sight at *all* times. They treated him reverentially. *Why wouldn't they if Keenan is a faery king?*

She thought, for a heartbeat, that she was going to be sick from the flood of fears and horrible images that came rushing over her. *A faery king . . . and he's stalking me.*

With no small effort, Aislinn managed to push down the rising worries as Leslie and Carla headed her way. Panic wouldn't help. A plan was what she needed; answers were what she needed. Maybe if she had answers, if she knew why he'd fixated on her, she could find a way to get rid of him.

As she watched Keenan walk toward her, Aislinn saw a

fleeting image of sunlight rippling over water, bouncing off buildings, strange flickers of warmth and beauty that made her want to run toward him. He looked at her, smiling invitingly, as he followed Rianne through the crowded cafeteria.

Rianne was chattering animatedly to him, looking for all the world like they were long-lost friends. Leslie laughed at whatever Keenan said, and Aislinn realized that her friends had all accepted him.

And why wouldn't they? As much as she wished they would ignore him, there was nothing she could say. She couldn't explain why she wanted him gone. She couldn't tell them how very dangerous he was. It wasn't a choice she had. Sometimes that lack of choices, the pressures of dealing with the fey, made her feel like she was smothering, like the secrecy was a physical weight bearing down on her. She hated it.

After her traitorous friends brought him to the table, she tried to ignore him. It worked—for a while—but he kept watching her, directing most of his comments to her, asking her questions. All the while he sat on the opposite side of the table staring at her with those inhuman green eyes.

Finally he pointed at over-steamed green beans and asked something inane and she snapped, "What? Too common for someone like you?"

Where's my control? More and more, her lifetime of emotional control seemed to be faltering, sliding away.

He was frighteningly still. "What do you mean?"

She knew better than to provoke a faery, especially a

faery king, but she barreled on, "You'd be surprised at what I know about you. And you know what? None of it impresses me. Not one little bit."

He laughed then—joyous and free, like the anger that'd flared in his eyes hadn't existed. "Then I shall try harder."

She shivered in foreboding, in sudden longing, in some uncomfortable mixture of the two. It was worse than the simple compulsion she'd felt to reach out toward him: it was the same disquieting tangle of feelings she'd felt at Comix when he'd first spoken to her.

Leslie whistled softly. "Give him a little something, Ash."

"Drop it, Les." Aislinn fisted her hands in her lap under the table.

"PMS." Rianne nodded. Then she tapped Keenan's hand and added, "Just ignore her, sweetie. We'll help you wear her down."

"Oh, I'm counting on that, Rianne," Keenan murmured. He was glowing—like a bright light radiated from inside his skin—as he spoke.

Aislinn could taste rose-heavy air, could feel the too-tempting warmth from him.

Her friends stared at him as if he were the most amazing thing they'd ever glimpsed. *I am so screwed.*

Aislinn stayed silent until it was time to go to afternoon classes, her fingernails digging small half circles— *like slivers of the sun*—into her palms. She concentrated on the pain of those suns, only partially visible in her skin, and wondered if she had any chance at all of escaping from Keenan's attention.

By the end of the day, Keenan's proximity had grown intolerable to Aislinn. A strange warmth seemed to permeate the air when he stood close to her, and after a few moments, it was near painful to resist touching him. Her mind told her to, but her eyes wanted to drift shut; her hands wanted to reach out.

I need space.

She'd learned to deal with seeing the fey. It was awful, but she did it. She could do this, too.

He's just another faery.

She concentrated, repeating the rules and warnings in her mind like a prayer, a litany to keep her focused. *Don't stare, don't speak, don't run, don't touch.* She took several calming breaths. *Don't react. Don't attract their attention. Don't* ever *let them know you can see them.* The familiarity of the words helped her push back the edge of desire, but it wasn't enough to make it anywhere near comfortable to be around him.

So when they walked in to Lit class and one of the cheerleaders offered him an empty seat—a seat gloriously far away from hers—Aislinn gave the cheerleader a big smile. "I could kiss you for that. Thank you."

Keenan flinched at the phrase.

The cheerleader stared back at Aislinn, not sure if it was a joke or not.

"Seriously. Thank you." Aislinn turned away from the less-than-pleased Keenan and slid into her seat, grateful to have a respite—however brief it was.

A few minutes later Sister Mary Louise came in and passed out a stack of papers. "I thought we'd take a Shakespeare break today."

Appreciative murmurs greeted her, quickly followed by groans when people saw the poetry on the handouts.

Ignoring the grumbling, Sister Mary Louise scrawled a title on the whiteboard: "La Belle Dame Sans Merci."

Someone in the back muttered, "Poetry and French, oh joy."

Sister Mary Louise laughed. "Who wants to read about the 'Beautiful Woman Without Pity'?"

Utterly unself-conscious, Keenan stood and read the tragic tale of a knight fatally entranced by a faery. It wasn't the words that had every girl in the room sighing: it was his voice. Even without a glamour, he sounded sinfully good.

When he was done reading, Sister Mary Louise seemed as stunned as the rest of them. "Beautiful," she murmured. Then she pulled her gaze away to drift over the room, pausing on the typically vocal students. "Well? What can you tell me?"

"I've got nothing," Leslie murmured from across the aisle.

Sister Mary Louise caught Aislinn's eye expectantly.

So after yet another steadying breath, Aislinn said, "She wasn't a woman. The knight trusted something inhuman, a faery or a vampire or something, and now he's dead."

Sister Mary Louise prompted, "Good. So what does that mean?"

"Don't trust faeries or vamps," Leslie muttered.

Everyone but Keenan and Aislinn laughed.

Then Keenan's voice cut through the laughter, "Perhaps the faery wasn't at fault. Perhaps there were other factors."

"Right. What's one mortal's life? He died. It doesn't matter if the faery, vamp, whatever it was felt bad or didn't mean to. The knight is still dead." Aislinn tried to keep her voice calm, and mostly succeeded. Her heartbeat was another matter entirely. She knew Keenan watched her, but she stared at Sister Mary Louise and added, "The monster's not suffering, is she?"

"It could be a metaphor about trusting the wrong person, right?" Leslie added.

"Good. Good." Sister Mary Louise added several lines to the scrawl on the board. "What else?"

The discussion veered onto several other topics, until Sister Mary Louise finally said, "Let's look at Rossetti's 'Goblin Market' for a moment and then we'll come back to this."

Aislinn was unsurprised that Keenan volunteered to read again; he had to know how his voice sounded. This time he stared straight at her as he read, barely glancing at the words on the page.

Leslie leaned toward Aislinn and whispered, "Looks like Seth has competition."

"No." Aislinn shook her head and forced herself to hold
Keenan's gaze as she answered, "No, he doesn't. There's
nothing Keenan could offer me that I want."

Her voice was low, but he heard her. He stumbled
briefly, confusion flitting across his too-beautiful face. He
stopped mid-poem.

Aislinn looked away before he could see how tempted
she really was, before she admitted to herself how much she
wanted to ignore all reason.

Sister Mary Louise stepped into the silence. "Cassandra,
please continue from there."

Please. Let him go away.

Aislinn didn't glance his way once for the rest of the
class. Afterward she all but ran from the room, hoping the
taxi would be waiting as promised. If she had to face much
more of Keenan's attention, she was afraid of what she
might do.

CHAPTER 12

Folks say that the only way to avoid their fury is to hunt a
branch of verbena and bind it with a five-leaved clover. This
is magic against all disaster.

—*Folk Tales of Brittany* by Elsie Masson (1929)

When Donia walked into the library, she saw Seth. *Aislinn's
friend, the one who lives in the den of steel walls.* It wasn't
quite late enough to see Aislinn, but if Seth was here, perhaps Aislinn was meeting him again.

He didn't seem to notice anyone around him, despite
the mortals and faeries who were all noticing him. And why
wouldn't they? He was lovely, tempting in ways so different
than Keenan: dark and still, shadows and paleness. *Don't
think of Keenan. Think of the mortal. Smile for him.*

She took her time, moving slowly and carefully with a
casual hand for support on the vacant tables she passed, a
moment's pause to catch her breath at the new book display.

He watched.

Let him speak first. You can do this. Her gaze—hidden behind dark glasses—lingered on him for a breath or two. He sat at one of the handful of computer terminals, a pile of printouts beside him.

When she was beside the desk, she smiled at him.

He folded his pile of papers, effectively hiding what he'd been researching.

She tilted her head, trying to see what he was reading on the screen.

He clicked on something on the screen and flicked off the monitor. He pointed at her. "Donia, right? Ash didn't introduce us last night. You're the one who helped her?"

She nodded and held out a hand.

Instead of shaking it, he lifted it and kissed her knuckles. *He has my hand.* It didn't burn like Keenan's touch.

She froze, like quarry before the Hunt, and felt foolish for it. *No one touches me. As if I still belonged to Keenan. Forbidden.* Liseli swore it would change when the new Winter Girl took the staff, but that was hard to believe sometimes. It'd been decades since anyone had truly held her.

"I'm Seth. Thank you for what you did. If anything happened to her . . ." For a moment he looked fierce enough to rival Keenan's best guards. "So, thanks."

He still had her hand; she trembled as she pulled it from his grasp. *He's hers, just like Keenan is now.* "Is Ash here?"

"Nope. Should be on her way from school soon." He glanced past her to the clock that hung on the wall behind her.

She stood, indecisive for a moment.

"Did you need something?" He stared at her, as if he would like to ask her a different question.

She pushed her dark glasses farther up the bridge of her nose. Looking past him, where several of Keenan's girls stood listening, she smiled wryly.

"Are you Ash's . . ." She waved her hand in the air.

Somberly he prompted, "Ash's what?"

"Beau?" she said, and then winced. *Beau. No one uses that anymore.* The years sometimes blurred, the words and the clothes and the music. It rolled together. "Her boyfriend?"

"Her beau?" he repeated. He poked his tongue at a ring in his bottom lip, and then he smiled. "No, not really."

"Oh." Catching an unusual scent, Donia sniffed slightly. *It can't be.*

Seth stood and picked up his bag. He stepped close to her, a handsbreadth from her, as if he were trying to make her step back, asserting some sort of male dominance. *That doesn't change over the years.*

She stepped back—just once—but not before she caught the slightly acrid scent of recently handled verbena, not overpowering, but there. *It is. In his bag.* Underneath it were the slight scents of chamomile and Saint-John's-wort.

"I look out for her, you know? She's a wonderful person. Gentle. *Good.*" He slung his bag over his shoulder and stared down at her.

"If anyone tried to hurt her"—he paused, scowled, and

continued—"there's *nothing* I wouldn't do to keep her safe."

"Right. Glad I could help with that the other day." Distracted, she nodded. *Verbena, Saint-John's-wort, what's he doing with* those? They were chief among the list of herbs thought to give a mortal faery sight.

Then he left, trailed by several of Keenan's girls. *I wonder if they'll notice what he carries in his bag.* She doubted it.

Once the door swung shut behind Seth and the Summer Girls, Donia sat down at the terminal and pulled up his search history: *Faeries, Glamour, Herbs for Seeing, Summer King.*

"Oh," she whispered. That couldn't be good.

When Keenan got to his loft on the outskirts of the city, Niall and Tavish were waiting. They lounged as if they were relaxing, but he didn't miss the assessing looks they gave him when he walked in.

"Well?" Tavish asked as he muted the television, silencing the weather report about a freak hailstorm.

Beira must have heard I spent the day with Aislinn. She often snarled over any progress he made with the mortal girls, but she couldn't—by rules of the contest—actively interfere.

"Not great." Keenan was loath to admit it, but Aislinn's resistance was wearing on him. "She doesn't react as they usually do."

Niall flopped into an overstuffed chair and grabbed a controller for one of the game systems. "Did you ask her out?"

"Already?" Keenan picked up a half-eaten slice of pizza

from the box on one of the geode tables scattered around the room. He sniffed it and took a bite. *Not too old.* "Isn't that too soon? The last girl . . ."

Niall glanced up from the TV. "Mortal habits change faster than ours. Try a casual 'friends' approach."

"He doesn't want to be her friend. That's not what the girls are for," Tavish insisted in his usual stiff manner. He turned and held out a hand for the box of leftover pizza. "You need protein, not that. Why you two insist on eating mortal food is beyond me."

Because I've had to live so long among them? But Keenan didn't say it. He handed over the pizza and sat down, trying to relax. It was easier here than most places they'd lived. Tall leafy plants dominated every possible space in the loft. A number of birds flitted through the room, squawking at him and retreating to nooks in the columns that supported the high ceilings. It made the room seem open, more like being outside. "So casual's what they like now?"

"It's worth a try," Niall said, his attention still on the screen. With a muttered curse, he tilted to one side and then the other in the chair—as if that would make the on-screen image move. It was hard to believe he could speak more languages than a faery would ever need: give him a toy, and he was hopeless. "Or perhaps try aggressive—*tell* her you're taking her out. Some of them like that."

Tavish returned with one of the green concoctions he was forever insisting Keenan drink. He nodded approvingly. "That sounds more fitting."

"Well, there you have it: sure wisdom on which to try"—Niall paused and shot a grin at Tavish—"casual."

"Indeed." Keenan laughed.

"How is this amusing?" Tavish sat the green protein drink on the table. His lengthy silver braid fell over his shoulder as he moved; he flicked it back with an impatient gesture, a telltale sign that he was agitated. He didn't let his temper slip, though. He never did anymore.

"When's the last time you dated?" Niall asked, still not looking away from the screen.

"The girls are more than adequate company—"

Niall interrupted, "You see? He's rusty."

"I am the Summer King's oldest advisor, and"—Tavish stopped himself, sighing as he realized that he was only underlining Niall's point—"try the boy's advice first, my liege."

And with the impeccable dignity he wore like a comfortable cloak, Tavish retired to the study.

Keenan watched him go with more than a little sadness. "One of these years, he's going to strike you for your belligerence. He *is* still summer fey, Niall."

"Good. He needs to find some passion in his old bones." Niall's humor fled, replaced with the cunning that made him every bit as important as Tavish in advising Keenan these past centuries. "Summer fey are made for strong passions. If he doesn't loosen up, we'll lose him to Sorcha's High Court."

"The search is hard on him. He longs for what the court

was like under my father." Feeling every bit as somber as Tavish, Keenan let his gaze drop to the park across the street.

One of his rowan-men saluted.

Glancing back at Niall, Keenan added, "What it still should be."

"Then woo the girl. Fix it."

Keenan nodded. "A casual approach, you say?"

Niall came to stand beside him at the window, staring down at the already frost-laden branches, more proof that if they didn't stop Beira's ever-growing power, it wouldn't be many more centuries until the summer fey perished. "And show her a exciting night, something different, something unexpected."

"If I don't find her soon . . ."

"You will," Niall assured him, repeating the same words he'd been repeating for almost a millennia.

"I need to. I don't know if"—Keenan drew a steadying breath—"I *will* find her. Maybe this one."

Niall merely smiled.

But Keenan wasn't sure either of them believed it anymore. He wanted to, but it became more difficult each time the game was played out.

When the Winter Queen bound his powers—making him unable to access much of summer's strength, freezing the earth steadily—she'd also begun crushing the hope of many of his fey. He might be stronger than most faeries, but he was far from the king they needed, far from the king his father had been. *Please let Aislinn be the one.*

CHAPTER 13

Everything is capricious about them. . . . Their chief occupations are feasting, fighting, and making love.
—*Fairy and Folk Tales of the Irish Peasantry*
by William Butler Yeats (1888)

After the taxi dropped her at the railroad yard, Aislinn paced outside Seth's door. A few faeries stood nearby, watching her, talking among themselves. They never stayed long so close to the old train cars and lengthy tracks, but others would come and replace them. Since Keenan had first spoken to her at Comix, faeries seemed to gather wherever she went.

"She pays too much attention to the mortal boy," a lanky faery with birdlike limbs grumbled. "The Summer King oughtn't put up with it."

"Times are different," said one of the female faeries. Like the others, she had flowering vines creeping over her skin, but unlike them, she wore a slate-colored suit instead of the sort of girly outfit the others seemed to prefer. Her vines started around her neck and snaked through her ankle-length hair, making her seem somehow both wild and sophisticated.

"She goes into his home every day." The bird-thin faery circled the female faery like a predator. "What's she doing in there?"

"I know what *I'd* be doing," she said. With a sly smile, she reached up and grabbed his face with both hands. "Might as well in case she ends up with Keenan for eternity."

Eternity?

Aislinn turned her back so they didn't see her face. She paced back across the dead grass, close enough to hear the faeries, but not so close that they would find it odd. *With Keenan for* eternity?

The female faery pulled the birdlike one down toward her until they were nose to nose and added, "Doesn't matter what she's been doing, though. She's changing already,"— she licked from the tip of his nose to his eye—"becoming one of our court. Let the girl have her fun with her mortal while she's still able. Soon it won't matter."

Where the hell is Seth? For the fourth time Aislinn pulled out her cell and hit 2 to speed-dial Seth's number.

It rang right behind her.

Stabbing the End button, she turned.

"Relax, Ash." He was walking toward her—holding out the now-silenced cell, strolling obliviously past the faeries.

"Where were you? I was worried that something . . ."

He lifted an eyebrow.

". . . that you forgot," she finished weakly.

I know better.

"Forget you?" He looped an arm around her middle and steered her forward. Opening the door, he motioned for her to go inside. "I'd never forget you."

The birdlike faery skittered over, sniffing Seth and wrinkling his nose.

"Answer your phone next time. Please?" Aislinn poked Seth in the chest. "Where were you?"

He nodded and followed her inside, closing the steel door in the faery's face. "I was talking to Donia."

"What?" Aislinn felt like her throat was closing.

"Not terribly friendly, prettier than I realized, though." Seth smiled, calmly, like he hadn't just told her that he'd been chatting up one of Them. "Not so pretty that I didn't tell her to watch her step. But still, she's almost as pretty as you."

"You did *what*?" Aislinn shoved Seth—gently, but he still winced.

"Talked to her." He put a hand on his chest where she'd touched when she shoved him. He pulled his shirt away and looked. A puzzled expression on his face, he said, "That stung."

"She might seem nice, but she's still one of them. You can't trust them." Aislinn turned to stare at the faeries loitering outside. One of them—the girl in the suit—was sorting a handful of leaves, folding them like origami.

Seth came up behind her and rested his chin on her

head. "How many are out there?"

"Too many." She turned so she was facing him, chest to chest, too close to glare up at him. "You can't do stuff like that. You can't risk—"

"Relax." He caught a length of her hair in his hand, letting it slowly sift through his fingers. "I'm not an idiot, Ash. I didn't say, 'nasty faery, stay away.' I thanked her for her help the other day and mentioned that it would be bad if anything happened to you. That's all."

He stepped back so he could look down at her upturned face. There were dark circles under his eyes. "Trust me, okay? I'm not going to do anything that could put you in more danger."

"Sorry." Feeling guilty for yelling, for doubting, for the shadows under his eyes, she took his hand and squeezed. "Sit down. I'll make tea."

"I made some progress in the research on faery sight and faery defense. Not a lot, but some." He settled into his favorite chair and pulled out a sheaf of papers.

When she didn't answer, he laid the papers in his lap and asked, "Or do you want to tell me what's got you spooked first?"

She shook her head. "No. Not now, at least."

All the talk of faeries, research on faeries, avoiding faeries. *How fair is that to him?* "I thought we could try talking about something else for a while. I don't know. . . ."

He rubbed his eyes. "Okay. Do you want to tell me about school?"

"Umm. Definitely not school if we're trying to avoid discussing faeries." She filled up the teakettle and opened the chamomile tea on the counter. Holding it up, she asked, "Does this taste awful?"

"I don't think so, but there's honey in the bottom cupboard if you want it." He stretched, exposing bare stomach where his shirt lifted, flashing the black ring in his navel. "We could talk about after, when life gets back to normal. I was thinking we should go out to dinner when this is all over."

She'd seen him without a shirt before, seen him in his shorts. They'd been friends for a while. *What did he say? Dinner? Dinner with Seth.* She stood in his kitchen, watching him toy with the ring in his lip. It wasn't quite that he was biting it, but sucking it into his mouth. He did that when he was concentrating. *It isn't sexy. He's not sexy.*

But he was, and she was staring at him like a fool. "Wow," she whispered.

She looked away, feeling stupid. *We're friends. Friends go to dinner too. It doesn't mean anything.* She opened the cupboard. The bottle of honey sat next to an odd assortment of spices and oils. "Dinner, right. Carla wants to go to the new place over on Vine. You could . . ."

"Wow, huh?" His voice was low, husky. His chair creaked as he stood. His footsteps seemed strangely loud as he closed the couple yards between them. Then he was beside her. "I can work with wow."

She turned away, quickly, squeezing the bottle and

squirting honey on the counter. "I didn't mean anything. Too much flirting lately, and that call, and . . . I know you probably have a dozen girls waiting. I'm just tired and . . ."

"Hey." His hand was on her shoulder, trying to turn her to face him. "There's no one else. Just you. No one for the last seven months."

He tugged gently on her shoulder again. "There's no one but you in my life."

She turned, and they stood there. She stared at his shirt; there was a button missing. She clutched the bottle of honey until he pulled it out of her grasp and set it down.

Then he kissed her.

She stretched up on her tiptoes, tilted her head, trying to get even closer. Seth slid a hand around her waist and kissed her like she was the air, and he was suffocating. And she forgot about everything: there were no faeries, no Sight, nothing—just them.

He lifted her onto the counter where she'd sat and talked to him countless times. But this time her hands were in his hair, wrapping her fingers in it, pulling him closer.

It was the most perfect kiss she'd ever had until she realized, *Seth. This is Seth.*

She pulled away.

"Definitely worth the wait," Seth whispered, his arms still around her.

Her legs were on either side of him; her ankles crossed behind him. She rested her forehead on his shoulder.

Neither of them said anything.

Seth doesn't date. This is a mistake. It'd be weird after: she'd been telling herself that for months. It hadn't made her stop thinking traitorous thoughts.

She lifted her head to look at him. "Seven months?"

He cleared his throat. "Yeah. I thought if I was patient . . . I don't know. . . ." He gave her a nervous smile, not at all like himself. "I hoped you might stop running away . . . that after all the talking and time, we . . ."

"I can't, I didn't. . . . I need to deal with this faery thing and . . . Seven months?" She felt awful.

Seth's been waiting for me?

"Seven months." He kissed her nose, like everything was normal, like nothing had changed. Then he gently lifted her off the counter and stepped away. "And I'll keep waiting. I'm not going away, and I'm not letting them take you away."

"I don't know . . . didn't know." She had so many questions: What did he want? What did "waiting" mean? What did she want? None of those were things she could ask.

For the first time that she could think of, she was more comfortable thinking about faeries than anything else. "I need to deal with this—Them—right now, and . . ."

"I know. I don't want you to ignore them, but just don't ignore this, either." He brushed back her hair and let his fingers linger on her cheek. "They've been stealing mortals away for centuries, but they can't have you."

"Maybe it's something else."

"I haven't found anything, *anything* that suggests they go

away once they find a mortal they like." He pulled her into
his arms, tenderly this time. "We're one up since you can
see them, but if this guy really is a king, I don't think he's
going to take 'no' very well."

Aislinn didn't say anything, couldn't say anything. She
just stood there in Seth's arms as he gave voice to her growing fears.

CHAPTER 14

Fairies seem to [be] especially fond of the chase.

—*The Folk-Lore of the Isle of Man* by A. W. Moore (1891)

By the end of the week, Aislinn was sure of two things—being with Seth had become beyond tempting, and avoiding Keenan was utterly impossible. She needed to do something about both situations.

The faery king could navigate the school just fine, but he still trailed her like a particularly devoted stalker. There would be no waiting him out, and her careful attempts at callousness and indifference were proving futile. She could barely stay upright by the end of the day, exhausted by the sheer effort of *not* touching him. She needed a new approach.

Faeries chase. That rule, at least, seemed unchanged. Like the lupine fey that prowled the streets, Keenan was chasing her. She might not be physically running, but it was the same thing. So—even though it terrified her—she decided to stop, let him think he could catch her.

In her childhood that was one of the hardest lessons. Grams used to take her to the park for short trips so she could practice not-running when they sniffed and chased, so she could practice making her sudden stops seem normal, uninfluenced by the faeries chasing her. She hated those lessons. Everything inside screamed *run faster* when they chased, but that was fear, not reason, compelling her. If she stopped running, they lost interest. So she'd stop running from Keenan, once she figured out how to make it seem somehow natural.

She tried a few tentative smiles at Keenan as they walked toward health class.

He responded without hesitation, directing such an intensely happy look at her that she stumbled.

But when he reached out to steady her, she flinched away, and a frustrated frown returned to his face.

She tried again after they left religion class. "So do you have big plans this weekend?"

The expression on his face was an odd one, somewhere between amused and surprised.

"I'd hoped to, but"—he stared at her until she felt that familiar panic and compulsion rise up—"I've been doubting that I'd have much luck."

Don't run.

Her chest hurt too much for her to offer an answer, so she just nodded and said, "Oh."

Silent then, he looked away, but he was smiling and quiet now. He waded through the crowd without another word. He still stayed too close, but the silence was a nice change. The lack of tempting warmth was incredible, like some odd calm radiated from him.

When they walked into Government, he was still smiling. "Can I join you at lunch?"

She paused. "You have every other day."

He laughed, a sound as musical as the chiming song of the lupine fey when they ran. "Yes. But you resented it every other day."

"What makes you think I won't resent it today?"

"Hope. It's what I live on. . . ."

She bit her lip, considering: he was too easily encouraged by a few friendly remarks, but when he wasn't trying so hard she seemed able to breathe around him, felt less overwhelmed by odd compulsions.

Tentatively she said, "I still don't like you."

"Maybe you'll change your mind if you spend more time with me." He reached out like he'd touch her cheek.

She didn't flinch, but she tensed.

Neither of them moved.

"I'm not a bad person, Aislinn. I just . . ." He stopped and shook his head.

She knew she was walking on precarious ground, but it was the closest to honest he'd sounded and the closest to peace she'd felt since he'd started attending Bishop O.C.

She prompted, "What?"

"I just want to get to know you. Is that so strange?"

"Why? Why me?" Her heart sped as she waited for him

to respond, as if he'd answer the real question. "Why not someone else?"

He stepped closer, watching her predatorily, his mood shifting rapidly once more. "Honestly? I don't know. There's something about you. From the first time I saw you, I just knew."

He took her hand.

She actually let him. *Play along.* It wasn't just playing, though: she'd been resisting the need to reach out to him since they first met. It wasn't logical, but it was definitely there.

At his touch, her Sight sharpened. It appeared as if the faeries around them had all donned human glamours simultaneously.

No one in the classroom reacted; no one screamed. Obviously, the faeries hadn't suddenly become visible.

What happened? She trembled.

Keenan was staring at her, too intently for comfort. "I don't know why certain people shine for others. I don't know why you and not someone else." He gently pulled her forward and whispered, "But it's you I think of when I wake each morning. It's your face in my dreams."

Aislinn swallowed. *That would seem odd even if he were normal.* And he wasn't. What he was—unfortunately—was completely serious.

She shivered. "I don't know."

Keenan stroked her hand with his thumb. "Give me a chance. Let's start over."

Aislinn froze. Years of Grams' warnings tumbled through her mind, a symphony of wisdom and worry. She heard her own voice telling Seth that the way things were done wasn't working. *Try something new.* She nodded. "Start over. Sure."

And he smiled at her, truly smiled—wicked and lovely and so tempting that the stories of faery kidnapping came crashing into her mind. *Kidnapping? Following by choice is more like it.* She all but collapsed into her chair. *He's a faery. Faeries are bad. But if I can find out what they want . . .*

Class was half over before she realized she hadn't heard a word of the lecture or—she glanced at the notebook she didn't remember opening—written any of it down.

Afterward, still in a daze, she walked beside Keenan to her locker.

He was talking, asking her something, ". . . carnival? I could pick you up or meet you. Your choice."

"Sure." She blinked, feeling like she was sleepwalking in someone else's dream. "What?"

The faery guards exchanged knowing looks.

"There's a carnival tonight." He held out a hand for her books.

Stupidly she started to hand them to him, but stopped herself. "What about your big plans?"

"Just say yes." He waited expectantly.

Finally she nodded. "As friends."

He stepped back as she closed her locker. "Of course. Friends."

Rianne, Leslie, and Carla came over then.

"Well?" Rianne prompted. "Did she say yes?"

"She shot him down, didn't you, Ash?" Leslie patted Keenan's arm consolingly. "Don't worry. She turns everyone down."

"Not everyone." Keenan looked entirely too pleased with himself. "We're going to the carnival."

"What?" Aislinn looked from Rianne to Keenan. *They knew?*

"Pay up." Rianne held a hand out to Leslie, who grudgingly pulled a crumpled bill out of her pocket, and then turned to Carla. "You too."

"Pay up?" Aislinn echoed, following them toward the cafeteria.

Behind her, she heard several guards laughing.

"I told them he'd be able to get you to go out." Rianne folded her winnings and tucked the bills into her blazer pocket. "Look at him."

"He's right here, Ri," Carla murmured, shooting Keenan an apologetic look. "We've tried to teach her manners, but . . ." She shrugged. "It's like housebreaking a dog. If we'd had her when she was still a puppy, maybe."

Rianne smacked her on the arm, but she was grinning. "Woof, woof."

Turning to Aislinn, Carla lowered her voice. "When we saw you two talking, she wouldn't let us come over until she was sure he had asked you. She actually grabbed Leslie."

"It's not a date," Aislinn muttered.

"Right. We're just going to talk, get to know each other," Keenan agreed. He paused, looking at each of them, glowing just a little as he did it. "In fact, you can join us if you want. Meet some of my old friends."

Aislinn's heart sped. "No."

"Sounds like a date to me. Don't worry. I'm not coming on your date, Ash." Rianne sighed, like something wonderful had just happened, and turned to Carla. "What do you think?"

Carla nodded. "Definitely a date."

"Aislinn is accompanying me as a friend," Keenan said with a contented look. "I'm simply honored that she's joining me at all."

Aislinn looked at him, at her friends who were staring at him adoringly.

He caught her gaze and smiled.

She didn't speed up as he kept pace with her. Now that Keenan seemed pleased, the compulsion she'd been feeling had faded to barely a whisper.

I can handle this.

But as he pulled out her chair with an unusual courtly gesture, she saw her reflection in his eyes, surrounded by a tiny halo of sun.

I hope.

CHAPTER 15

They live much longer than we; yet die at last, or [at] least vanish from that State.

—*The Secret Commonwealth* by Robert Kirk
and Andrew Lang (1893)

When Donia returned home from her evening walk, Beira was waiting on the porch, reclining in a chair fashioned of ice.

Almost idly the Winter Queen sculpted screaming faces on a sheet of ice beside her. It looked like the faeries in the sculpture were trapped alive, writhing and shrieking.

"Donia, darling," Beira gushed, coming to her feet with such grace that it looked like she'd been pulled upright with invisible strings. "I was beginning to wonder if I should send Agatha after you."

The hag in question grinned, exposing gaps where a number of her teeth should've been.

"Beira. How very . . ." Donia couldn't find a word that wouldn't be a lie. *Unexpected? Pleasant? No, neither of those.*

"What can I do for you?"

"Such a good question, that one." Beira tapped her chin with one finger.

"Now, if only my son had the good manners to ask that"—Beira frowned petulantly—"but he doesn't."

Across the yard, at the edge of the trees, several guards saluted. The rowan-man waved.

"Do you know what that boy did?"

Donia didn't answer; it wasn't really a question. *Just like Keenan.* It'd be a relief not to be stuck between them.

"He went to the girl's school. Enrolled there, like a mortal. Can you imagine?" Beira began pacing, the staccato rhythm of her steps cracking like falling sleet on the battered porch. "He's spent the week with her, trailing behind her like that dog of yours."

"Wolf. Sasha is a wolf."

"Wolf, dog, coyote, whatever. The point"—Beira paused, standing so still she could've been carved of ice— "the point, Donia, is that he's found an *in.* Do you understand what that means? He is making progress; you are not. You're failing me."

Agatha cackled.

Beira turned, slowly, deliberately. She crooked a finger. "Come here."

Not yet realizing her error, Agatha stepped onto the porch with her grin still in place.

"Is it amusing then that my son could win? That he could undo everything I've built?" Beira put one finger under Agatha's chin, her long manicured fingernail cutting into the hag's skin. A line of blood trickled down her throat. "I don't find it the least bit funny, Aggie dear."

"'S not what I meant, my Queen." Agatha's eyes widened. She glanced at Donia, imploring.

"Aggie, Aggie, Aggie"—Beira *tsk-tsk*ed—"Donia won't help you. She *couldn't* even if she wanted to."

Donia looked away, staring instead at the ever-present rowan-man. He shuddered in sympathy. They'd all seen Beira's temper before, but it was still awful.

Holding the hag tightly in her embrace now, Beira put her lips to Agatha's withered mouth and blew.

All the while Agatha tried to escape, her hands pushed against Beira's shoulder, clutched at the Winter Queen's wrists. Sometimes the Winter Queen relented; sometimes she did not.

Today she did not.

Agatha fought, but it was futile: only another monarch could stand against Beira.

"Well then," Beira murmured as Agatha's body slumped forward, limp in Beira's embrace.

Agatha's spirit—a shade now—stood beside them, wringing her hands, weeping soundlessly.

Beira licked her lips. "I feel better."

She dropped Agatha's body to the ground.

Agatha's shade knelt beside her now lifeless body. Ice crystals fell from the corpse's open mouth, trailed down her sunken cheeks.

"Go on, now." Beira shooed the soundlessly weeping shade with a gesture, like she'd brush off an insect. Then she turned to Donia. "Work faster, girl. My tolerance wears thin."

Without waiting for an answer, Beira walked away—the shade of Agatha trailing behind her—leaving Donia to deal with the corpse on the porch.

Donia stared at Agatha—*at the body that used to be Agatha.* The ice had melted, leaving a puddle soaking the hag's hair.

That could be me. It will *be me someday if I fail Beira. . . .*

"May I help?" the rowan-man stood close enough that she should've known he was there long before he spoke.

She glanced up at him. His gray-brown skin and dark-green leafy hair made him almost a shadow in the dark. If it weren't for his bright red eyes, he'd almost blend into the growing evening.

Evening? How long have I been standing here? She sighed.

He gestured to the other guards who waited back at the tree line. "We could take her with us. The soil is moist; her shell would fade quickly in the loam."

Donia swallowed the sickness that threatened to rise.

"Does Keenan know yet?" she whispered, embarrassed that she still worried over how he felt.

"Skelley already went to tell him."

Donia nodded.

Skelley? Which one is he? She tried to focus, think about

the guardsmen. *Better that than thinking about Agatha.*

Skelley, he was one of the court guards, thin, like the Scrimshaw Sisters, gentle. He'd wept when she'd frozen the guards before. Still he stayed, taking his turns guarding her, doing as Keenan ordered.

"Do you need extra guards?" The rowan-man did not wince when he offered, although she knew he remembered the temper tantrums she'd thrown when such a thing was offered in the past. "We could at least come closer."

Frozen tears rolled down her face and landed in the puddle on the porch. *I don't weep for her. Would he still offer such kindness if he knew that—that even now with Agatha at my feet, I weep for myself?*

She looked away, to where the other guards stood, waiting, ready to protect her even though she'd never shown them a single reason to do so. *Of course they would. Keenan wills it.*

"Donia?"

She looked up. "That's the first time you've said my name."

With another soft rustling sound, he stepped onto the porch. "Let us take her away."

Still watching him, Donia nodded.

He motioned to the others, and in barely a moment they'd taken the body away, leaving only a giant wet spot where Agatha had lain.

Closing her eyes as if that would shut out the images, Donia drew several deep breaths.

"Shall I stay closer?" the rowan-man whispered. "Just one guard nearer to you. If she returns . . ."

Eyes still closed, she asked, "What do they call you?"

"Evan."

"Evan," she murmured. "She's going to kill me, Evan, but not tonight. Later. If I let the new girl take up the staff, she'll kill me. I'll join Agatha." She opened her eyes and held his gaze. "I'm afraid."

"Donia, please . . ."

"No." She turned away. "She won't be back tonight."

"Only one extra guard?" He held an arm as if he'd pull her into an embrace. "If you were harmed . . ."

"Keenan would get over it. He has a new girl. She'll give in. We all do." She folded her arms over her chest and turned to go back inside. Back still turned, she added softly, "Let me think. Tomorrow I'll figure the rest out."

Then she went inside and closed the door, calling to Sasha, burying her face in his soft fur and trying to breathe.

Keenan was in great spirits when he got home. The guards had already filled in Niall and Tavish, so he wasn't surprised to see them smiling when he walked in the door.

"Almost record time," Tavish nodded approvingly, holding out a glass of summer wine. "I told you: nothing to worry over. Mortals are like that, especially these days. Get her in line, get back to business."

"Get her in line?" Niall laughed and poured himself a

glass too. "I'd love to see you say that to a mortal girl."

Tavish scowled and carried the decanter into the living room. Several cockatiels perched on a long tree branch that spanned the left side of the room. "I've spent centuries with the Summer Girls. They were mortals, and they're not that complex."

Niall turned to Tavish and said, slowly, as if the older faery were a very, very young child, "Once they're Summer Girls, their inhibitions are gone. Remember Eliza when she was a mortal? Not the least bit affectionate." He took a long drink and sighed. "Now she's much more receptive."

"Aislinn's different," Keenan interrupted, feeling immeasurably angry over the idea that his Aislinn could be like Eliza, could join the Summer Girls, could warm other faeries' beds. "I can feel it. She could be the one."

Tavish and Niall exchanged a look. They'd heard the selfsame words before, and he knew it.

She could be, though. She could be the one.

He dropped onto the sofa and closed his eyes. *I hate this, how damnably important these games are.* "I'm going to go grab a shower. Clear my head."

"Relax." With a solemn expression, Tavish topped off his glass and handed it to him. "She might be the one. One of them has to be. Sooner or later."

"Right." Keenan took the glass of wine. *If not, I'll spend eternity doing this.* "Send a couple of the girls. I could use some help relaxing."

A couple hours later Keenan looked at the clock for the third time in the past half hour. *Two more hours.* This was the first time his people would see them together, the first chance they had to see him speak with the girl who might be the Summer Queen, the girl who might change everything. No matter that there'd been others. It was always the same: that precious bubble of hope that *this one* would be his queen.

Niall leaned against the wall in the doorway to the bedroom. "Keenan?"

Keenan held up a pair of gray trousers. *Too formal.* He rummaged in his closet. *Jeans. Black ones. She'd like that.* It was quicker if he simply became what they wanted, made a few changes to act like what they found appealing. "I need black jeans, not new looking, but not too faded."

"Right." Niall passed the message on to one of the Summer Girls. When she left, he came farther into the room. "Keenan?"

"What?" Keenan found a T-shirt he didn't remember owning. He pulled out a dark blue shirt, silk from the desert spiders, much nicer. He could only change so much.

"The mortal boy that Aislinn . . ."

"He'll be gone soon." Keenan slipped off his shirt and put on the new one. Then he looked through the jewelry the girls had brought over earlier. It was nice to have a gift handy if things went well. Mortal or fey, they liked that sort of thing.

"I'm sure he will, but in the meantime . . ."

The tiny heart seemed nice. *Too personal, too soon?* The sunburst was a nice choice. He set it aside while he looked through the others. "After tonight he'll be busy elsewhere."

"Why?"

"I asked the girls to find someone to distract him. He's in the way." He picked up the gold sunburst. *Later, it'll mean more to her if she's the one.* He slipped it into his pocket. *The sunburst it is.*

CHAPTER 16

They transgress and commit Acts of Injustice, and Sin. . . .
For the Inconvenience of their Succubi, who tryst with Men,
it is abominable.

—*The Secret Commonwealth* by Robert Kirk
and Andrew Lang (1893)

Seth stirred the pasta absently. He glanced at her. "You want
to tell me what you're thinking?"

He didn't say anything else, just waited, quietly and
patiently. Since their kiss—and the conversation afterward—
he'd been as good as his word, waiting for her to make the
next move.

She went over and watched him, trying to figure out
how to tell him about the carnival. She'd tried to start that
sentence several times since she'd arrived. It hadn't worked.
This time she just blurted out, "I'm meeting Keenan
tonight."

Seth didn't look away from the boiling water as he asked,

"You're going out with the faery king? The guy who's stalking you?"

"It's not a date." She was close enough to touch him, but she didn't. "He asked me to go to a carnival. . . ."

He did look at her then. "He's dangerous."

She took the spoon out of his hand and pulled his arm gently so he turned toward her. "If I don't figure out what he wants, Grams is going to take away the little bit of freedom I still have. I need to figure out a way to make him leave me alone."

Seth had that same strange panicked look he'd had after he heard about the guys—*the human guys*—outside the library. He nodded, slowly, like he was thinking, processing what she was saying.

She kept talking. "Maybe there's something I can do or say . . . or overhear." She leaned against him, needing his comfort, his support. She was afraid, but she couldn't just sit around waiting for someone to save her. She had to try to save herself, try to figure it out.

He didn't say anything.

So she said softly, "Do you have a better idea?"

"No."

He sighed and pulled her close, holding her tightly. "His timing sucks."

She laughed—because it was either that or weep. "You think?"

The pasta started boiling over behind them, hissing and spattering. She picked up the wooden spoon and stirred.

He stood behind her, his hands resting on her hips. "After dinner I wanted to check out some of the ointments in those recipes, so I can see them too."

"Okay." She looked over her shoulder at him.

He dropped a quick kiss on her cheek. It was sweet, tender.

His next remark, however, was anything but sweet. "You need to move out of the way."

"What?"

He nudged her to the side. "No wonder you eat all that yogurt. Your cooking skills"—he sighed—"pitiful."

She laughed for real then, grateful that he was teasing, grateful that he wasn't letting her admission spoil what was left of their evening. She smacked his arm lightly. "I can stir pasta. It's not a special skill."

"Half of it will be stuck to the pan if you keep trying to do it. Come on. Out of the way."

Still smiling, she moved to the side and opened the minifridge. A six-pack of some microbrew sat there—no cheap drinks for him. *Only Seth.* He didn't share his beer, though. Any drinking done at his place was strictly BYOB. *Doesn't hurt to ask.* She pulled one out. "Can I?"

"You don't drink well, Ash." He frowned. "Thought you'd want a clear head."

She stopped herself before she told him how afraid she was. Instead she closed the fridge, still holding the bottle. "Split it with me?"

With another disapproving look, he handed her a plate

of already sliced bread. "So where is this carnival?"

"Down at the river." She set the plate on the table and held out the bottle to him.

"You could cancel—postpone even, at least until we know more." He twisted the cap off, took a drink, and handed it back. "Do you know how many stories there are of them stealing people? Hundreds of years, Ash, people being gone hundreds of years."

"I know." She took a drink, looked at him, and took another.

Seth took the bottle out of her hand and pointed at the bread. "Eat something, then we'll try some of those recipes."

He glanced at the clock as he started rinsing the pasta. "I need to be able to see them so I can find you if something does go wrong."

After dinner Aislinn called to check in with Grams. She assured Grams she was in a safe place. "I'm with Seth. I'll be here for a while. . . ."

She didn't tell Grams that she wasn't staying at Seth's. She felt guilty for it, but Grams already worried too much. After murmuring a few more assurances—and feeling guiltier—she hung up.

I wish I could just stay here. Careful not to bump Boomer, she stretched out on the sofa and closed her eyes for a minute.

Seth leaned down and kissed her forehead. He did that

a lot lately, little touches, careful signs of affection—
reminding her that he cared. Of course, he still flirted until
the tension was exhilarating.

And real, not some faery trick. Seth is real. She hadn't
asked *what* he wanted, didn't know how, but she was almost
positive he wasn't looking for a fling.

She opened her eyes. For a moment it almost looked like
her skin was glowing.

I'm just tired. She blinked.

He sat on the other end of the sofa, putting her feet on
his lap. Then he held out a stack of recipes. "I've got three
teas, a couple salves, a few tinctures, and one poultice.
What do you think?"

She sat up and scooted closer. "A poultice?"

His hand tangled in her hair, lifting a long strand out
and twisting it around his fingers. "Something you put on
an injury, like putting steak on a black eye."

"Umm, yuck." She took the papers, scanned them.

Seth's playing with my hair. His fingertips brushed against
her collarbone, and she realized she was holding her breath.
Breathe.

She let her breath out slowly and tried to focus on the
words on the page. Everything felt somehow more important when she thought about where she was going that
night and with whom.

She held out the paper she'd been trying to read. "This
one has to sit for three days."

"A few are like that." He took that page with his free

hand, the one that wasn't tracing circles on her skin. "The tinctures are to 'steep' for seven to ten days. I'll start a couple later tonight when you're out. I just wondered if any of them seemed, I don't know, familiar?"

She dropped the other pages on the stack in his lap. "I was born like this. Grams, my mom, that's just what happens in my family—something in the genes. Like being short or whatever."

"Right." He wasn't looking at the papers, but at her hand, which was still resting on his leg. Abruptly he stood up and walked away. "Let's try a salve. They seem quicker."

She followed him to the counter, where he had spread out the herbs, some bowls, a knife, and a piece of white pottery with a matching stick. She picked it up.

"Pestle."

She looked at him. "What?"

"It's a pestle. Here." He put some of the herbs into the white bowl and held out his hand.

She gave him the pestle, noticing how much distance he was suddenly giving her.

He used it to grind the herbs, crushing them into tiny pieces. "Like this."

Then he handed it back.

"Saint-John's-wort. Pulverize it and dump it here." He pointed at an empty cereal bowl.

"Right." She started crushing the strange-smelling plants.

Beside her, Seth filled a pan half full of water and set it

on a burner. He got out two more pans and sat them on the counter.

"So about the other day, about us . . ." She glanced at him, more anxious than she expected. She needed to be sure what it really meant to him, but she was afraid he'd be hurt when she asked.

His tone wasn't insulted, though. Instead he sounded nervous too. "Yeah?"

"Are you, I don't know, going to ask me out or something? Or is it just casual, wanting to . . ."

"Just tell me what you want." He took the bowl out of her hand and pulled her up against him, hip to hip. "Dinner? Movie? A weekend at the beach?"

"A weekend? Aren't you moving a bit fast?" She put her hands on his chest, keeping a little distance between them.

"Not as fast as I want to." He bent down so his mouth was almost touching hers. "But I'm trying to wait."

She didn't even think about it; she nipped his bottom lip.

And they were kissing again, slow and soft and somehow more maddening than the first time. Somewhere between telling him she was meeting Keenan and asking him where they stood, the stakes had shifted.

Her hands found the bottom of his shirt, slid under it, over skin and the rings that decorated his chest. Any objections she used to remember had melted.

I found the uncrossable line. She almost giggled at the thought.

"Seth? You in there?" The doorknob jiggled.

"Seth, we know you're in there," Mitchell, one of Leslie's exes, yelled. He knocked again, loudly. "Come on, open up."

"Ignore him," Seth whispered, his lips against her ear. "Maybe he'll go away."

The doorknob jiggled again.

"It's probably a good thing." Aislinn pulled back further, feeling almost lightheaded. "We're not thinking very clearly."

"I've done nothing but think about this for months, Ash"—Seth put a hand on either side of her face—"but just say the word and we stop. You set the pace. I won't push you. Ever."

"I know that." She blushed. It was a lot easier to give in to the temptation than it was to talk about it—surprisingly easy. "I'm not sure how far that is, though."

He hugged her closer and stroked his hand down her hair. "So we take it slow. Right?"

"Right." She nodded, feeling both relieved and disappointed. There were too many diseases out there to be casual, but just letting go of control, of logic, of what she should and shouldn't do . . . *Tempting* was an understatement.

His voice was low and steady as he said, "And yes, dating. There's nothing casual about what I want."

She didn't say anything, couldn't.

From outside Jimmy yelled, "Open the damn door, Seth. It's freezing out here."

Seth titled her head up so she was looking at him and said, "You're worrying me here. We good?"

She nodded.

"You thinking about running again?"

Her heart thumped too fast. She blushed. "No. I'm thinking the exact opposite."

He ran his fingertips over her cheek—pausing at the corner of her mouth—and stared at her. "No pressure."

Finally she leaned her face on his chest, hiding her expression. "I need to think. If we're going to try this . . . *us* together. I don't want to mess it up, mess *us* up."

"It wouldn't, but"—he swallowed audibly before adding—"we don't need to rush. I'm not going anywhere."

The knocking grew louder again until finally Seth let go of her. He straightened his clothes, turning his back to her to do so. Then he went to the door and yanked it open. "What?"

"Christ, man, it's cold out there." Mitchell pushed past Seth.

Jimmy, another one of the guys who had graduated last year, came in behind him. With him were three girls Aislinn didn't know.

Aislinn went back to the counter and resumed crushing herbs. Jimmy stopped just inside the door and looked over at her with a wide grin. "Well, hello, Ash."

She lifted the bowl in greeting, but she didn't say anything. Her lips were tender; her hair felt like it was a mess. It had to be obvious they'd interrupted something.

Keeping her attention on the salve was easier than dealing with them. She poured the powdered herbs into an empty bowl, added more, and kept grinding them.

Jimmy nudged Seth. "What happened to the 'only friends in the house' rule?"

"Ash is a friend." Seth narrowed his eyes at Jimmy and added, "The only one who has an open door here."

Still grinning, Jimmy came over and looked at the bowl Aislinn clutched. "Well, this is interesting. What you got?" He picked up the bowl of already pulverized Saint-John's-wort and sniffed. "Nothing I've smoked."

He was a loudmouth; Mitchell was even worse, especially since Leslie had told everyone who'd listen that he was a lousy lay. He set a six-pack of beer on the counter.

The girls were over by Boomer, staring at the boa, but not getting too close. All three were dressed in clothes that meant they would be freezing outside—tight skirts, cleavage-baring shirts—the sort of thing that'd be uncomfortable even if it weren't autumn. *Three?* She looked over at them, looked at Jimmy, who was making himself at home, picking at the leftover pasta.

"Thought I asked everyone to let me have a few days to myself." Seth poured the first bowl of crushed herbs into the boiling water and set a timer. "Ash, can you grab the olive oil when you finish those?"

She nodded.

"Time to yourself, huh?" Mitchell grinned. "You don't look like you're by yourself."

"We were." Seth raised his eyebrow and inclined his head toward the door. "We still could be."

"Nope." Mitchell popped the top on a can.

Seth took several deep breaths. "If you're going to be here for a while, turn on some tunes."

"Actually, we thought you might want to go out," the girl who'd been clinging to Jimmy said.

One of the other girls—the one watching Seth—moved to the side, just a little, and Aislinn caught a glimpse of tiny horns poking through her hair, of leathery wings curled behind her.

How did she *walk in here? Looking like that?* Only the strongest of the fey could be surrounded by this much steel and hold on to a glamour. That was one of the rules that had given Aislinn the most comfort over the years.

The winged girl moved toward Seth slowly, like each step took a lot of concentration. "We can't really stay long. Come with us? There's supposed to be a good band down at the Crow's Nest." She offered Aislinn a catty smile. "I'd invite you, too, but they're being strict about the age thing after the raid. Eighteen only, you know?"

Slowly Aislinn set the bowl down and went over to stand in front of Seth, between him and the faery. "Seth isn't available."

Seth put his hands on her hips, touching her but not restraining her.

Glaring at the faery, Aislinn leaned back against Seth. *How dare she come here? Who sent her?* The idea of Seth being vulnerable to them made her almost violently angry.

"Well, this is fun," Mitchell said.

Nodding, Jimmy sat down with the pan of half-cold pasta and a fork. "My money's on Ash."

The faery kept coming toward the kitchen.

Aislinn put her arm out in front of the faery. "I think you need to leave."

"Really?" She wrinkled her nose.

"Yes." Aislinn put a hand on the faery's wrist, not gripping it, but resting her fingers there. Just like at school, contact with the faery made Aislinn's Sight clearer.

Aislinn pushed, gently.

The faery winced and stumbled. Her eyebrows shot up as she gave Aislinn a strange look.

Recovering quickly, the faery murmured, "Another night, then."

"No." Seth slid his arms around Aislinn's waist. "I'm exactly where I want to be."

Jimmy and Mitchell exchanged another goofy grin.

"Man, you need to share your secrets." Mitchell got up and picked up his beer. At a quick glance in his date's direction, she came over to stand next to him.

Mitchell continued, "Not like you ever have trouble getting—" He cleared his throat, and his date smacked him on the arm. He grinned.

"All I'm saying is whatever he's doing"—he inclined his head toward the back of the train where Seth's bedroom was—"must work. Ash hardly ever even speaks. He's got her ready to start a fight over him."

The faery hadn't moved. She trailed her fingertips down

her cleavage, slowly. "You'd have fun. More than you'll get here."

Aislinn stepped away from Seth. She wrapped her fingers around the girl's wrist and walked over to the door, tugging the faery behind her. For such a strong faery, she was unbelievably easy to drag along. *Maybe she's weak from all the steel.*

"Go." Aislinn opened the door and shoved the faery forward. "Stay out."

The faeries outside were all watching. Several giggled gleefully.

The vine-girl in the suit was there again. She looked up from her newest menagerie of origami animals—which were now walking around as if they were alive. "Told you, Cerise," she said, and went back to folding more leaves. "That sort of approach doesn't work if they're already in love."

Aislinn let go of the encroaching faery. "Stay away from him."

"For the night"—the faery looked back inside, her wings opening and closing behind her, slowly, like a butterfly at rest—"but really, I think he could do so much better."

Freaking faeries. Aislinn opened her mouth to say something else.

"Not interested," Seth called from behind her.

"Bitch," said one of the girls to Aislinn as she left. She stomped out like she had a right to be offended. "You didn't need to grab her like that. She was just flirting."

The other said, "Guys don't like pushy girls. They like ladies."

At the door Jimmy paused and deadpanned, "Yeah. It's really not a total turn-on." Then he cracked up. "You get tired of Seth . . ."

Mitchell shoved him. "Shut up."

Invisible to everyone but her and the faeries, several of the ever-changing group of fey things outside scurried off.

Aislinn shut the door and leaned against it.

Seth was already back at the nasty-smelling concoction, stirring it. "Since you don't seem the jealous sort, I'm guessing she was a faery."

"Wings and all." She went over, pulled him down to her, and kissed him. "But I might be a bit more the jealous sort than I realized."

He grinned. "Works for me."

He put down the spoon and followed her over to the counter. "Thought they didn't like steel."

"They don't. That's why she was trying to get you to go out. She was strong enough to come in, but not strong enough to stay long. She couldn't even hold her glamour very well." She picked up another handful of herbs to crush. "Do me a favor?"

"Always."

"Stay home tonight." She picked out a few thicker stems. She glanced back at the door, a suddenly thin barrier against the growing number of faeries outside.

"I could ask you the same," he murmured. He held her tightly.

She closed her eyes and leaned her cheek on his chest. "If

I don't get answers soon, Grams is going to pull me out of school. I can't stall her much longer, and I don't want to lie to her and say they've gone away."

"I could come with you. . . ."

"He's not going to talk to me if I bring you along. I need him to think I'm believing him." She stretched up so she could kiss him, and then added, "If this doesn't work, we'll try something else."

He looked worried, afraid—things she didn't want to see, didn't want him to feel—but finally he nodded. "Be safe, okay?"

"I'll do my best. . . ."

Because if she didn't, everything would be taken away—school, friends, Seth, everything. Keenan needed to let something slip. The faeries needed to say something that could help her figure out how to get rid of him. They simply *had* to.

CHAPTER 17

Once they take you and you taste the food . . . you cannot come back. You are changed . . . and live with them for ever.
—*The Fairy Faith in Celtic Countries*
by W. Y. Evans-Wentz (1911)

A half hour later Aislinn walked down Sixth Street, feeling more apprehensive with each step. Thinking about the faery coming into Seth's home didn't make matters any better. *What if I hadn't been there? Would they hurt him?* She hadn't wanted to leave Seth, or meet Keenan, or deal with the whole debacle, but she needed answers. Keenan had them.

He stood outside the entrance to the carnival, looking so normal that it was hard to remember that he was one of them, and not just court fey but a king. He reached out as if he'd embrace her. "Aislinn."

She stepped backward, easily dodging him.

"I'm so glad you came." Keenan looked terribly serious.

At a loss for what to say, she shrugged.

"Shall we?" He held out his arm, like they were at a formal dance or something.

"Sure." She ignored his arm—and his brief frown—as she followed him toward the maze of booths that had seemingly sprung up overnight.

People milled around, an impossibly large crowd. Families and couples played games on every side. Many of them had sweet-smelling drinks—some sort of golden slushy thing.

"You're just so"—he stared at her, smiling that inhuman smile—"I'm just so honored that you joined me."

Aislinn nodded, like he made sense. He didn't. *This is ridiculous.* His too-eager comments made her feel increasingly uncomfortable.

Beside her, a group of girls tried to throw tiny plastic balls onto glass platters. Overhead the lights of the Ferris wheel sparkled. People laughed and cuddled close to one another as they walked by.

Then Keenan took her hand, and suddenly her Sight was so clear that she gasped. Everywhere she looked, glamours faded. The workers running the booths, the concessions, the rides . . . *They're all fey.* All the carnies and quite a few of the guests were faeries. *Oh my God.* She'd never seen such a large crowd of faeries before.

Everywhere she looked, disguised faeries smiled back at her, friendly and happy.

Why are so many faeries wearing human faces?

Some real humans milled about, playing rigged games

and riding rickety rides, but the faeries didn't stare at them. She was the one they all watched.

Keenan waved to a group of faeries who had called out to him. "Old friends. Do you want to meet them?"

"No." She bit down on her lip and looked around again, feeling her chest tighten.

He frowned.

"Not right now." She forced a smile, hoping he'd think her nervousness was just shyness.

Control. She took a deep breath and tried to sound friendly. "I thought we were going to get to know each other."

"Right." He smiled like she'd given him some rare and precious gift. "What can I tell you?"

"Umm, what about your family?" Aislinn stumbled, feet as unsteady as her breathing.

"I live with my uncles," he said as he led her forward, past a group of faeries that—until a moment ago—looked like they could go to Bishop O.C.

Several gestured toward her, but no one approached. In fact, the others moved out of Keenan's path as he led her toward a row of booths where the now-revealed faeries ran carnival games.

"Your uncles?" she repeated, feeling increasingly doubtful that coming was a wise idea. She pulled her hand free. "Right, the guys who were at school."

Faeries. Just like almost everyone here. She felt dizzy.

She tried again. "What about your parents?"

"My father died before I was born"—he paused, looking

not sad, but angry—"but everything I am is his gift."

Did faeries die? She wasn't at all sure how to respond to his odd comment, so she simply said, "My mom is gone too. Childbirth."

"I'm sorry." He took her hand again, squeezed it affectionately, and intertwined his fingers with hers. "I'm sure she was a good woman. And she must've been lovely to be your mother."

"I'm not much like her." Aislinn swallowed hard. All she had was pictures. In the pictures Grams had around the house, her mother always looked haunted, like she couldn't quite handle the things she could see. Grams never spoke of her mother's last year, as if it hadn't existed.

"What about your father? Is he a good man?" He stopped, holding her hand while they stood there, surrounded by faeries, talking about their families.

If she hadn't been able to see the oddly shaped eyes and strange smiles on the faeries who listened, it might seem so very normal. It wasn't.

She started to walk away, going toward one of the concession stands where they were selling those sweet-smelling drinks.

"Aislinn?"

She shrugged, more comfortable talking about a father she knew nothing of than the mother who'd given her the Sight. "Who knows? Grams doesn't know who he is, and Mom's not here to tell us."

"At least you have your grandmother." He reached up

with his free hand and stroked her cheek. "I'm glad you
have had that, a loving caretaker."

She started to answer, but headed toward them were
Pointy-Face and about six of the other faeries who liked to
linger at Shooters, harassing the regulars, chasing her away
from the pool hall with their very presence. She froze,
unable to move, years of instinct overriding logic.

"Aislinn? What's wrong?" He moved in front of her,
blocking her view of everyone and everything but him.
"Have I offended you?"

"No. I'm just"—she offered him what she hoped was a
convincing smile and lied—"chilly."

He shrugged off his jacket and draped it over her shoulders, gently. "How's that?"

"Better." And it was. If he were what he pretended to
be—kind and considerate—she might've felt bad that she
was here on false pretenses.

But he wasn't. He wasn't real at all.

"Come on. Let's walk. There's always some interesting
games here." He took her hand again, bringing her Sight
back in full force.

Beside them, a woman stood in a child's wading pool
calling, "Three darts for a prize."

A thick braid dangled like a rope past her knees. Her
face was like one of those angels in old paintings, innocent
with a spark of danger in her eyes. Aside from the goats' legs
that peeked out of her long skirt, she was gorgeous, but no
one approached her.

At the next tent a steady line of faeries and humans waited. Faces Aislinn had glimpsed around the city mingled with faeries she could never have imagined—wings and thorn-crusted skin and all manners of dress. It was too much to process.

Aislinn paused, overwhelmed by the sheer number and variety of faeries around her.

"The fortune-tellers here always put on a good show." Keenan pulled the flap of the tent back farther so she could look inside. There were three women with rheumy white eyes. Behind them stood a row of statues—like gargoyles without wings. They were freakishly muscular. *And alive.* Their gazes flitted around the tent, as if they were trying to find someone to answer unspoken questions.

The faeries all stepped aside, and Keenan led her to the front of the tent.

She stepped closer to one of the statues. It looked wide-eyed, almost afraid as she reached out her hand.

One of the women reached out and snatched Aislinn's still uplifted hand. "No."

The women spoke all at once, not to her or to Keenan, but softly—as if to themselves—in a sibilant whisper. "He's ours. Fair exchange. Not yours to interfere."

The one gripping her hand winked at Aislinn. "Well, then, sisters? What say we?"

Aislinn tugged backward; the woman held tight.

"So you're the young one's"—the fortune-teller looked at Keenan with her seemingly blind eyes—"new ladylove."

Behind them, faeries pushed closer, scuffling and chattering.

The old woman gave Keenan a searing look—her white eyes shining—and said, "She's different than the others, dear. Special."

"I already knew that, mothers." Keenan wrapped an arm around Aislinn's waist, half hugging her, like he had a right to pull her closer.

He doesn't.

Aislinn stepped away as far as she could with the woman holding her hand.

All three women sighed, simultaneously. "Fierce, isn't she?"

The one still holding Aislinn's hand asked Keenan, "Shall I tell you just how different she is? How special this one will be?"

Every faery there suddenly stopped talking. They were all watching openly, transfixed and gleeful, as if a horrible accident were happening in front of them.

"No." Aislinn pulled her hand free and grabbed Keenan's arm.

He didn't move.

"As special as I've dreamed?" Keenan asked the blind women, his voice carrying clearly to the faeries who pushed forward.

"There are none you will meet so rare as she." The three women all nodded, eerily in sync with one another, like three bodies with one mind.

Grinning, Keenan tossed a handful of unfamiliar bronze

coins to the women, who unerringly snatched them out of the air, their hands moving in precisely the same arcs at exactly the same moment.

I need out of here. Now.

But she couldn't run. If not for the Sight, she wouldn't have reason to react so strongly: the women weren't any stranger than most carnies.

Don't expose yourself. Remember the rules.

She couldn't panic. Her heart still beat madly. Her chest felt tight, like she couldn't breathe. *Hold it together. Focus.* She needed to get out of there, get away from them, back to Seth. She shouldn't have come. It felt like she'd walked into a trap.

She stepped away from the women and pulled on Keenan's arm. "Let's get a drink. Come on."

He pulled her closer to him and went with her to the door, past the crowd of murmuring faeries.

"She *is* the one."

"Did you hear?"

"Send the message."

"Beira will be furious."

As the evening wore on, faeries he hadn't seen in years arrived at the carnival. *It's a good turnout—even with the hags here to spy for Beira.* Emissaries from the other fey courts came, some for the first time in centuries. *They know.*

"Keenan?" One of the guards from Donia's house came toward him and bowed.

Keenan shook his head. He spun Aislinn to him in a loose embrace, far from graceful, but effective nonetheless. She glimmered faintly in the dark, the sunlight of her changing body already filling her. Sometimes it was like that; the change came on so quickly that the mortal girls grew suspicious. It made sense that his queen—for surely she could be none other—would change even quicker.

Behind Aislinn's back, a rowan-man in a mortal glamour intercepted Donia's guard.

"What?" Aislinn started, staring up at Keenan, eyes wide, lips parted as if she waited for a kiss.

Too soon for that. But he did move closer to her, holding her in his arms as if they were at a ball. *And we shall have one, show her the splendor of* our *court. As soon as she ascends to the throne.*

Glancing past Aislinn's shoulder to where the rowan-man had stopped Donia's guard, Keenan said, "I don't want anything to spoil tonight. Should the world end tonight, I wouldn't want to know."

And it was true. He had his queen in his arms; after centuries of searching, she was finally in his arms. The Eolas had all but said it.

He tilted her head up and whispered, "Dance with me."

She shook her head, something very close to fear in her eyes. "There's no room, no music."

He spun her, wishing she had on proper skirts, missing the sway of silk and rustle of petticoats. "Of course there is."

No one strayed into their path. No one jostled them.

Instead the crowd moved around them, parting to clear a space so he could have his first dance with her, his queen.

At the very edge of the river, he saw his summer faeries—*our faeries now*—fade from view, shed their glamours, and join the dance. Soon, with Aislinn beside him, he'd be able to protect them, take care of them as a true King of Summer should.

"Can you truly not hear the music?" He led her past a crowd of bog faeries, who hadn't bothered to shed their glamours, but were dancing all the same. Their luminous brown skin sparkled with light that lay trapped just under the surface, looking like long-lost cousins to the selchies. Several of the Summer Girls had begun to swirl in place, waif-thin dervishes of blurring vine and skirt and hair.

With one hand on the small of Aislinn's back and the other holding her tiny hand, he led her through the swirling crowds of invisible fey. Mouth against her ear, he sing-songed, "Laughter, the roll of the water, the soft whir of traffic, the hum of insects. Can't you hear it, Aislinn? Just listen."

"I need to leave." Her hair flung across his face as he spun her away and back, closer still this time. She sounded terrified when she said, "Let go."

He stopped. "Dance with me, Aislinn. I hear enough music for both of us."

"Why?" She was still and stiff in his arms, looking around them, staring into faces hidden under mortal masks. "Tell me why. What do you want?"

"You. I've spent my life waiting for you." He paused,

looking at the joy on the faces of the summer creatures, those who'd suffered under Beira's reign for so long. "Give me this dance, this night. If it's in my power, I'll give you whatever you ask in return."

"Whatever I ask?" she repeated incredulously. After all the worries, the research, the panic, he offered her an out in exchange for a simple dance.

Could it be that easy? One dance and she could leave, get out of here, away from all of them. But if there was truth in any of the stories, faeries only offered exchanges that would benefit them.

"Give me your vow." She stepped several paces back so she could look him in the eye—an impossible task from up close.

He smiled that earthshaking smile, and her words caught in her throat.

She shivered, but she didn't back down.

"Swear it in front of all these witnesses." She gestured at the waiting crowd. They were mostly faeries, but a few humans stood by watching, not knowing what the spectacle was about, but watching all the same.

The faeries—those invisible and those wearing glamours—gasped and murmured.

"She's a clever one . . ."

". . . getting a king's vow without knowing what he is, *who* he is."

"Will he?"

"She'll make a wonderful queen."

Then Keenan raised his voice so everyone could hear him, "In front of all before us, I give you my vow of honor, Aislinn: anything you ask of me that I can offer is yours." He dropped to one knee and added, "And from this day forward, your wishes shall be as my own as often as I am able."

The faeries' murmurs rose, tumbling together, like discordant songs, "What if she's not the one? How could he be so foolish. . . ? But the Eolas said . . ."

Still kneeling, Keenan bowed his head to her, hand outstretched. His eyes twinkled dangerously as he looked up and asked, "Will you dance with me now? Just take my hand, Aislinn."

All she had to do was dance with him—join the faery revelry for this one night—and she could ask him to leave her alone. It was a small price for such a reward. He'd never even have to know she knew what he was, never know about the Sight.

"I will." She slipped her hand into his, almost giddy with relief. Soon it would all be over.

The throng cheered and laughed, raising such a din that she laughed too. Maybe they weren't cheering for the same reason, but it didn't matter: they echoed her rejoicing.

One of the smiling girls with vines around her arms held out plastic cups filled with the sweet golden drink that most everyone seemed to be drinking. "A drink to celebrate."

Aislinn took one and sipped. It was amazing, a heady mix of things that shouldn't have a flavor—bottled sunlight and spun sugar, lazy afternoons and melting sunsets, hot breezes and dangerous promises. She downed it all.

Keenan took the cup from her hand. "May I have my dance?"

She licked the last taste from her lips—*like warm candy*—and smiled. She was strangely unsteady on her feet. "With pleasure."

Then he led her through the crowd, spinning her in dances old and new, from a stylized waltz to modern moves without any choreography at all.

Somewhere in the back of her mind, she knew that something was wrong, but as he twirled her through the dance, she couldn't remember what. They laughed, and drank, and danced until Aislinn no longer cared why she'd been worried.

Finally she put her hand on Keenan's wrist and gasped, "Enough. I need to stop."

He scooped her up in his arms and—holding her aloft—he sat back on a tall chair carved with sunbursts and vines. "Never stop. Only pause."

Where did the chair come from? All around them, faeries danced and laughed.

I should go. The humans had all gone home. Even the bone girls—*Scrimshaw Sisters*—danced. Groups of Summer Girls spun by, swirling far too fast to ever be mistaken for humans.

"I need another drink." Sitting on his lap, Aislinn leaned her head on Keenan's shoulder, breathing hard. The more she tried to make sense of her flashes of unease, the less clear they were.

"More summer wine!" Keenan called, laughing as several young lion-boys tumbled over themselves to bring tall goblets to them as she sat in his lap. "My lady wants wine, and wine she shall have."

She took hold of one of the etched goblets, spinning it in her hand. Delicate scrollwork traced the surface, surrounding an image of a dancing couple under a bright sun. The colors in the wine spiraled and shifted like a tiny sunrise burned inside the cup. "Where'd the plastic cups go?"

He kissed her hair and laughed. "Beautiful things for a beautiful lady."

"Whatever." She shrugged and took another long drink.

With an arm securely around her waist and a hand between her shoulder blades, Keenan dipped her backward. "Once more around the faire?"

Her hair fell onto the dew-damp grass as she looked up at him—the faery king who held her in his arms—and wondered that she was having so much fun.

He swung her back up and whispered, "Dance with me, Aislinn, my love."

Her legs ached; her head spun. She hadn't had so much fun since . . . *ever.* "Definitely."

On every side, faeries laughed—dancing in ways that were graceful, wild, and sometimes shocking. Earlier they'd seemed sedate, like couples in old black-and-white movies, but as the night wore on, it had changed. *When only the fey remained.*

Keenan swung her up into his embrace and kissed her neck. "I could spend eternity doing this."

"No"—she pushed him away—"no kissing, no . . ."

Then they were moving again. The world spun by, a blur of strange faces lost in a cloud of music. The sawdust-covered paths of the carnival were hidden under shadows; the lights of the rides were darkened.

But dawn was coming, light spilling out over the sky. *How long have we danced?*

"I need to sit down. Seriously."

"Whatever my lady wants." Keenan lifted her into his arms again. His doing so had stopped seeming strange several drinks ago.

One of the men with skin like bark spread out a blanket by the water. Another brought over a picnic basket. "Good morrow, Keenan. My lady."

Then, with a bow, they left.

Keenan opened the basket and pulled out another bottle of wine, as well as cheese and strange little fruit. "Our first breakfast."

Definitely not carnival food. Oops, faire *food.* She giggled. Then she looked up—behind him the carnival was gone. As if they'd never been there, all the faeries had left. It was just the two of them. "Where did they all go?"

Keenan held out the goblet again, filled with the same

liquid sunrise. "It's just us here. Later, after you've rested, we'll talk. Then we can dance every night if you will it. Travel. It'll all be different now."

She didn't even see the invisible faeries that always lingered at the river. They were truly alone. "Can I ask a question?"

"Of course." He held a piece of fruit up to her lips. "Bite."

Aislinn leaned in—almost toppling over as she did—but she didn't bite the strange fruit. Instead she whispered, "Why don't all the other faeries glow like you do?"

Keenan lowered his hand. "All the other *what*?"

"Faeries." She gestured around them, but it was as empty of faeries as it was of humans. She closed her eyes to try to stop the world from spinning so madly and whispered, "You know, *fey things*, like the ones dancing with us all night, like you and Donia."

"Fey things?" he murmured. His copper hair glittered in the light that was creeping over the sky.

"Yeah." She laid down on the ground. "Like you."

It sounded like he said, "And soon, like you . . ." But she wasn't sure. Everything was blurry.

He bent over her where she lay on the ground. His lips brushed hers, tasting like sunshine and sugar. His hair fell onto her face.

It's soft, not like metal at all.

She meant to say stop, to tell him she was dizzy, but before she could speak, everything went dark.

CHAPTER 18

They are not subject to sore Sicknesses, but dwindle and decay at a certain Period. . . . Some say their continual Sadness is because of their pendulous state.

—*The Secret Commonwealth* by Robert Kirk
and Andrew Lang (1893)

Early the next morning, Donia awakened on the floor, Sasha's body between her and the door. No one had brought her a message from Keenan. No guards had knocked on her door.

"Has he forsaken me?" she whispered to Sasha.

The wolf laid his ears back and whined.

"When I actually might welcome his presence, he's not here." She wouldn't weep, though, not for him. She'd done enough of that over the years.

She'd expected him to hear of Agatha's death, to come demanding she accept his help. She couldn't, but it would've been easier—safer—than what she'd have to do now.

"Come, Sasha." She opened the door and motioned Evan to her. *At least* he's *here waiting.*

The rowan-man joined her, keeping a respectful distance, standing in the withered grass in front of the porch until Donia said, "Come inside."

She didn't wait to see if he'd follow. The idea of inviting one of Keenan's guards into her home—even Evan, whose presence had been steadfast the past few decades—unsettled her.

Gesturing to the seat farthest from her, she asked, "Has Keenan been told about Agatha?"

"He was out when Skelley arrived at the loft. One of the others went to the faire to find him." Evan cleared his throat, but his stare was bold. "He was preoccupied with the new queen."

She nodded. *So it's truly her.* Beira would be furious, a force to fear.

It'd been so long since Donia had much to truly fear. Between Keenan and Beira, she was cosseted, safer than most any fey or mortal.

"I'd ask that you allow a few guards closer." Evan dropped to his knees, showing a respect his kind rarely offered any fey other than Keenan. "Let me stay here with you."

"Fine," she murmured, ignoring both his brief look of shock and her irritation at it. *I can be reasonable.* Then she said the words she'd never said to any of Keenan's guards: "Tell Keenan I need him to come. Now."

It didn't take long for Skelley to summon Keenan—not long enough for Donia to prepare for the pain of seeing him in her home. When Evan led Keenan in, she stayed in her rocking chair—curled into herself, arms folded tightly over her chest, feet tucked up beneath her.

Before Evan had closed the door behind him—returning to the guards outside—Keenan was across the room, standing beside her.

Sasha moved closer, pressing his body against her, trying to soothe her. Donia absently petted his head.

She glanced at Keenan and said, "I wasn't sure you'd come."

In a strange mimicry of Sasha's position, Keenan dropped to the floor. "I've waited decades for you to want me around, Don, begged to be in your presence."

"That was before her." She felt foolish for it, but as much as she wanted Aislinn to take up the staff, she was jealous. *Aislinn* was the one; she'd spend eternity with Keenan.

"Things are different now." Donia tried to keep all of her emotions out of her voice, but she failed.

"I'll always come when you want me. How many times have I told you that?" he whispered, his words carrying that warm breath of summer. "That won't change. Ever."

She reached out, putting her hand over his lips before he could say anything else. A thin layer of frost formed where she touched him, but he didn't complain.

He never does.

She didn't pull away, although his breath burned her. "I heard the news from the faire, that she's the one."

When Evan had told her, she'd almost wept, imagining eternity in this pain, alone, watching them dance and laugh. *Unless Beira kills me.*

"Don . . ." His lips moved against her fingers, gentle even as they hurt her—just like the words he'd say if she didn't stop him.

When there were no witnesses, he'd let himself be the person he'd been before she knew he was a king—the person she fell in love with. It was why she avoided being alone with him.

"No," she said, not wanting the gentle side of him, not now. Today she needed him to be the Summer King, to set aside the person he could be without the crown. She needed him to be arrogant and assured, able to do what needed doing.

Steam rose against her hand as he exhaled, the breath of summer melting her frost. Sometimes, in secret dreams she'd never tell him, she wondered what would happen if her frost and his sun truly clashed, if they touched as they had in those few weeks before she became the Winter Girl, when he was pretending to be a mortal for her. Would she melt away? Burn up?

She shivered—excited at the thought—and felt the cold well up inside her as her emotions raged like a blizzard. If she didn't keep calm, she'd need to let that awful cold out.

"Beira was here last night. You need to know what she's doing."

He nodded, weariness on his face, as she told him almost everything—about Beira's initial visit when Aislinn was chosen, about the attack on Aislinn outside the library, about her belief that the attack was at Beira's behest, about Agatha's death, about Beira's threats, about her insistence that Aislinn not lift the staff.

Donia kept quiet about Seth's research—fearing for the mortal's safety—but beyond that, she was more honest with Keenan than she'd been in a very long time. When she stopped talking, he stared at her, silent and struggling to contain the temper he rarely freed.

She clenched her hands so tightly that icicles formed on the tips of her fingernails. *Now comes the hard part.*

"Let's go." He looked over at Sasha, then past the wolf to the tiny mementos handed down by the other Winter Girls. "The guards will bring your things. We can turn the study into a private chamber and—"

"Keenan," she interrupted before she could be tempted.

He'd see the logic of what needed to be done if he thought clearly; she needed to assure that he did so. She opened her hand. Icicles fell and shattered at her feet. "I'm not going anywhere."

"You can't stay here. If something happened to you"— he bowed his head, letting his forehead rest on her knee— "please, Don, come with me."

Where is the Summer King? But it wasn't the king who laid his head in her lap, pleading.

She didn't move away. It burned her, froze him, but she stayed still. "I can't come with you. It's not my place. I'm not the one you're looking for."

He looked up at her, an ugly frostbitten bruise forming where his skin had touched her knee. "I'm not strong enough to stop her, but I will be soon. Stay with me until we get this sorted out."

"And what would she do to me when I left?"

"I'll be strong soon." He was almost frightening in his insistence. His eyes darkened to that unearthly green hue she still dreamed of; if she stared long enough, she'd see flowers blooming there, a promise of what he could become once his queen freed him.

She couldn't look away.

He whispered, "Stay with me. I'll keep you safe."

"You can't." She wished he could, but it was impossible: there was no winning, not for her. "I want you to win. I always have, but I still have to try to convince Aislinn not to believe in you, that you're not worth the risk. Those are the rules. I gave my word when I lifted the staff. We both did."

He put a hand on either side of her, his fingertips burning her skin through her clothes. "Even if it means Beira wins? Even if she kills you? We can work together, find a way."

She shook her head. For all his centuries—far more than she'd ever see—he could still be so reckless. It usually infuriated her. Today she found it saddening. "If she wins, she won't kill me. It's only if you win that I'll die."

"Then why tell me? I need to win." He looked awful, pale and sickly like he'd been skewered by iron spikes. He moved farther away from her—crouched on the floor, head bowed—where they couldn't touch. He sounded as broken as he looked. "If you stop Aislinn, I lose everything. If you don't, you die. What am I to do?"

"Hope I lose," she suggested softly.

"No."

She stood up and walked over to him. "I'm terrified of Beira, but I truly do hope that Ash is the one. For both of your sakes."

"You'll still be a shade. That doesn't fix anything."

Where is the Summer King? She sighed as she watched him struggle between what he wanted and the inevitable. *Not all dreams come true.* If it'd make things easier, she'd be cruel. It wouldn't help, though.

She leaned over him, holding her hair back so it didn't fall against him. "It fixes a lot of things."

"It . . ."

"Make me lose, Keenan. Convince her you're worth the risk"—she kissed his cheek—"because you are." It was easier to say it, knowing Beira would kill her, knowing she wouldn't spend eternity with him knowing she still loved him.

"I can't. . . ."

She put her hand over his mouth. "Convince her."

She pulled her hand away and—lips firmly closed to keep the icy air from his mouth—kissed him. "Then kill Beira."

CHAPTER 19

[Faeries] are partly human and partly spiritual in their nature. . . . Some of them are benevolent. . . . Others are malevolent . . . abducting grown people, and bringing misfortune.

— *The Folk-Lore of the Isle of Man* by A. W. Moore (1891)

Keenan was shaken when he left Donia; he walked aimlessly through the city, wishing, wanting an answer. There wasn't one. Unless Aislinn was his missing queen and he was able to convince her to trust him, to accept him, there was nothing he could do. He simply wasn't strong enough to stand against Beira.

If I were . . . He smiled at that thought: stopping Beira, maybe in time to save Donia. That was the only recourse they had.

But if Aislinn's Sight was that thing which the Eolas spoke of—and that would be in their nature—it was all for nothing. Donia would die, and he would still be bound.

The small trickle of summer that he could call was nowhere near enough to stand against Beira.

He rested his head against an oak tree, eyes closed. *Breathe. Just breathe.* Aislinn was different, perhaps different enough; perhaps she was the one.

But she might not be.

The Eolas' proclamation—which the fey had heard as a herald of the Summer Queen's discovery—could be nothing more than a revelation that she was Sighted. *She might not be the one.*

He'd just turned toward the greener part of the city when he heard Beira's hags approach. They followed at an almost respectful distance until he reached the river.

At the river's side, he sat—feet on the soil, sun on his back—and waited.

Better here than at the loft.

The last time she'd visited, Beira had frozen as many of his birds as she could when he left the room. He'd returned to find them dead on the ground, or affixed to branches, hanging like awful ornaments at the tips of icicles. Unless he could stop her, one of these times it could be the Summer Girls or his guards who felt her temper.

Beira stood in the shadow of a garish awning held over her by several of her nearly-naked guards—Hawthorn-people and one slick-skinned troll, all sporting fresh bruises and frostbitten skin.

"What, no hug? no kiss?" Beira held out a hand. "Come here, dearest."

"I'll stay out here." Keenan didn't bother getting up; he just glanced up at her. "I like the warmth on my skin."

She wrinkled her nose and made a little moue of distaste. "Nasty stuff, sunlight."

He shrugged. Talking to her now—after seeing Donia, after all the doubts about Aislinn—was the last thing he wanted.

"Do you know that there's a market these days for SPF cloth?" She sat back on a blindingly white chair that the hags dragged up for her. "Mortals are such strange beasts."

"Do you have a point, Beira?" He never enjoyed her presence, but she'd threatened Donia—feigning civility was more of a struggle than usual.

"Is it so hard to believe I just wanted to visit with you? Chat with you?" Without looking behind her, she held out a hand; a collared wood-sprite slipped an icy drink into her outstretched fingers. "You so rarely visit."

Keenan reclined on the grass, relishing the strength of the earth's warmth seeping into his body from the soil. "Perhaps because you're vicious and cruel?"

She waved her hand as if brushing away his comment. "You say potato; I say potahto. . . ."

"I say integrity; you say deceit."

"Well, it's such a *subjective* idea, integrity." She sipped her drink. "Can I offer you a refreshment, dear?"

"No." He ran his fingers over the soil, sending his warmth down to the resting bulbs. Small flower sprouts rushed out toward his touch; delicate shoots poked up between his opened fingers.

"I hear you shared quite a bit of refreshment with the new Summer Girl. Poor dear was dizzy with it." She *tsk*ed at him with a censorious look. "Haven't I taught you better? Getting the poor lamb intoxicated to convince her to *you know.*"

"That wasn't what it was," he snapped. "Aislinn and I danced and celebrated her new life. It wasn't a seduction."

She stepped out from under her awning, sending her guards scurrying to keep it over her as she moved. If they failed, they'd suffer, regardless of whose fault it was.

As the shade blocked his comforting rays, Keenan was torn between waiting and simply setting the awning to flame. He stood to face her.

"Well, if you want my opinion, a mother's wisdom, I say she's not worth it." She glanced at the flowers; they froze in her sight. She stepped forward and—with a grating noise—ground them under her boot. "Poor Deborah shouldn't have any trouble convincing her to stay away from you. You didn't ask her to go easy on the mortal, did you?"

"It's Aislinn's choice. She'll either take up the staff or not." He wanted to tell her that threatening Donia wouldn't change anything, but he couldn't. "I spoke to Donia—which you so obviously know—about the Eolas' announcement."

"Oh?" She paused, wide-eyed as if she were surprised. "What announcement?"

"That Aislinn is special."

"Of course she is, sweetling. They're *all* special—at least the first few nights. After that, the"—she looked back at a cowering sprite—"novelty just isn't there, you know?"

He forced a laugh.

"Poor Delilah, I imagine she's bitter. It wasn't so long ago that she was the one dancing with you." Beira swayed as if she were dancing with an invisible partner, looking elegant even though she was alone. "Mortals are such fragile things. Just tender feelings walking around exposed in their delicate shells . . . Easy to crush."

His heart sped. The rules prevented her from contacting the mortal girl, and until now Beira'd never broken that rule—to the best of his knowledge—but she was already breaking other rules. "What do you mean?"

"Nothing, love." She stopped and curtsied to him, pulled out a fan, and fluttered it in front of her face, sending cold air toward him. "I'm just wondering if you should pick another girl for the game; let this one join the rest of the other discarded girls. I'll even go girl-watching with you. We could pick up Delia and make a bonding experience of it."

He let all the bitterness he felt show in his voice and said, "Well, at the rate Donia's going, I may need to. Aside from one drunken dance, I'm getting nowhere."

"There'll be other girls, darling." Beira sighed, but her eyes glimmered with a sheen of ice—a sure sign she was pleased.

But they aren't the Summer Queen, are they?

"Perhaps I just need to try harder," he said as he sent a

hot breath toward Beira's awning—catching it on fire—
then he walked away, leaving her there shrieking at the
guards to keep the sunlight away from her.

Someday I'll truly be able to stand against her.

For now, he took pleasure in the moment.

Keenan wandered the city, up Fifth Avenue away from the
river until he got to Edgehill, following it until he reached
the seedier shops. The din of the city was a welcome buzz,
reminding him of the mortals who thrived where his kind
could not.

*That's what this is all about: these mortals and his summer
faeries.*

"Keenan?" Rianne stepped out of a music store and all
but ran into him. She gaped at him. "What's up with your
hair?"

In his distraction, he had been walking around plainly
visible, his hair its normal shade, reflective copper.

"Dye." He smiled at her, lightening his hair until the
metallic glimmer was gone.

She reached out and caught a few strands, holding it up
to the sunlight, moving it from side to side. "For a minute
it almost looked like strips of metal."

"Hmm." He pulled back, freeing his hair from her hand.
"Have you seen Aislinn today?"

She laughed. "Nope. Thought maybe she was still with
you."

"No." He looked beyond Rianne, to where several of the

Summer Girls were flirting with an off-duty rowan-man. "I escorted her home this morning."

"Morning, huh?" She shook her head, still smiling. For all of her posturing, she smelled like innocence to him, untouched and sweet. Her words were at complete odds with her attitude. "I knew you were a good bet."

"We were just dancing."

"It's a start, right?" She glanced around, looking down the street and back inside the shop. For a moment her illusory lasciviousness vanished, and her genuine personality slipped through. "Between you and me, Ash could use a bit more fun in her life. She's too serious. I think you'll be good for her."

Keenan paused. He hadn't thought about *that* very much; all that mattered was that she was good for him, for the summer fey.

Was he good for her? Between the sacrifices she'd need to make and difficulty of what stood before them if she were the true queen, he wasn't sure. *Probably not.* "I'll try to be, Rianne."

"You've already got her out till dawn dancing: sounds like a good start to me." Rianne patted him on the arm, consoling him for something she couldn't begin to grasp. "Don't worry so much."

"Right."

After she walked away, Keenan faded back to his normal state—invisible to mortals—and resumed walking to the loft. If there was ever a time when he needed the wisdom of his advisors, this was it.

Keenan felt the music before he even walked into the loft. He took a deep breath and stepped inside, a false smile on his face.

After only a cursory glance at him, Tavish removed Eliza's arms from around his neck and went toward the study. "Come."

At times like these, Keenan felt as if having Tavish's presence was almost like having a father. The older faery had been the last Summer King's advisor and friend; he'd been there waiting when Keenan had come of age and left Beira's household. While Tavish would never presume to act like a father, he was far more than a servant.

Noticing their movement, Niall opened his mouth.

With a brief shake of his head, Keenan said, "No. Stay with the girls."

"If you need me . . ."

"I do. Always." Keenan squeezed Niall's shoulder. "Right now, I need you to keep everyone out here."

This wasn't the place to talk. If word got out that he suspected Beira of trickery or maliciousness, if rumors spread that Aislinn had the Sight, it could go badly for all of them.

As he wound his way through the room—embraced by the Summer Girls who were spinning dizzily with off-shift guards—Keenan kept his face clear of any doubt. *No hint of problems. Smile.*

By the time he reached Tavish, he was ready to bar the door for the rest of the day. He believed the girls and his guards were trustworthy, but one never knew, not really.

Tavish poured a glass of wine. "Here."

Keenan took the glass and sank onto one of the heavy leather chairs.

After Tavish settled on an opposite chair, he asked, "What happened?"

So Keenan told him—about Aislinn's Sight, about Beira's threats, all of it.

Tavish stared into his glass like it was a reflecting mirror. He spun it by the stem. "She may not be the queen, but Beira fears her. To me, that is reason enough to keep hope—more reason than we've had ever before."

Keenan nodded, but did not speak yet. Tavish was rarely direct in his points.

Instead of looking at Keenan, Tavish let his gaze drift around the room, as if he were reading the spines of the books that lined every wall of the study. "I have waited with you, but I've never suggested that one of the girls was *her*. It is not my place."

"I value your opinion," Keenan assured him. "Tell me what you think."

"Do not let Aislinn refuse the challenge. If she is the one, and she does not . . ." Tavish's gaze stayed on the heavy books behind Keenan. "She *must* accept."

The older faery had been somber so long that his vehemence was disquieting.

Keenan asked, "And if she refuses?"

"She cannot. Make her agree." Tavish's eyes were as black

as pools in shadowed forests, eerily captivating, when he finally held Keenan's gaze. "Do whatever you must, even if it is . . . *unpalatable* to you or her. If you heed only one word I ever say, my liege, make it this one."

CHAPTER 20

[They offered] him drink . . . after, the music ceasing, all the company disappeared, leaving the cup in his hand, and he returned home, though much wearied and fatigued.

—*The Fairy Mythology* by Thomas Keightley (1870)

When Aislinn woke—the clock's red numbers proclaiming it past 9:00—the evening's events came crashing down on her. *The weird drinks, dancing, telling Keenan she knew what he was as they watched the sunrise, him kissing her.* That was the last thing she remembered. *What else happened? How did I get home? When?* She bolted out of bed, barely making it to the bathroom before she threw up. *Oh my God.*

She sat with her face against the cold porcelain until she was sure she could stand without vomiting again. Her whole body trembled, like she had the flu, but it wasn't the flu making her feel so awful. It was terror. *He knows I see them. He knows. They'll come for me, and Grams. . . .* The thought of her Grams fighting faeries almost made her sick again. *I need to get out of here.*

After brushing her teeth and washing her face, Aislinn hurriedly slipped on jeans and a shirt, shoved her feet into boots, and grabbed her bag.

Grams was in the kitchen, staring at the coffeepot, a bit less observant before her morning jolt.

Aislinn pointed at her ear.

Grams turned on her hearing aid and asked, "Everything okay?"

"Just running late, Grams. Overslept." Aislinn gave her a quick hug and turned to leave.

"But breakfast . . ."

"Sorry. I need to, umm, meet Seth. I thought I told you? We were to have a breakfast thing, date. . . ." She tried to keep her voice steady.

Don't let her see how worried I am.

Grams was already too fearful after their talk the other night; adding to that would be selfish.

"You know you aren't fooling me, Aislinn, dodging me so I don't ask about that *issue*. We're going to talk about it." Grams scowled. "It isn't any better, is it?"

Aislinn paused. "Just a few more days, Grams. Please?"

For a minute Grams looked like she was going to balk: she pursed her lips and put her hands on her hips. Then she sighed. "Not a few days. *Tomorrow* we'll talk. You understand?"

"Promise." Aislinn kissed her good-bye, grateful to put it off even one day more. She wasn't sure she could handle that conversation, not now.

I need Seth. I didn't even call him last night.

"I can't believe I did that." Aislinn put her head between her knees and concentrated on not vomiting on her feet. "I told him I knew they were faeries."

Seth sat on the floor beside her feet. He was patting her back, making small soothing circles. "It's okay. Come on. Breathe. Just breathe."

"It's not okay, Seth." Her voice was muffled by her decidedly uncomfortable posture. She lifted her head enough to scowl at him. "They used to *kill* people, gouge out their eyes for knowing what they were."

The nausea rose again. She closed her eyes.

"Shh." He moved closer, comforting her the way he'd always done when she fell apart. "Come on."

"What if they blind me? What if . . ."

"Stop. We'll figure it out." He pulled her into his lap, cradling her like a child.

Just like Keenan did last night.

She tried to stand up, feeling guilty, like she'd betrayed Seth even though all she did was dance—she hoped.

What if I, Keenan, we . . . She started to sob again.

"Shush." Seth rocked her, murmuring reassuring words.

And she let him—until she started to think about faeries again and dancing with Keenan and kissing him and not knowing what else might have happened.

She pulled away and stood.

Seth stayed on the floor. He propped his head up on one hand, his elbow on the seat of the chair where she'd been sitting.

She ducked her head, unable to look at him. "So what do we do about it?"

He came to stand beside her. "We improvise. He promised you a favor. If the books are right, vows are like laws."

She nodded.

He stepped in front of her and leaned forward until the longer strands of his hair fell like a web over her face. "The rest we'll deal with too."

Then he kissed her—softly, tenderly, lovingly—and said, "We'll get this figured out. Together. I'm here with you, Ash, even after you tell me what else happened."

"What do you mean?" Aislinn felt the world swim again.

"You drank something that messed you up, danced until dawn, and woke up in your bed sick." He cradled her face in his hands. "What else happened?"

"I don't know." She shivered.

"Okay, how did you get home?"

"I don't know." She remembered the taste of sunshine, the feel of sunbeams falling onto her as she stared up at Keenan's face, as he leaned toward her. *What happened?*

"Did you go anywhere else?"

She whispered, "I don't know."

"Sleep with him?" He looked straight at her as he asked it, the question she'd been trying—and failing—to answer.

"I don't know." She looked away, feeling sicker with the

words hanging there like something awful. "I'd know, right? That's something I'd remember. Right?"

He pulled her into his arms, tucking her under his chin, as if he could keep her safe from all the bad things by keeping her close enough. "I don't know. Are there any flashes of memories? Anything?"

"I remember dancing, drinking, sitting on some strange chair, and then the carnival was gone. He kissed me." She shivered again. "I'm so sorry."

"It's not your fault." He stroked his hand over her hair. She tried to pull away.

He didn't force her to stay, but he kept his hands on her arms. He looked so serious, so adamant. "Listen to me. If something happened, it wasn't your fault. He gave you some drug, some faery booze. You were drunk, high, whatever, and what happened afterward isn't your fault."

"I remember laughing, having fun." She looked down at her hands, clenched tightly so they didn't shake. "I was having fun, Seth. What if I *did* do something? What if I said yes?"

"Doesn't matter. If you're fucked up, you can't consent. It's that simple. He shouldn't have done anything, Ash. If he did, he's the one who's wrong. Not you." He sounded angry, but he didn't tell her that he had been right, that she shouldn't have gone. He didn't say anything awful to her. Instead he tucked her hair behind her ear and let his hand rest on her face, gently tilting her head so she looked at him. "And we don't know that anything did happen."

"I just wanted the first time to be with someone special, and if I, if we, it's just *wrong*." She felt half foolish for worrying about it—exposed to the wrath of a faery king and she worried about her virginity. He could take her life; he could take her eyes. Her virginity shouldn't matter so much.

But it does.

She walked away, going over to curl up in the comfort of Seth's sofa. "I'm sorry. You were right, and I—"

He interrupted, "There's nothing for *you* to be sorry for. You're not wrong. I'm not upset with you. It's him—" He stopped. He didn't move, just stood there in the middle of the room, watching her. "You're what matters."

"Hold me? If you still want to, I mean." She looked away.

"Every day"—then he was there, lifting her into his arms, holding her like she was fragile and precious—"I want to hold you every day. Nothing will ever change that."

CHAPTER 21

The Fairy then dropped three drops of a precious liquid on her companion's left eyelid, and she beheld a most delicious country. . . . From this time she possessed the faculty of discerning the Fairy people as they went about invisibly.

—*The Fairy Mythology* by Thomas Keightley (1870)

Donia walked past the faeries outside Seth's home—a few familiar guards, the demi-succubus Cerise, and several Summer Girls. Without Keenan beside her, none of them smiled. They still bowed their heads, but there was no affection in their respect. To them she was the enemy—never mind that she'd risked everything for him, everything the girls hadn't been willing to risk. They conveniently forgot that.

At the door she braced herself for the inevitable weakness that such awful walls would bring about. She knocked. Pain seared her knuckles.

She didn't react when Aislinn opened the door, but it

took effort. From the hollow look on her face, Donia was sure that her memories of the faire were far less clear than Keenan's. All he'd admitted was that he'd let her drink far too much summer wine, caught up in the moment, the revelry, the dancing. It was his way: too easy to rejoice, to believe. For him, it worked.

Aislinn looked awful.

Clutching her hand, looking both angry and wary, was her mortal, Seth. "What do you want?"

Aislinn's eyes widened. "Seth."

"No. It's fine, Ash." Donia smiled; for all her wishes of success to Keenan, she saw the look on Seth's face and couldn't help but respect him. A mortal stood against the considerable temptation of the Summer King, and it was the mortal holding Aislinn's hand.

Donia added, "I just want to talk."

Behind her Cerise came closer, announcing her approach by flapping her wings—as if she could frighten Donia.

"Maybe take a walk." She glanced back at Cerise and blew a breath of cold air at her, not enough to wound, but frigid enough to remind her to watch her step.

Cerise shrieked, the mere touch of cold sending her fluttering backward.

Donia started to smile: there weren't enough good moments lately. Then she realized that Aislinn had jumped at Cerise's outburst. Seth hadn't moved, hadn't heard it: faeries could raise such a cacophony that mortals' heads ached, but they didn't respond in any other way, didn't hear it.

The exclamations behind her confirmed that the others had seen Aislinn's reaction as well.

Donia looked at Aislinn. "You can see them."

Aislinn nodded.

Cerise trembled behind a rowan-man. The Summer Girls gaped.

"I see faeries. Lucky me," Aislinn added, sounding as weary as she looked. "Can you come in here or is there too much iron?"

Donia smiled at the girl's bravado. "I'd rather walk."

Nodding, Aislinn lifted her gaze to the head guard and told the rowan-man, "Keenan already knows, and now Donia does too, so if there's anyone else you need to scurry off and tell, now's your chance."

Donia winced. *Not bravado, recklessness.* She would be a good match for Keenan.

Before anyone could respond, Donia walked past the Summer Girls and stood before the rowan-man. "If anyone here tells Beira, I'll find you. If loyalty to Keenan isn't enough to keep your lips sealed, I'll seal them for you."

She stared at Cerise until the demi-succubus growled, "I would never betray the Summer King."

"Good." Donia nodded. Then she returned to Aislinn's side.

Only the sound of Cerise's wings flapping madly broke the silence until Donia asked, "Shall I tell you about Keenan's infidelity, about his lasciviousness, about how foolish it'd be to trust him?"

Blanching even more, Aislinn looked away. "I may already know."

Donia said softly to Seth, "You say you aren't her beau, but she needs you. Maybe we can talk about herbs as well?"

"Hold on." Seth pulled Aislinn back inside to talk for a moment, closing the door on Donia.

As she waited outside for their inevitable agreement, she gave the Summer Girls her coldest smile, hoping it was enough, hating the game she had to play.

I gave my vow.

From behind the rowan-man, Cerise hissed at her.

"Why?" one of the youngest Summer Girls—Tracey—asked, coming far closer to Donia than the others usually did. "He still cares for you. How can you do this to him?" Tracey looked genuinely confused, a familiar frown on her face.

With her reed-thin body and soft voice, Tracey was one of the ones Donia had tried hardest to convince not to risk the cold. She was too fragile, too easily confused, too gentle to be either Winter Girl or Summer Queen.

"I made a vow." Donia'd tried to explain it often enough, but Tracey's view was black and white. If Keenan was good, Donia must be bad. Simple logic.

"It hurts Keenan." Tracey shook her head, as if she could make the troubles go away by saying no.

"It hurts me, too."

The other girls pulled Tracey back to them, trying to distract her before she began weeping. She never should've

been chosen. Donia still felt guilty for it; she suspected
Keenan did too. The Summer Girls were like plants needing the nutrients of the sun to thrive: they couldn't be away
from the Summer King for long, or they'd fade. Tracey,
however, never seemed to thrive, even though she stayed
with Keenan year-round.

The door opened again. Seth stepped outside; Aislinn
followed close behind him.

"We'll come." Aislinn's voice was stronger, but she still
looked far from well. There were dark hollows under her
eyes, and her face was almost as pale as Donia's. "Can you
tell them they can't follow us?"

"No. They are his, not mine."

"So they'll hear everything?" Aislinn looked like she
needed someone to help her make decisions, not like her
usual self at all.

What didn't Keenan tell me?

"They can't come into my home. We'll go there," Donia
offered before she could think it through. Then, before she
had to hear the comments that followed the gasp of surprise, she walked away, leaving Aislinn and Seth rushing to
catch up with her.

More strangers in my home. She sighed, hoping it wouldn't
soon become Aislinn's home, hoping that Keenan was right.
Let Aislinn be the one.

At the edge of the yard where they came upon the natural
barrier that protects a fey domicile from mortal intrusion,

Seth's eyes widened, but Aislinn didn't flinch. Perhaps she'd always been immune; perhaps it was only her Sight that made her oblivious to it. Donia didn't ask. Instead she whispered the words to ease Seth's aversion and led them—still silent—into her home.

"Are we the only ones here?" Seth looked around the room, although his mortal eyes would see nothing if the three of them weren't alone. He still held Aislinn's hand and made no move to let go anytime soon.

"We are." Aislinn's gaze lingered on the simple natural wood furnishings in the small room, the massive fireplace that took up most of one wall, and the gray stones that finished out that wall. "It's just us."

Donia leaned against the stones, enjoying their warmth. "Not quite what you pictured?"

Aislinn leaned on Seth; they both looked thoroughly exhausted. She crooked her mouth in a half-smile. "I don't think I pictured anything. I didn't know why you were talking to me, still don't. I just know it's got something to do with him."

"It has everything to do with him. Beyond here, to those who wait out there"—Donia motioned to the door—"what he wants is the most important thing. Nothing else matters to them. You, me, we are nothing in their worlds other than what we can be to him."

Leaning her head against Seth's arm, Aislinn asked, "So what about in here?"

Seth wrapped his arms around her and pulled her to the

sofa, murmuring, "Sit down. You don't need to stand to talk to her."

Donia came closer then, standing across from them, gazing at Aislinn. "In here, what matters is what I want. And I want to help you."

Trying to contain her emotions, Donia paced through the room; she paused periodically, but she made no move to continue the conversation. *How do I say what needs saying?* They were weary, and she couldn't blame them for it.

"Donia?" Aislinn curled into Seth's arms, half asleep and lethargic. She was vulnerable from whatever Keenan had done.

Donia ignored her. Turning instead to the shelf that held the mortal- and faery-authored books that the Winter Girls had collected over the past nine centuries, she ran her fingers over some of her favorites—Kirk and Lang's *The Secret Commonwealth*, the complete collection of *Tradition of the Highest Courts*, Keightley's *The Fairy Mythology*, and Sorcha's *On Being: Faery Morality and Mortality*. She slid her fingers past these, past an old copy of *The Mabinogion*, past a collection of journals the other girls had kept, past the tattered book holding letters Keenan had sent them over the centuries—always in that elegant script of his, even if the language wasn't always the same. There she stopped.

Her hand lingered on a well-worn book with a torn green cover. In it, handwritten in the strangely beautiful words of an almost lost language, were two recipes known to give the Sight to a mortal.

It was forbidden to allow those recipes to be read by a mortal. If any of the courts learned that she'd done so, Beira's threat would be a minor worry. Many fey had grown fond of being a hidden people; they'd be loath to lose that should mortals begin to see them again.

"Are you okay?" Seth didn't come toward her, staying protectively at Aislinn's side, but his voice held worry.

For me, a stranger.

He was worthy of protection. She knew fey history well enough, having spent long hours poring over these books. Once the courts might have given him a gift for what he did, defending the one who would be queen. "I am. I am surprisingly fine."

She pulled the book out. After sitting down across from them, she rested the book in her lap and gingerly flipped the pages. Several slid loose of the binding, coming free in her hands. She spoke barely above a whisper but she said it, "Write this down."

"What?" Aislinn blinked and straightened up, pulling away from the circle of Seth's arms.

"It's a crime with the most serious of punishments if they learn I've given you this. Keenan may look the other way if no one else knows, but I want him"—she inclined her head ever so slightly at Seth—"to stand a fair chance in what will follow. To leave him defenseless and blind . . . it would be wrong."

"Thank—"

She cut him off, "No. Those are mortal words, made empty by casual use. If you are to walk among our kind, remember that: they are an insult of sorts. If one does you a good turn, an act of friendship, remember it. Do not lessen it with that shallow phrase."

She told him then, gave him the words that would let him make the salve to *see*.

He raised an eyebrow as he wrote it down, but he did not ask questions until she'd closed the book and returned it to its place on the shelf. Then he asked only, "Why?"

"I've been her." Donia looked away, staring at the spines of the worn books on her shelves, feeling shaky as the weight of what she'd just done settled on her. Would even Keenan forgive her? She wasn't sure, but—like him—she believed Aislinn truly was the Summer Queen. Why else would Beira be so adamant that she stay away from the staff?

Donia pulled her gaze from the shelves and looked at Aislinn as she said the rest: "I was a mortal. I had no idea what he was; none of us ever do. You're the first one to see him, see any of them for what they are. What I am now."

"You were mortal?" Aislinn repeated shakily.

Donia nodded.

"What happened?"

"I loved him. I said yes when he asked me to choose to stay with him. He offered me forever, love, midnight dances." She shrugged, unwilling to think too long about dreams she had no right to still have, especially with Aislinn looking back at her. Someday Seth would fade away, but Keenan would not. If Aislinn were the Summer Queen, it was merely a matter of time until she fell in love with Keenan. Once she saw his true nature—the person he could be . . .

Donia shook her head and added, "There was another girl who tried to talk me out of it, a girl who had believed in him once."

"Why didn't you listen?" Aislinn shivered, moving closer to Seth.

"Why does Seth sit here?"

Aislinn didn't answer, but Seth did. He squeezed Aislinn's hand and said, "Love."

"Choose wisely, Aislinn. For Seth, he can choose to leave you, choose to walk away—"

"I won't," Seth interrupted.

Sparing him a smile, Donia said, "But you could. For us, if we choose Keenan, there's no walking away. If we don't—"

"It's not a problem then. I don't want Keenan." Aislinn lifted her chin, looking defiant despite her trembling hands.

"You will, though," Donia said gently.

Donia remembered the first time she'd seen him as he truly was, in the clearing when she stood waiting to lift the Winter Queen's staff. He was so incredibly perfect that she had to remind herself to breathe. How could any mortal deny him when he could be himself?

"Now that he knows of your Sight, he can be himself in front of you. You'll forget your own name."

"No." Aislinn shook her head. "I've seen him as he is, and I'm still saying no."

"Really?" Donia stared at her, hating that she had to say it, but knowing that Aislinn needed to hear the truth. "Were you saying it last night?"

"That was different," Seth ground out. He stood up and stepped forward.

Donia didn't even move. She blew gently, thinking: *ice.* A wall of ice formed around Seth, like a glass cage. "All I know is that he believes Aislinn is the one destined to be his. Once he believed I was, and this is the result of his love."

She reached out and touched the ice, shivering as it retracted back into her skin. "That's all I can tell you tonight. Go make your salve. Think about what I said."

CHAPTER 22

[A] woman of the Sidhe (the faeries) came in, and said that the [girl] was chosen to be the bride of the prince of the dim kingdom, but that as it would never do for his wife to grow old and die while he was still in the first ardour of his love, she would be gifted with a faery life.

—*The Celtic Twilight* by William Butler Yeats (1893, 1902)

When Sunday morning came, Aislinn wasn't surprised to find Grams up and alert. At least she waited until after breakfast to pounce.

Aislinn sat down on the floor beside Grams' feet. She'd sat there so often over the years, letting Grams comb out her hair, listening to stories, simply being near the woman who'd raised and loved her. She didn't want to fight, but she didn't want to live in fear, either.

She kept her voice level as she said, "I'm almost grown, Grams. I don't want to run and hide."

"You don't understand. . . ."

"I do, actually." Aislinn took Grams' hand in hers. "I really, really do. They're awful. I get that, but I can't spend my life hiding from the world because of them."

"Your mother was the same way, foolish, hardheaded."

"She was?" Aislinn paused at that revelation. She'd never had any real answers when she asked about her mother's last years.

"If she hadn't been, she'd still be here. She was foolish. Now she's dead." Grams sounded feeble, more than tired—exhausted, drained. "I can't bear to lose you too."

"I'm not going to die, Grams. She didn't die because of the faeries. She . . ."

"Shh." Grams looked toward the door.

Aislinn sighed. "They can't hear me in here even if they're right outside."

"You can't know that." Grams straightened her shoulders, no longer looking like the worn-out woman she had become, but like the stern disciplinarian of Aislinn's childhood. "I'm not letting you be foolish."

"I'll be eighteen next year. . . ."

"Fine. Until then, you're still in my house. With my rules."

"Grams, I—"

"No. From now on, it's to and from school. You can take a taxi. You will let me know where you are. You will not walk around town at all hours." Grams' scowl lightened a little, but her determination did not. "Just until they stop following you. Please don't fight me, Aislinn. I can't go through that again."

And there wasn't much else to say after that.

"What about Seth?"

Grams' expression softened. "He means that much to you?"

"He does." Aislinn bit her lip, waiting. "He lives in a train. Steel walls."

Grams looked at Aislinn. Finally she relented and said, "Taxi there and back. Stay inside."

Aislinn hugged her. "I will."

"We'll give it a little longer. They can't reach you in school or in here. They can't reach you in this Seth's train." Grams nodded as she listed the safety measures, restricting but not yet impossible. "If it doesn't work, though, you'll need to stop going out. You understand?"

Although Aislinn felt guilty for not correcting Grams' mistaken beliefs about school and about Seth's, she kept her emotions as securely hidden as she did when the fey were near, saying only, "I do."

The next day, Monday, Aislinn went through school like a sleepwalker. Keenan wasn't there. No faeries walked the halls. She'd seen them outside, on the steps, on the street as the taxi drove by them, but not within the building.

Has he already had what he wanted? Was that all this was?

The way Donia had talked there was far more to it, but Aislinn couldn't focus on anything other than the blank spot in her memories. She wanted to know, needed to know what had happened. It was all she could think about as she went through the motions of classes.

At midday, she gave up and walked out the front door, not caring who saw.

She was still on the steps when she saw him: Keenan stood waiting across the street, watching her. He was smiling, gently, like he was happy to see her.

He'll tell me. I'll ask, and he'll tell what happened. He has to. She was so relieved that she went toward him, dodging cars, almost running.

She didn't even realize he was invisible until he said, "So you truly can see me?"

"I . . ." She stammered, stumbled over the words she'd been about to say, the questions she needed to have answered.

"Mortals can't see me unless I will it." He acted as calm as if they'd been talking about homework, as if they weren't discussing something that could get her killed.

"You see me, and they"—he pointed to a couple walking their dog down the street—"don't."

"I do," she whispered. "I've always seen faeries."

It was harder to say this time, to tell *him*. Faeries had terrified her as long as she could remember, but none so much as Keenan. He was the king of the awful things that she'd fled from her whole life.

"Walk with me?" he asked, although they already were.

He faded into what she now thought of as his normal glamour—dulling the shimmer of his copper hair, the rustling sound of wind through trees—and she fell in step with him, silent now, trying to think of how to ask him.

They had just passed the park when she turned to him and blurted, "Did you? Did we? Sex, I mean?"

He lowered his voice, like he were sharing secrets with her. "No. I took you home, saw you to your door. That's all. When the revelry ended, when they all left, and it was just us . . ."

"Your word." She trembled, hoping he wasn't so cruel as to lie. "I need to know. Please."

As he smiled at her reassuringly, she could smell wild roses, fresh-cut hay, bonfires—things she didn't think she'd ever been around, but knew nonetheless in that moment.

Solemnly he nodded. "My word, Aislinn. I swore to you that your wishes would be as my own as often as I am able. I keep my vows."

"I was so afraid. I mean, not that you would"—she broke off and grimaced, realizing what she'd implied—"it's just that . . ."

"What can you expect of a faery, right?" He gave her a wry grin, looking surprisingly normal for a faery king. "I've read the mortals' stories of us, too. They aren't untrue."

She took a deep breath, tasting those strange summer scents on her tongue.

"But the fey I . . . hold sway over don't. Will not do that—violate another." He acknowledged the bows of several invisible faeries with a nod and a quicksilver smile. "It is not the way of my fey. We do not take the unwilling."

"Thank . . . I mean, I'm glad." She almost hugged him, her relief was so great. "You don't like those words, right?"

"Right." He laughed, and she felt like the world itself rejoiced.

She rejoiced. *I'm a virgin.* She knew there were other thoughts she should ponder, but that one precious sentence was all she could think. Her first time would be one she would remember, one she would choose.

As they walked on, Keenan took Aislinn's hand in his. "In time I hope you'll come to understand how much you mean to me, to my fey."

The scent of roses—*wild roses*—mingled with a strange briny scent: waves crashing on rocky shores, dolphins diving. She swayed, feeling the pull of those faraway waves, as if the rhythm of something beyond her was creeping inside her skin.

"It is a strange thing, this chance for openness. I've never courted anyone who could truly know me." His voice blended with the tug of foreign waters, sounding more musical with each syllable.

Aislinn stopped walking; he still held her hand, like an anchor to keep her from leaving. They were standing outside The Comix Connexion.

"We met here." He caressed her cheek with his free hand. "I chose you here. In this spot."

She smiled languidly, and suddenly she became aware that she was happier than she should be.

Focus. Something was wrong. *Focus.* She bit her cheek, hard. Then she said, "I gave you your dance, and you gave me your word. I know what I want from you. . . ."

He ran his fingers through her hair. "What can I give you, Aislinn? Shall I weave flowers in your hair?"

He opened his hand, letting go of her hair. An iris blossom sat in the palm of his hand. "Shall I bring you necklaces of gold? Delicacies mortals can only dream of? I'll do all those things anyway. Don't waste your wish."

"No. I don't want any of that, Keenan." She stepped back, putting more distance between them, trying to ignore the cry of gulls that she heard under the rhythm of waves. "I just want you to leave me alone. That's all."

He sighed, and she wanted to weep at how sad she suddenly felt. *Faery tricks, it's all faery tricks.*

She scowled. "Don't do that."

"Do you know how many mortals I've wooed in the past nine centuries?" He stared through the window at a display for the release of yet another vampire movie.

A wistful expression on his face, he said, "I don't. I could ask Niall, probably even ask Donia."

"I don't care. I'm not interested in being one of them."

The ocean faded under the acrid taste of desert winds, searing her skin, as anger flared on his face. "How very fitting."

He laughed, softly then, like a cool breeze on her burning skin. "To finally have found you, and you don't want me. You see me, so I can be as I truly am—not a mortal, but a faery. I am still bound by other rules: I cannot tell you *why* you matter to me, who I am—"

"The Summer King," she interrupted, moving away

from him, ready to run. She tried to keep her te
check. He'd done the right thing by her, but that cha...g
nothing. He was still a faery. She shouldn't have let herself
forget that.

"Aaah, so you know that as well." In an inhumanly
quick move, he stepped closer until they were chest to
chest. In less time than it took to blink, he stood there as he
truly looked—not wearing his glamour. Warmth rained
over them, as if sunbeams fell from his hair like warm
honey pouring slowly over her.

She gasped, feeling like her heart would burn out from
racing so fast. The warmth rolled across her skin, until
she was almost as dizzy as she'd been when she danced
with him.

Then he stopped it, like turning off a faucet. There were
no breezes, no waves, nothing but his voice. "I promised
you I would do anything you asked of me *within my power*.
What you ask is not within my power, Aislinn, but there is
much that is."

Her knees felt like they'd give out; her eyes wanted to
close. She had the awful temptation to ask him to do that—
whatever it was—just once more, but she knew that didn't
make sense.

She shoved him away, as if distance would help. "So you
lied."

"No. Once a mortal girl is chosen, she cannot be un-
chosen. At the end you may reject me or accept me, but
your mortal life is behind you." He cupped his hand in

f her, scooping the empty air and coming up with a
ful of creamy liquid. Swirls of red and gold shivered in
it; flecks of white floated among the other colors.

"No." She felt her temper—her lifetime of anger at
faeries flare up. "I reject you, okay? Just go away."

He sighed and poured the handful of sunlight out,
catching it in the other hand without looking. "You're one
of us now. Summer fey. Even if you weren't, you'd still be
mine, still belong with us. You drank faery wine with me.
Haven't you read *that* in your storybooks, Aislinn? Never
drink with faeries."

Though she didn't know why, his proclamation made
sense. Somewhere inside she'd known she was changing—
her hearing, the strange warmth just under her skin. *I am
one of them.* But that didn't mean she had to accept it.

Despite her growing anger, she paused. "So, why did
you let me go home?"

"I thought you'd be angry if you woke up with me,
and"—he paused, mouth curled in a sardonic half-smile—
"and I don't want you angry."

"I don't want you at all. Why can't you just leave me
alone?" She fisted her hand, trying to restrain her temper, a
thing that she was finding more and more difficult the past
week.

He took a step closer, letting the sunlight drip onto her
arm. "The rules require you to make a formal choice. If you
don't agree to the test, you become one of the Summer
Girls—bound to me as surely as a suckling child to its dam.

Without me, you'll fade away, become a shade. It is the nature of the newly-made fey and the limitation of the Summer Girls."

Her temper—so well controlled after all these years—beat against her like a cloud of moths pushing against her skin, aching to be set free.

Control. Aislinn dug her fingernails into her palms to keep from slapping him. *Focus.* "I will not be a faery in your harem or anywhere else."

"So be with me, and only me: it's the only other choice." Then he bent down and kissed her, lips open against hers. It was like swallowing sunshine, that languorous feeling after too many hours on the beach. It was glorious.

She stumbled back until she bumped into the window frame.

"Stay away from me," she said, letting all that anger she'd been feeling show in her tone.

Her skin began to glow as brightly as his had. She stared down at her arms, aghast. She rubbed her forearm, as if she could wipe it away. It didn't change.

"I can't. You've belonged to me for centuries. You were born to belong to me." He stepped closer again and blew on her face as if he were blowing the head off a dandelion gone to seed.

Her eyes almost rolled back; every pleasure she'd felt under the summer sun combined into one seemingly endless caress. She leaned against the rough brick wall next to them. "Go away."

She fumbled in her pocket for the packets of salt Seth had given her and cracked them open. It was a weak throw, but the salt sprinkled over him.

He laughed. "Salt? Oh my lovely, you're such an exquisite prize."

It took more strength than she thought she had, but she pushed away from the wall. She pulled out the pepper spray: it worked on anything with eyes. She flicked the safety off, exposing the nozzle, and aimed it at his face.

"Courage and beauty," he whispered reverently. "You're perfect."

Then he faded away, joining the rest of the invisible faeries walking down the street.

He paused halfway down the block and whispered, "I'll allow this round to you, but I shall still win the game, my beautiful Aislinn."

And she heard it as clearly as if he were still beside her.

CHAPTER 23

[T]heir gifts usually have conditions attached, which detract from their value and sometimes become a source of loss and misery.

—*The Science of Fairy Tales: An Enquiry into Fairy Mythology* by Edwin Sidney Hartland (1891)

Donia knew who it was before she reached the door. No faery would dare pound on her door like that.

"A game?" Aislinn stormed into the room, her eyes flashing. "Is that what this is to you too?"

"No. Not in the same way, at least." At Donia's side Sasha bared his teeth and laid his ears back, welcoming Aislinn as he'd once welcomed Donia. He knew that—despite the waves of anger flowing off Aislinn—she meant no harm.

She stood there, glimmering as Keenan did when he was angry, and prompted, "How then?"

"I am a pawn, neither king nor queen," Donia said with a shrug.

Anger gone as quickly as it'd come, Aislinn stopped.

As volatile as he is too.

Aislinn bit her lip, silent for a moment. "One pawn to another, will you help me?"

"Indeed. It is what I do."

Glad to look away from terrible brightness hurting her eyes, Donia walked over to the old wardrobe and opened it. Intermingled with her daily wear were clothes she'd no use for: velveteen tops with impossibly beautiful embroidery, shimmering blouses that looked like nothing more than a net of stars, dresses fashioned of sheer scarves that bared as they concealed, and leather clothes of every cut a girl could want.

She held out a crimson bustier that Liseli said she'd once worn to the Solstice Ball, the year after she'd become Winter Girl. *He wept, tears of sunlight,* she'd told Donia. *Show him what he cannot ever have.*

Donia had never been able to be so callous, but she'd wanted to.

Aislinn's eyes widened as she looked at the bustier. "What are you doing?"

"Helping you." Donia hung the top back up and held out a strange metal halter, strung with black gems.

Aislinn pushed it away with a frown. "This is helping?"

"It is." Donia found it then, the one that fit Aislinn: a Renaissance chemise that had been altered into a blouse, strikingly white with an almost lurid red ribbon lacing from bosom to waist. "Faeries respond well to confidence. I learned that too late. You must show him that you are not meek, that you will not be commanded. Go there—act as his equal, not a subject—and tell him you want to negotiate."

"For what?" Aislinn took the blouse, fingering the soft cotton.

"For some sort of peace. He's not going away. Your mortality isn't coming back. Don't start eternity with him believing he can tell you what to do. Start by putting him off kilter: dress for battle."

Donia sorted through the skirts and overdresses. They all seemed too regal, too formal. Aislinn would need to remind him she was not like the others, bound to do his bidding. She was a girl who'd grown up in a world where women had choices. "Be more aggressive than he is. Summon him to you. If he takes too long, don't wait. Go to him."

Aislinn looked helpless, standing there clutching the blouse. "I'm not sure I can."

"Then you've already lost. Your modernity is your best weapon. Use it. Show him that you are entitled to some sort of choice. You know what he is now, so demand that he talk to you. Negotiate for what control you can wrest from him." Donia drew out pants, sleek and modern. "Go change. Then we'll talk more."

Aislinn took the slick black pants with a shaky hand. "Is there a way to win?"

"The Summer Girls believe they've won." Donia hated saying it, but it was true. The girls were happy: they didn't see their dependence as a burden.

Aislinn twisted the cotton blouse in her hands, wringing it like a wet cloth. "What's the alternative? There has to be another choice."

Donia paused. She put a hand on Aislinn's wrist, shook off her glamour, and revealed the snow falling in her eyes. "Me."

Although the winter chill was awful for the summer fey—which she now was—Aislinn didn't look away.

So Donia let the cold slip into her fingertips, leak out until frost blossomed on Aislinn's arm, forming small icicles that dangled on her elbow, then fell to the floor with a clatter. "This."

Wincing finally, Aislinn pulled back. "I want neither."

"I know." Donia reigned the cold in, trembling with the effort. "But given the two . . . They are free in ways that I'm not. To be a Summer Girl is to live forever, to dance and play, and have the freedom from almost everything. It's a life of eternal summer. They have no responsibility; they leave that behind with their mortality, and he"—she almost choked on the words but she still said them—"takes care of them. They want for nothing."

"I don't want that."

Donia wanted to tell Aislinn to refuse it, but it wasn't her place. That was *his* job. Instead Donia told her, "It's what you're becoming already. Surely you've noticed?"

At that, Aislinn's shoulder's slumped.

Donia remembered it—that strange dissociative feeling that accompanied the changes. It wasn't a pleasant memory, even now with the cold settled deep inside her. She kept the pity from her voice and said, "To not join them, you must take the test."

"What kind of test?" Aislinn sounded even younger then, frightened.

No one had asked it before. By the time the test was an issue, the girls were already decided. They might not have verbalized it, but their choice—to risk everything to be with Keenan or not—was already made in their hearts. In Donia's time, none had loved him enough to attempt it. Nor, for that matter, had he truly loved them—at least that was what she'd told herself each time he wooed them.

"That's for him to say. I cannot. He'll hold out a third choice, the prize, as it were. In nine centuries, no one has ever become that third thing. If you take the test and lose, you become what I am. If you do not take the test before the next season comes upon us, that too is a choice: you simply join the other girls." Donia gave Aislinn a gentle push toward the bedroom. "Go change."

Aislinn stopped in the doorway. "Is there any way out of whatever mess this is? To just walk away? I want to go back to my life. Isn't there someone we can talk to?"

Donia carefully closed the wardrobe door, not looking at Aislinn. No one had ever asked that, either.

Still facing the wardrobe, she said, "Only one girl has ever avoided choosing."

"How?"

Turning, Donia caught Aislinn's gaze and killed the hope that had crept into her voice. "She died."

CHAPTER 24

He is no less a personage than the King of Faerie. . . . Very numerous indeed are [his subjects] and very various are they in their natures. He is the sovereign of those beneficent and joyous beings . . . who dance in the moonlight.

—*The Mabinogion* (notes) by Lady Charlotte Guest (1877)

Keenan stirred his drink idly. The Rath usually cheered him, but all he could think about was how to convince Aislinn that she was essential. He had let his emotions go earlier, let his power leak all over her, and she'd swooned—recognizing it as it called to her own changed self—but he'd need another tactic for their next meeting.

Never the same move twice.

"If you aren't going to talk, go dance, Keenan." Tavish spoke calmly, as if he weren't worried. "It will do them well to see you smiling."

Beyond him, the girls were dancing, spinning in that dizzying way that they liked, and giggling. Guards—on and off duty—circulated through the crowd. Though it was his club, the winter fey and the dark fey both frequented it more and more, making his own guards increasingly necessary as time passed. Only the high court fey seemed able to follow house rules somewhat regularly. Even his own summer fey weren't well behaved most nights.

"Right." Keenan slammed back the rest of his drink and motioned to Cerise.

His cell rang, and it was her. *Her voice. Her. My resistant queen.* "Aislinn?"

He made a writing motion in the air. Tavish held out a napkin; Niall scrambled for a pen.

"Sure . . . No, I'm at the Rath. I could come now. . . ." He hung up and stared at the phone.

Tavish and Niall looked expectantly at him.

Keenan motioned for Cerise to go back to the floor. "She wants to meet and talk."

"See? She'll fall in line like the rest of them," Tavish said approvingly.

"Do you need us or can we go"—Niall snagged Siobhan around the waist as she walked by—"relax?"

"Go dance."

"Keenan?" Cerise held out a hand.

"No, not now." He turned away, watching the cubs run through the crowd, barely avoiding being trampled under the dancers' feet.

He let his sunlight trickle out over the crowd, setting several illusory suns to rotate over the dancers. *My queen sought me out.* It would all be as it should, soon. *My queen, finally beside me.* He laughed joyously, seeing his fey frolic in front of him, the fey who'd waited with him. Soon, he'd be able to restore the court to order. Soon, all would be right.

Aislinn walked down to the abandoned building by the riverside, murmuring Donia's advice over and over with each step: *Take the offensive.* She tried to believe she could do it, but the mere idea of going into their den made her feel ill. She'd seen enough faeries going into Rath and Ruins over the years that she'd known to avoid it at all costs.

But here I am.

She knew where he was, knew that he'd come if she beckoned, but Donia thought this was wiser. *Be aggressive. Strike first.*

Aislinn clung to the hope that there was a way to keep her life, at least as much of it as she could.

I still don't even know what he wants, not really. So she was going to ask—*demand*—that he talk to her, that he tell her what he wanted, and why.

I can do this. She stopped at the door.

In front of her, half leaning on a stool, was one of the club's bouncers. Under the glamour, he was a terrifying sight—curled tusks spiraled out on either side of his face, ending in sharp points. He looked like he spent all of his time lifting weights, a fact he didn't hide with his glamour.

She stopped several steps away from him. "Excuse me?"

He lowered his magazine and looked over his sunglasses. "Members only."

She looked up at him, catching his gaze as best she could, and said, "I want to see the Summer King."

He laid the magazine aside. "The what?"

She straightened her shoulders. *Be assertive.* It sounded a lot easier than it felt.

She tried again. "I want to see Keenan. He's in there. And I know he wants to see me. I'm the"—she forced the words out—"new girl in his life."

"You shouldn't come here," he grumbled as he opened the door and motioned to a boy with a lion's mane standing just inside. "Tell the . . . tell *Keenan* that . . ." He looked at her.

"Ash."

"That Ash is out here."

The lion-boy nodded and scampered off, disappearing through a doorway. His glamour made him seem cherubic, his lion's mane a wild twist of sandy-blond dreads. Of the fey around town, the lion-maned ones were among the few that never seemed to cause trouble on purpose.

The guard let the door fall closed with a thud. He picked up his magazine, but he kept glancing at her and shaking his head.

Her heart thudded. Trying to feign nonchalance, she glanced back at the street. Only a few cars had driven by so far; it wasn't a busy area.

If I'm going to go for aggressive, why not start now? A practice run. The next time he looked back at his magazine, she said, "For what it's worth, you're sexier with the tusks."

He gaped at her. The magazine hit the damp ground with a soft *smack.* "With the *what*?"

"Tusks. Seriously, if you're going to go with a glamour, add bars in place of your tusks." Aislinn gave him an appraising look. "Bit more menacing, too."

His grin was a slow thing, like sunrise creeping over the horizon. He altered his glamour. "Better?"

"Yeah." She stepped closer to him, not touching, but closer than she'd have believed she could get without panicking. *Pretend it's Seth.* She tilted her head so she was looking up at him. "Works for me."

He laughed, nervously, and glanced over his shoulder. The messenger wasn't back yet. "I'm liable to get flogged if you keep doing that. It's one thing to go for a mortal, but you"—he shook his head—"you're off limits."

She didn't move, not closing that last little gap, but not backing up, either. "Is he that cruel? To beat people?"

The guard almost choked on his laugh. "Keenan? Hell, no. But he's not the only player. The Winter Girl, Keenan's advisors, the Summer Girls"—he shuddered, lowered his voice—"the Winter Queen. You never know who's going to get pissy about what once the game's in motion."

"So what's the prize for the game?" Her heart thumped so loudly now, she felt like she'd have chest pains any minute.

Keenan and Donia weren't telling her everything; maybe

he would. Donia might say she was trying to help, but she was one of the players.

The messenger was coming back, leading two of the vine-decorated faeries she'd seen in the library.

Focus. Don't panic whatever *he says.*

He leaned down so his tusks framed her forehead and whispered, "Control. Power. You."

"Oh."

What does that mean?

She mutely followed the vine-covered girl, wondering if the fey ever gave a straight answer.

Aislinn—*my queen, here*—followed Eliza through the crowd; they parted for her as they did for him. She was lovely, a vision come true. The Summer Girls spun like dervishes. Winter fey sulked. And the dark fey licked their lips, as if in anticipation. Others—solitary fey and the rare high court fey who mingled in the crowd—looked on, curious, but not invested in the outcome. It was as if his life, his struggle, were nothing more than a tableau for their amusement.

Eliza stepped up, bowed her head. "Your guest, Keenan."

He nodded, then pulled out a chair for Aislinn. She wasn't smiling, not happy at all. She wasn't here to accept, but to fight.

And everyone's watching.

He felt curiously ill at ease. He'd always chosen the field of battle, always set the stage, but she was here—in his club,

surrounded by his people, and he hadn't a clue about how
to deal with it.

She came to me. Not for the reason he'd like, though; her
posture was proof enough that she was there to deny him.
As strategies go, it was a good one. Even if she wasn't the
queen, she was the best game he'd had in a long time. If she
weren't so terrified of him, it would be a lovely start to the
evening.

"Let me know when you're done staring at me." She
tried to sound blasé and failed.

She turned away and flagged down one of the innumerable cubs that scampered around. "Can I get something
normal that mortals drink? I don't want any of that wine I
had at the faire."

The cub bowed—his mane bristling when another faery
tried to step closer—and went in search of her drink, not
slowing for the fey clustered around him, becoming lost in
the throng of dancing faeries.

From the edge of the dance floor, Tavish and Niall
watched openly, using the guards to form a barricade of
sorts to keep the girls farther away. They rarely had sense
about what should and shouldn't be said. Tonight they were
almost impossible to deal with, believing their queen was
finally among them.

"I'm done staring," he murmured, but he wasn't. He
didn't think he ever would be if she dressed like that very
often. She had on some sort of vinyl pants and a very old-
fashioned blouse that laced up with a red velvet ribbon. If

he tugged that ribbon, he was fairly certain the whole thing would come undone.

"Do you want to dance before we talk?" His arms almost ached to hold her, to dance as they had at the faire, to swirl in the fey—*our fey.*

"With you? Not likely." She sounded like she was laughing at him, but her bravado was forced.

"Everyone is staring." *Staring at both of us.* He needed to assert himself or the fey would think him weak, subservient to her. "Everyone but you."

So he dropped his glamour, letting all the sunlight he carried illuminate him, making himself shine like a beacon in the dim light of the club. It was one thing for a mortal to see a faery; it was another to sit before a fey monarch.

Aislinn's eyes widened; her breath caught on a gasp.

Leaning forward across the table, Keenan darted a hand out to grab one of her tightly clenched hands.

In a move too fast for mortal eyes to see, Aislinn yanked away—then scowled down at her hand, as if she could quell the reminder of how changed she already was.

Then the cub Aislinn had sent for refreshments was back, holding a tray of drinks; three of his pride followed him, each carrying a tray of the sugary mortal snacks the fey preferred.

With a friendliness she denied feeling for the fey, Aislinn smiled at them. "That was quick."

They stood straighter, tawny manes puffed in pleasure.

"For you we'll do anything, my lady," the eldest one answered in that gravel voice the cubs all had.

"Thank"—she caught herself before she said those uncomfortable mortal words—"I mean, it's kind of you."

Keenan smiled as he watched her. Maybe her changing attitude was a result of her own changing body; maybe it was a product of her inevitable acceptance of the fey. He didn't care, though, as long as she was smiling at their faeries.

But when she glanced away from the cubs—compelled to look at his glowing face—she stopped smiling. Her pulse beat in her throat like a trapped thing. Her gaze skittered away from him; she swallowed several times.

It isn't the cubs that make her blood race, that make her face flush. It's me. Us.

The cubs sat their trays on the table: ice cream, cakes, and coffees; desserts from local bakeries and sweet drinks with no alcohol in them. They snarled at each other as they pointed out delicacies.

"Try this."

"No, this."

"She'll like this better."

Finally Tavish came over to the table with one of the guards to remove them. "Go away."

Aislinn watched silently. Then, with visible decisiveness, she turned back to Keenan. "So let's talk about your little game. Maybe there's an answer we can find that'll let us both get back to our lives."

"You are my life now. This"—he waved a hand dismissively around him at the club—"the fey, everything, it all falls into place once you accept me."

None of it mattered without her beside him. *If she says no, they all die.*

He whispered, "I need you."

Aislinn clenched her fists. *This wasn't working.* How was she to reason with him when he sat there shining like a celestial object? He wasn't threatening her, wasn't doing anything but tell her things that should sound sweet.

Is it so awful? She wavered as he looked at her so intently—seeming for all the world like he was a good person.

He's a faery. Never trust a faery.

His harem stood behind her, other girls who'd been where she was. Now they mingled in the crush of bodies around her, faeries themselves. It wasn't a life she wanted.

"That's not the sort of answer that helps." She took a deep breath. "I don't like you. Don't want you. Don't love you. How can you think there's any reason to . . ." She tried to find the right words. There weren't any.

"To court you?" he prompted, half smiling.

"Whatever you call it." The smell of flowers was overwhelming her, dizzying. She tried again. "I don't understand why you're doing this."

"It's already done." He reached out.

She pulled away. "Don't."

He leaned back in his seat. The blue lights of the club heightened his inhuman appearance. "What if I told you that you were the key—the grail, the book—that one object that will rescue me? What if I said you were what I need to defeat one who freezes the earth? If your acceptance would save the world—all these faeries, your mortals, too—would you do it?"

She stared at him. Here was the answer that they'd been hiding from her. "Is that what this is about?"

"It might be." He walked around the table, slowly enough that she could've stood and put the chair between them.

She didn't.

"There's only one way to find out, though." He stepped just close enough that she'd need to shove him away to stand. "You have to choose to stay with me."

She wanted to run.

"I don't want to become one of them"—she motioned to the Summer Girls—"or some ice faery like Donia."

"So Donia told you about that." He nodded, as if this too were normal.

"The detail you didn't mention? Yeah." She tried to sound reasonable, as if being told her options were harem girl or ice faery was an average thing. "Look. I don't want to be one of your playthings, and I don't want to be what Donia is."

"I don't think you will be either of those. I told you earlier. I want you to choose to be with me." He pulled her to her feet, leaving her standing far too close to him. "If you are the one—"

"Still not interested."

He looked weary then, as unhappy as she felt. "Aislinn, if you're her, the key I need, and you turn away, the world will continue to grow colder until the summer fey—including you, now—die of it, until mortals starve." His eyes were reflective, like an animal's eyes under the weird lights of the club. "I cannot allow that to happen."

For a moment Aislinn stood there, unable to find a word to say. Donia had been wrong: she wasn't able to talk to him, try to reason with him. He wasn't reasonable.

"I need you to understand." His tone was frightening, the warning growl of a predator in the dark. Just as quickly, he sounded desperate as he added, "Can't you at least try?"

And Aislinn felt herself nodding, agreeing that she'd try, desperate to end his unhappiness.

Focus. That wasn't what she came here to do. She gripped the edge of the table until it hurt.

Seeing him, knowing that he was real, knowing what the world he was offering her truly looked like—it wasn't making it any easier to resist. She'd thought it would, thought the horrible things she'd seen would make her stronger, more resolute. But as he stared imploringly at her, all she could think of was the desire to give him what he wanted, anything to make that sunlight flare over her again.

She tried concentrating on the faeries' awfulness, thinking about the cruel things she'd seen them do. "Your faeries aren't important enough to be worth me giving up my life."

He didn't answer.

"I have seen them. Don't you understand? The ones

here"—she lowered her voice—"I've seen them groping girls, heard them, watching them pinch and trip and mock. And *worse*. I've heard them laughing at us. My whole life, every day, I've seen your people. I don't see anything worth saving."

"If you accept me, you would rule them—be the Summer Queen. They would obey you as they do me." His eyes implored her, not faery wiles now, just a look of desperation.

She lifted her chin. "Well, if the way they act is any indication, they don't obey very well. Unless you don't object to their actions."

"I've been too powerless to do much other than count on their better natures to make them listen. If you rule them, you could change that. We could change so much. Save them." He made a sweeping gesture to the crowds of dancing faeries. "Unless I become king in truth, these faeries will die. The mortals out there in your city will die. They're dying already. You'll be around to watch it happen."

She felt the tears in her eyes, knew he saw them, and didn't care. "There has to be another way. I don't want this, and I won't become one of the Summer Girls."

"You will. You *are* unless you choose to be with me. It's a simple thing. Really, it's laughable how quick the process is."

"And if I'm not this grail of yours? I spend eternity like Donia?" She pushed him away. "How is that a good plan? She's miserable, in pain. I've seen it."

He winced and looked away when she mentioned Donia,

seeming so much more real for it. It made her pause. He might have a lot to gain, but from the look of pain that raced over his face, he'd lost a few things that mattered.

"Just tell me you'll think about it. Please?" He leaned in and whispered, "I'll wait. Just tell me you're considering it. I *need* you."

"Can't you find another way?" she asked, although she knew the answer, knew that there wasn't another answer. "I don't want to be your queen. I don't want *you*. There's someone else I—"

"I know." Keenan accepted a drink from a cub who'd scurried under the legs of one of the innumerable guards that followed Keenan. With another sad smile, he added, "I am sorry for that as well. I do understand, far better than I'm able to say."

The inevitability of it all was starting to set in. She thought about it: the things that would change, the things she wanted to keep unchanged. She had so many questions. "Is there another way? I don't want to be a faery at all, and I certainly don't want to rule them."

He laughed, mirthlessly. "Some days I don't either, but neither of us can change what we are. I'll not lie and say I wish I could undo it for you, Aislinn. I believe you're the one. The Winter Queen fears you. Even Donia believes you are the one." He held out his hand. "I wish it didn't trouble you. But I'm begging you to accept me. Simply tell me what you want, and I'll try."

In a moment uncannily like the faire, he waited with his

hand outstretched, asking her to accept him. At the faire she thought it was almost over; now she had the sinking feeling it was only beginning.

How do I tell Seth? Grams? What do I tell them? Simply willing it all away had never worked with the Sight, and she was beginning to believe that this was much the same. She knew she was changing, despite how much she'd been trying to deny it.

I'm one of them.

If she were to survive, she needed to start thinking about figuring out the faery world.

Then she realized that both the guard and Keenan had mentioned another ruler, another player in this game of theirs. She looked at him and asked, "Who's the Winter Queen? Could she help me?"

Keenan choked on his drink. In that blurringly quick way he moved, he clutched her arms. "No. You cannot let her know that you see us, that you know any of what is transpiring." He shook her slightly. "If she were to know . . ."

"If she can help me . . ."

"No. You must believe me. She's more vicious than I can begin to explain. I might not strike out at you for seeing us, but there are others who would, including the Winter Queen. She's why I am powerless. Why the earth freezes. You must not seek her out." His fingers dug into her arms until she began to glow too. He seemed terrified, a thought she didn't want to consider too closely.

He considers himself powerless?

Mutely she nodded, and Keenan let go of her arms, smoothing out her wrinkled sleeves.

Aislinn leaned in closer, her lips almost on his skin since the music and noise were growing louder by the moment. "I need to know more than this. You're asking too much for me to . . ." She couldn't continue for a moment, thinking of what he was asking her to give up, to become. *What I'm already becoming.* "I need more answers if you want me to think about any of this."

"I can't tell you everything. There are rules, Aislinn. Rules that have been in place for centuries . . ." He was almost yelling to be heard over the noise. "We can't talk here amid their excitement."

All around them the faeries were cavorting, moving in ways clearly not mortal, even with their glamours in place.

He held out his hand again. "Let's go to the park, coffee shop, wherever you want."

She let him take her hand, hating how inevitable her choice was beginning to seem.

Keenan felt her tiny hand in his, as soothing as the touch of the sun. She hadn't said yes, but she was considering it, accepting the loss of her mortality. Sure, she would mourn, but it was often like that for the newly fey girls.

He led her toward the door, well aware that the summer fey were watching with approving looks. They danced nearer, brushing close and smiling at Aislinn.

And she held her head high, as bold as she'd been when

she walked through the crowd to see him. He suspected that she saw them as they were: not their glamours, but their true faces. She did not dance, but she did not flinch away when they came near. For a sighted mortal, it was a truly courageous thing.

He knew she heard the murmurs of those who—unaware of her Sight—chose to stay invisible, who wandered even closer and brushed a hand against her hair.

"Our lady."

"The queen is here."

"Finally come to us."

They hadn't heard her doubts or desperation. They only heard that the mortal girl had sought him out; they only knew that she left with him. After the Eolas' words at the faire, they believed she was the one who would free him, rescue them. He hoped they were right.

"The Summer Girls in the library, they said"—she looked away and blushed before rushing through the rest of her words—"they sounded like they, umm, *dated* mortals."

It hurt, her asking that. He hadn't ever thought that when he found his queen, she'd be so uninterested in him. He ground his teeth, but he answered, "They do."

"So I could . . ." She paused as they approached the door.

The guard—who'd added strange metal rings to his glamour since Keenan had arrived—grinned at her. "Ash."

Bold once more, she grinned at him. "Later."

Shocked by her easy smile at the guard, Keenan turned to ask her what had transpired between them—far better that than discuss her desire to continue to have a relationship with a mortal.

They stepped outside, and he felt it: the bone-aching wave of cold.

"Beira." Hurriedly he whispered, "Please, stay near me. My mother is coming toward us."

"I thought you lived with your uncles."

"I do." He stepped in front of Aislinn, putting himself between them. "Beira is supremely unqualified to care for anyone."

"Now, now, sweetling, that's not very kind." Beira stepped out of the darkness like a nightmare he couldn't ever stop remembering.

Her glamour revealed her usual strand of pearls resting on a gray dress. It revealed the thick fur jacket she wore. It didn't reveal her snow-filled eyes or the sparkle of frost on her lips. Keenan knew Aislinn saw it, though. He knew that she saw his mother's true face. The thought didn't comfort him.

Beira let her icy breath float toward his face as she sighed and said, "I just thought I should meet the girl who's got everyone talking."

Then the Winter Queen leaned closer still and kissed him on both cheeks.

Keenan felt the bruises, the frostbite, forming where her lips had touched his skin, but he didn't speak. Fortunately, neither did Aislinn.

"Does the *other* girl know you're out with her?" Beira stage-whispered, pointing at Aislinn and wrinkling her nose.

He balled his hand into a fist, wishing he could let his temper reign, thinking of Beira's threats to Donia. Now, with Aislinn beside him—vulnerable still—he dared not. "I wouldn't know."

"*Tsk, tsk,* temper is so unattractive, don't you think?"

He didn't rise to the bait.

She clapped her hands together, sending a wave of cold toward him, and gushed, "Aren't you going to introduce us, darling?"

"No." He stayed in front of Aislinn, keeping her out of Beira's reach. "I think you need to leave."

Beira laughed, letting her chill roll through the sound, making him ache.

He tried to keep Aislinn shielded safely behind him where that icy air wouldn't touch her, but she stepped up beside him and stared at Beira disdainfully.

"Let's go." Aislinn took his hand then, not in love or affection, but in a sign of solidarity. This wasn't the anxious girl he'd been talking to at Rath. No, she looked more like a warrior, one of the old guard who forgot to smile even in moments of bliss. She was glorious.

While he stood there, fighting not to falter under the chill Beira had released, Aislinn pulled him down and kissed each of his bruised cheeks, her lips soft as balm on the painful bruises. "I can't stand a bully."

Warmth shot through his hand, burned on his cheeks.

It can't be.

Keenan looked from Aislinn to his mother. They stood

facing each other like they were ready to wage a war the likes of which fey hadn't seen in millennia.

Unable to focus, Keenan stared at the Dumpster down the alley, the half-asleep man curled in a nest of frayed cloth and boxes, and listened to the sound of his advisors and guards approaching behind them.

Beira moved closer, her bone-white hand lifting toward Aislinn's cheek. "She has a familiar face."

Aislinn stepped out of Beira's reach. "No."

Beira laughed, and Aislinn felt something cold and vile sliding down her back.

Whether or not she was angry about becoming one of them no longer mattered; it had stopped mattering when Beira bruised Keenan. An instinct to protect him flared to life in her—an urge she'd felt often enough for her friends but never for a faery. Maybe it was the way he'd looked in the club, the growing sense that he was as trapped as she was.

Beira couldn't stand against us both. Not both the Summer King and Queen. As much as she didn't like that possibility, it sounded *right* as she thought it.

"Until we meet again, lovelies." Beira waved and two withered hags stepped forward, flanking her much the way ladies-in-waiting did in paintings of royalty. Under their glamours, these faeries shared none of Beira's dark beauty; they simply looked like someone had sucked the life out of them, leaving empty shells, haggard and glassy-eyed.

Without glancing back, the three strolled down the alley.

Shards of ice, cracked and angled like broken glass, glittered in Beira's footsteps.

Aislinn looked over at Keenan. "What a bitch. Are you okay?"

But he was looking at her with awe in his eyes. He put a hand to his cheek; the bruises were fading as she watched—leaving a red imprint where her lips had touched his skin.

His two "uncles" came up on either side of him. His guards moved out around them. *Too little, too late.* Several of the faeries were speaking at once.

"Beira's gone?"

"Are you. . . ?"

But Keenan ignored them. He lifted Aisinn's hand to his cheek, holding it there. "You did that."

One of the faeries stepped closer. "What did she do? Are you injured?"

"She didn't see, did she? Beira?" Keenan asked.

His eyes widened, and Aislinn saw tiny purple flowers blossoming inside them.

She pulled her hand away, shaking her head. "This doesn't mean anything, doesn't change a thing. I was just . . . I don't know why I even did that."

"You did, though," he whispered, taking both of her hands in his. "You see how different it is now."

She trembled.

He was looking at her as if she were the grail he'd spoken of, and her only thought was to run, far and fast, run until she could run no farther.

"We were going to talk. You said . . ." Her words vanished as the weight of it hit her. *It's true. I'm the* . . . She couldn't even think it, but she knew it was true, and *he* knew it too. She shook her head.

"Is someone going to fill us in here?" The quieter faery uncle stepped up.

Still holding fast to her hands, Keenan tilted his head to motion them forward. His voice a low whisper, like the rumble of thunderstorms, he announced, "Aislinn healed the Winter Queen's touch."

"I didn't mean to," she protested, trying to tug free of his grasp. Any flash of friendship, of protective instinct, had vanished as he gripped her hands too tightly in his.

"She kissed Beira's frost, and it's gone. She unmade Beira's touch. She offered me her hand—by choice—and I was stronger." He let go of one of her hands to touch his cheek again.

"She did what?"

"She healed me with a kiss, shared her strength with me." Still holding one of her hands, Keenan dropped to his knees, staring up at her, golden tears running down his face like rivulets of liquid sunshine.

The other faeries dropped to their knees beside him in the dirty alley.

"My Queen." Keenan let go of her other hand to reach up toward her face.

And she ran. She ran like she'd never run in her life,

crushing the still-shimmering ice under her feet, fleeing the sunlight gleaming in Keenan's skin.

Keenan knelt on the ground for several moments after Aislinn ran away. No one else rose.

"She left." He knew he sounded weak, but he couldn't find the strength to care. "It's her, and she left. She knows, and she left."

He stared down the alley where she'd vanished. She hadn't moved as quickly as the fey, but she'd been moving far quicker than a mortal could. He wondered if she'd even noticed.

"Shall we retrieve her?" one of the rowan-men asked.

Keenan turned to Tavish and Niall. "She left."

"She did," Tavish said as he motioned the guards back.

They faded into the shadows, close enough to hear should they be summoned, but not so close that they'd overhear a softly spoken conversation.

Niall took Keenan's arm. "Give her tonight to let it settle on her."

Tavish moved to Keenan's other side.

"She was going to think about it. She said that inside." Keenan looked from Tavish to Niall and back. "She still will. She has to."

Neither faery answered as they led him forward, his guards following behind them silently.

CHAPTER 25

The fairies, as we know, are greatly attracted by the beauty of mortal women, and . . . the king employs his numerous sprites to find out and carry [them] off when possible.

—*Ancient Legends, Mystic Charms, and Superstitions of Ireland* by Lady Francesca Speranza Wilde (1887)

Aislinn didn't stop running until she was at Seth's door. She pushed it open, calling his name, and stumbled to a stop when she saw the small crowd gathered there.

"Ash?" He was across the room and had her in his arms before she could think of what to say.

"I need . . ." She was still panting, her hair stuck to her face and neck. The noise of clinking bottles and moving bodies barely registered as she tried to catch her breath.

No one commented, or if they did, she didn't hear it as Seth led her through the doorway to the second train car, where the tiny bathroom and his bedroom were. They stood in the hallway, outside the closed door of his room.

"Are you hurt?" He was running his hands over her arms, looking at her face and arms, checking for rips in the ridiculous clothes Donia had given her.

She shook her head. "Cold. Scared."

"Take a shower. Warm up while I get rid of everyone." He opened the door and turned on the little heater in the room. The soft whir filled the room as the heater started to glow.

She hesitated, and then nodded.

He kissed her briefly and left her there.

When Aislinn came out of the tiny bathroom, the house was silent; everyone was gone. She stood in the doorway—feeling safer now that she was here with Seth. Grams had done her best, but her fear of the faeries had made them too central—as if even the mundane things were somehow dependent on the faeries' reactions.

Seth was stretched out on his sofa, his hands over his head, his feet dangling over the arm. He didn't seem alarmed or even surprised by her panicked arrival.

Do I look different to him now?

She thought, *invisible,* and walked over to him. He didn't get up, didn't look at her, or speak.

He really can't see me.

She ran her fingers over his arm, pausing on his biceps.

"Is it easier to be aggressive when you're like that?" He looked right at her.

She yanked her hand away. "What? How . . ."

"The stuff in Donia's recipe. You're all shadowy, like the faeries outside, but I still see you." He didn't move, staying exactly as he had been when she walked into the room. "I don't mind, you know."

"I'm already as bad as them."

"No." He rolled onto his hip so there was room on the sofa for her too. "You weren't touching some stranger on the street. It's me."

She sat down on the far end of the sofa. He wrapped his legs around her—one behind her back, the other resting on her lap.

"Keenan is convinced I'm the Summer Queen."

"The what?"

"The one who can give him back the powers he lost. If he doesn't find his queen, it'll just keep getting colder. He says everyone, humans too, will die. That's what this is all about. He thinks I'm her, this queen who'll change it all." She leaned forward just a little so Boomer didn't get tangled in her hair as he made his way across the back of the sofa. "They made me a faery. I'm one of them."

"I got that when you did the invisible thing."

"They did this to me, changed me, and I'm . . . I don't want to be their freaking queen."

He nodded.

"I think I am, though. . . . I don't know what to do. I met the other one tonight—the Winter Queen." She shivered, thinking of the terrible cold, the ache of it. "She's awful. She just walked up and attacked Keenan, and I wanted to hurt her. I wanted to bring her to her knees."

She told him about the ice that Beira left in her wake, the hags, the kiss that made everyone so convinced that she was their queen. Then she added, *"I don't want this."*

"So we find a way to undo it." He used his legs to pull her toward him so she was lying on his chest. "Or we figure out how to deal with it."

"What if I can't?" she whispered.

Seth didn't answer; he didn't promise it would be all right. He just kissed her.

She felt herself warming up, like a small glow starting somewhere near her stomach, but she didn't think anything of it until Seth pulled back and stared at her.

"You taste like sunshine. More and more every day," he whispered. He ran his fingertip over her lips.

She walked away, wanting to weep. "Is that why things changed with us? Me becoming something else?"

"No." He was calm, slow, like approaching a frightened animal.

"Seven months, Ash. For seven months, I've been waiting for you to see me. This"—he picked up her hand, which glowed like Keenan had earlier—"is not why. I fell in love with you before this."

"How was I to know?" She twisted the edge of the stupid blouse Donia had given her. "You didn't say anything."

"I said lots of things," he corrected gently. "You just didn't hear them."

"So, why now? If it's not this, why?"

"I waited." He undid the bow on her blouse, twirling the ribbon around his finger. "You kept treating me like a friend."

"You were my friend."

"Still am." He put one finger in the topmost lace and tugged the ribbon looser. "But that doesn't mean I can't be other things, too."

She swallowed hard, but she didn't move away.

He pulled the next cross of ribbon free.

"He didn't. We didn't, I mean," she stammered.

"I know. You wouldn't have gone there looking like this if you had." He looked at her, slowly letting his gaze travel up over the vinyl pants and slightly gaping blouse, until he was looking at her flushed face. "Unless you want him. If you do, Ash, tell me now."

She shook her head. "No. But when he, it's not him, it's some faery thing. . . ."

He tipped her head up. "Don't give up. Don't leave me before you're even here."

"If I, if we . . ." She took a deep breath and tried to keep her words from tumbling over each other as she said, "If I wanted to stay here, be with you tonight?"

He stared at her for several seconds. "This stuff with them, it's not the right reason."

"Right." She bit the inside of her lip, embarrassed.

But like an echo, she heard Keenan's silence earlier at Rath and Ruins, his careful avoidance of her questions when she asked about faeries and mortals. There was a chance that if she was their queen, she'd lose Seth. She closed her eyes.

"Ash, I want to. I want *you*, but because of *us*, not because of something they do or don't do."

She nodded. He was right; she knew it. It didn't feel fair, though. None of it felt fair or right. The only thing that felt right was Seth.

"That doesn't mean you can't stay. Just no sex." He spoke softly, like he'd done the other morning when she was freaking out. "That still leaves a lot open."

Seth took Aislinn's hand as they walked back to the other train car, the one that he'd turned into a bedroom, but he barely held on. If she wanted to, she could turn and go the other way. She didn't. She wrapped her fingers around his so tightly it probably hurt him.

But now that they stood in the doorway, with a bed that stretched from one side of the narrow room to the other, she almost panicked. "It's . . ."

"Comfortable." He let go of her hand.

It really wasn't that big, a queen at most, but that left only a couple feet on either side of it. Unlike the Spartan interior of the front car, this room was a bit more dramatic. Dark purple, almost black, pillows were piled on the bed; a few had tumbled onto the floor, like shadows on the black rug. On either side of the bed were small black dressers. A sleek black stereo sat on one; a candelabra sat on the other. Wax trailed down the candles and onto the dresser.

"I could sleep out on the sofa." Seth kept his distance when he said it, smiling gently. "Give you space."

"No. I want you here. It's just that it's"—she motioned

to the room—"so different from the rest of the house."

"You're the only girl who's been invited back here, ever." He walked to the stereo, his back toward her, and flipped through the discs in the wall-rack. "Just so you know."

She sat on the edge of the bed, folding a leg up in front of her, leaving the other foot on the floor. "It feels weird. Like it's more important now that I'm here."

"It should be." He stood on the opposite side of the bed, holding a clear jewel-case. "I've done it the other way, with people who didn't matter. It's not the same."

"Then why did you do it?"

"Felt good." He didn't look away, even though he seemed uncomfortable. He shrugged. "Drunk. All sorts of reasons, I guess."

"Oh." Aislinn did look away.

"It got old. There's, umm"—he cleared his throat—"some papers over there. I wanted to give them to you before . . . I was going to bring it up the other day . . . but, and, now . . ." He pointed.

Aislinn reached out and pulled the papers off the table with the candles. On the top sheet she read "Huntsdale Clinic." She looked over at him. "What?"

"Tests. I had them earlier this month. I get them regularly. Thought you'd want to know. I want you to know." He picked up one of the pillows, flipping it over in his hands. "I haven't been, you know, unsafe in the past, but still . . . things happen."

Aislinn skimmed them, test results for everything from

HIV to chlamydia, all negative. "So . . ."

"I planned on talking about this before. . . ." He squeezed the pillow between his hands, mashing it. "I know it's not all romantic."

"It's good." She bit her lip. "I've never . . . you know."

"Yeah. I know."

"There's been nothing that would, umm, put me at risk." She picked at the comforter, feeling increasingly shy.

"Why don't I go . . ."

"No, please, Seth"—she climbed across the bed and pulled him toward her—"stay with me."

Several hours later Aislinn felt her hands curling, gripping the comforter. She'd been kissed before but not like that, not *there*. If sex was any better than that, she wasn't sure she'd survive it.

All the stress, the worry, had faded away under Seth's touch.

Afterward he held her. He still had his jeans on, scratchy against her bare legs.

"I don't want to be one of them. I want this." She put her hand on his stomach. She slipped her pinky nail in the edge of his belly ring. "I want to be here, with you, go to college. I don't know what I want to be, but it's not a faery. Definitely not a faery queen. I *am*, though; I know it. I just don't know what to do now."

"Who says you can't still do all that even if you are a faery?"

She lifted her head to look at him.

"Donia uses the library. Keenan goes to Bishop O.C. now. Why can't you still do the things you want?" He slid a handful of her hair forward, making it fall over her shoulder onto his chest.

"But they do those things because of this game of theirs," she protested, but even as she said it, she wondered. Maybe it didn't have to be all or nothing.

"So? They had reasons; you have different reasons. Right?"

It sounded so much easier when he said it—not easy, but not impossible, either. Could she really keep her life? Maybe Keenan hadn't answered her questions because he didn't like the answers.

"I do." She laid her head back down on him, smiling. "More reasons every day."

CHAPTER 26

If we could love and hate with as good heart as the faeries do,
we might grow to be long-lived like them.
—*The Celtic Twilight* by William Butler Yeats (1893, 1902)

"It's her." Beira stomped her foot, setting frost rippling over
Donia's yard like a glistening wave. "You *cannot* let her near
the staff. Do you hear me?"

Donia winced at the bite in Beira's voice. She didn't
speak or move as Beira's wind ripped through the yard,
shredding trees, uprooting the fall flowers still clinging to
life.

Beira tossed the staff on the ground and said, "Here. I
brought it. Followed the rules."

Donia nodded. In all the times Beira had brought the
staff to her, in all the times they'd played this game, there
had never been any real doubt in the Winter Queen.

This time it's different. This girl *is different.*

Beira's eyes had bled to pure white, her temper so close

to uncontrollable that Donia couldn't speak.

"If she comes for it, lifts the staff"—Beira held out her hand and the staff moved toward her like a living thing going to its master—"you can stop her. I *cannot.* Those were the terms Irial dictated when we bound the whelp: if I actively interfere, the mantle that makes that mortal the Summer Queen is unavoidably manifest. I lose my throne; she gains hers and frees Keenan."

Beira caressed the staff as she spoke. "I cannot act. *Balance,* damnable balance, those were Irial's terms when we placed the limits on Keenan."

Donia could not speak much above a whisper, but she tried, "What are you saying?"

"I'm saying that those pretty blue lips of yours could solve my problem." Beira tapped a finger twice against her own far-too-red lips. "Is that clear enough?"

"It is." Donia forced herself to smile. "And if I do that, you'll free me?"

"Yes." Beira bared her teeth in a cruel snarl. "If it's not done in the next couple days, I'll send the hags to her, and then I'll be back for you."

"I understand." Donia licked her lips and tried to match the cruelty in Beira's face.

"Good girl." Beira kissed Donia's forehead and pressed the staff into her hands. "I knew I could count on you to do the right thing. It'll be fitting for you to be the one to bring Keenan to his knees after all he's done to you."

"I haven't forgotten anything Keenan's done." Donia did

smile then, and she knew by Beira's approving look that she looked as cruel as Beira did.

Holding the staff so tightly it hurt her hands, Donia added, "I'm going to do exactly what I should."

Keenan dismissed the guards, the girls, everyone but Niall and Tavish. The guards who'd followed Aislinn confirmed his suspicion of where she went. *She knows now. How can she still turn away? Go to him?*

Niall counseled patience as Keenan paced through the loft. It was what he had offered Aislinn earlier, but now, now that he knew, how could he wait?

"I've been patient for centuries." Keenan felt frantic. As he paced, his queen—the one he'd waited for his whole life, for *centuries*—was in the arms of another, a mortal no less. "I need to talk to her."

Niall stepped in his path. "Think about this."

Keenan pushed Niall aside. "Do you see her coming here? I'm here. I didn't follow her to his house, but she didn't come to me."

"A few hours?" Niall spoke calmly, as he'd done countless times before when Keenan's temper made him act foolishly. "Just until you're calmer."

"Every moment I wait, Beira has a chance of learning what happened, where she is." He went to the door. "She already knows of what the Eolas said. That's why she came out tonight. If she learns what Aislinn can do already, what we can do together . . ."

"Listen to yourself." Niall put a hand on the door, keeping it closed. "You aren't going to convince her when you're like this."

"Let him go, Niall," Tavish said, not raising his voice, but sounding even more assertive than usual. His gaze was terrifying as he told Keenan, "Remember what we spoke of. Nothing is too far to go in pursuit of this one. We all know it's her."

A horrified look came over Niall's face. "No."

Keenan shoved Niall aside, wrenched open the door, and promptly collided with Donia. A hiss of steam rose from their bodies as he stood pressed against her frigid body for that too-brief moment.

As undisturbed as the winter's first snow, she came into his loft—of her own volition, no less—and said placidly, "Close the door. We need to talk."

Donia stepped past Keenan, exposing her worried expression to his advisors rather than to him. He didn't need to see that, not as upset as he already was.

Once she heard the door close, she said, "She wants Ash dead. She wants me to kill her." She stood inside the doorway, further in the room than she'd like, with him standing between her and the exit. "You need to do something."

He didn't answer, just stared at her with a panicked look.

"Keenan? Did you hear me?" she asked.

He made a dismissive gesture to Niall and Tavish. "Leave me alone with Don."

They both left, but only after Niall caught her eye and told her, "Be gentle."

Keenan knelt on the sofa. "She ran away from me."

"She did what?" She came closer to Keenan, ducking as one of his damnable birds swooped down at her.

"Ran." He sighed, and the room filled with the rustle of leaves. "It's her. She unmade Beira's frost, healed me with a kiss."

"You can convince her," Donia said in a low voice. She didn't need Tavish and Niall and whatever Summer Girls lurked in the loft to overhear her sounding so gentle to Keenan. "Let her have tonight to think, but tomorrow . . ."

"She ran to him, Don. The rowan-men went there, to see." He looked stricken, his beautiful eyes haunted. "It's her. She knows it, but she left to go to the mortal. I'm going to lose if . . ."

Donia took his hand, ignoring the pain at his touch, the steam that rose like a cloud from their hands. "Keenan, give the girl a moment to think. You've known forever. This is all so new to her. . . ."

"She doesn't love me, doesn't even *want* me." His voice held such sadness that a small rain shower began in the room.

"Make her." Donia let her gaze rake over him, challenging him, trying to spark that arrogance that seemed so lost lately. "What? You've suddenly run out of ideas? Come on, Keenan. Go talk to her tomorrow. If that doesn't work, drop your glamour. Kiss her. Seduce her. Just do it quickly, or she'll be dead."

"What if—"

She cut him off. "No. I bought you a couple days at most. Beira thinks I'll do her bidding—kill Ash—but it won't take long for her to realize I'm not hers to control."

Before he could answer, she raised her voice, to be heard over the clatter of the ice that rolled off her where Keenan's raindrops touched her skin: "If you don't win Aislinn, she'll lose her life. Make her listen, or everyone loses."

CHAPTER 27

Citizens of Faery have one supreme quality in common—
that of single-mindedness.

—*Fairies* by Gertrude M. Faulding (1913)

When Aislinn woke the next morning—still curled in Seth's arms—she knew it was time, past time really, to tell Grams the whole truth. *How? How do I tell her any of it?*

Aislinn had checked in last night, a brief call to ease her grandmother's worries. Grams hadn't objected to Aislinn staying at Seth's place, only reminded her to be careful, to "use precautions and good sense." And Aislinn realized that her grandmother knew *why* Aislinn was staying. Despite her age, Grams was a believer in all sorts of women's equalities—a detail that had been shockingly apparent in her "birds and bees" talks not too many years ago.

Aislinn slipped out of bed for a quick bathroom trip. When she returned, Seth was propped up on one arm.

"You okay?" There was obvious worry in his voice. "With us?"

"Very." She climbed back onto the bed and snuggled close to him. Being with him was the one thing she truly felt right about. "I still need to go soon."

"After breakfast . . ." His voice was low, almost a growl, as he slid his hand under the edge of the T-shirt she was wearing, the one he'd had on last night.

"I should go. I need to talk to Grams about things and . . ." She swallowed as he pulled her onto his chest and sighed against her throat.

His breath was warm on her skin, tickling her. "You sure? It's early still."

She let her eyes drop closed again, let herself relax in his arms. "Ummm . . . just a few minutes."

His laugh was dark, different in a way she couldn't have imagined, filled with unspoken promises. It was wonderful.

Almost an hour later, she got dressed and assured him she didn't need him to walk her home.

"Come back later?"

"As soon as I can," she whispered.

I will, too. She wasn't giving Seth up. It wasn't an option. *If I'm really their queen, who has the right to tell me what to do?*

She was still smiling when the faeries outside bowed to her. Several of the ones who seemed to be guards followed her as she walked across the city, keeping a slight distance, but undeniably there. Behind them trailed the scarred faery who'd posed as Keenan's uncle at school.

In the bright morning light—after a long night with Seth—it seemed somehow less awful, not easy, but possible. She just needed to talk to Keenan, tell him she'd take his test *if* she could still keep her real life, too. The other option—giving up her mortal life to be either a Summer Girl or the Summer Queen—didn't work. Now she needed to figure out how to tell him and where to find him.

But she didn't need to find him: he sat in the hallway outside her apartment—invisible to her neighbors.

"You can't be here," she said, more irritated than fearful.

"We need to talk." He had a weary look on his face, and she wondered if he'd slept at all.

"Fine, but not here." She grabbed his arm and pulled. "You need to go."

He got to his feet, but he didn't leave. He glowered at her. "I've waited most of the night, Aislinn. I'm not going until we talk."

She pulled him away from the door, away from Grams' home.

"I know, but not here." She folded her arms over her chest. "This is my grandmother's house. You can't be here."

"So walk with me." His voice was quiet, filled with that desperation she'd heard at Rath and Ruins.

She'd worried that he'd be angry after she ran, that he'd be unwilling to compromise, but instead he looked as overwhelmed as she felt, if not more. His gleaming copper hair looked dull, as if the shine had vanished. He scrubbed his hands over his face. "I need you to understand. After last night—"

Grams opened the door and stepped outside. "Aislinn? Who are you talking—"

Then Grams saw him. She moved forward as quickly as she could, grabbed Aislinn, and pushed her backward. "You."

"Elena?" Keenan started, eyes wide, hands held open in a nonthreatening way. "I mean no harm."

"You are not welcome here." Her voice shook.

"Grams?" Aislinn looked from the near-panic in Keenan's eyes to the fury in Grams'. This wasn't going well.

Grams pulled Aislinn through the open door and started to push it shut.

Keenan stopped the door with his foot as Grams shoved on it with all her strength.

He stepped inside and pushed the door shut behind him. "I'm sorry about Moira. I wanted to tell you before. . . ."

"Don't. You have no right to even say her name. Ever." Grams' voice cracked. She pointed at the door. "Get out. Get out of my home."

"In all these centuries, I've never walked away for another, only for her. Only Moira. I offered her time." Keenan reached out as if he'd take Grams' hand.

Grams slapped his hand away. "You killed my daughter."

Aislinn couldn't move. *How could Keenan have killed my mother? She died in childbirth. . . .*

"No. I didn't," he replied in a low voice, sounding as

assured as he had the first night Aislinn had met him, sounding the way he had at Bishop O.C. He laid a hand on Grams' shoulder. "She ran from me, lay down with all those mortals. I tried to stop her, to—"

Slap.

"Grams!" Aislinn grabbed Grams' hand and tugged, pulling her away from Keenan, steering her to her chair.

Keenan didn't even flinch. "Once the mortal girl is chosen, there's no way to un-choose her, Elena. I'd have taken care of her, even after the baby was born. I waited, stopped seeking her when she was with child."

Grams was weeping now. Her tears rolled over her cheeks, but she made no move to wipe them away. "I know."

"Then you know I didn't kill her." He turned to Aislinn, his eyes pleading with her. "She chose death by her own hand rather than joining the Summer Girls."

Grams stared at the wall where the few existing pictures of Moira and Aislinn were. "If you hadn't hunted her down in the first place, she'd be alive."

Aislinn turned to Keenan; her voice came out half stran-gled when she said, "Go."

Instead he crossed the room, coming toward her, walking past the portraits of her mother without even a glance. He put a hand under Aislinn's chin and forced her to look up at him. "You're my queen, Aislinn. We both know that. We can talk now or later, but I cannot let you turn away from me."

"Not now." She hated how her voice shook, but she didn't back away from him.

"Tonight then. We need to speak to Donia, arrange for your guards, and"—he looked around the apartment—"decide what you'll want to move, where you want to live. There are other, lovelier places we can live."

This was the faery who'd stalked her—confident and compelling. As quickly as lightning across the sky, he'd gone from pleading to demanding.

She stepped behind Grams' chair, out of his reach. "I live with Grams."

Smiling beatifically, Keenan dropped to his knees in front of Grams. "If you want to join her in our home, I'll have your things brought over. It'd be our honor."

Grams said nothing.

"I am sorry that Moira was so afraid. I've waited so long, I'd almost given up. If I'd known that Moira would be the mother of our queen"—he shook his head—"but all I knew was that she was special, that she drew me to her."

The whole time he'd been speaking, Grams had not moved: she'd clenched her hands in her lap and glared at him.

Aislinn reached over and gripped Keenan's arm. "You need to leave. Now."

He let her pull him to his feet, but the look on his face was awful. Gone were all traces of kindness, of pleading, of anything but raw determination. "You *will* come to me tonight, or I will find you—find your Seth. That isn't how I want to do this, but I'm running out of choices."

Aislinn stared at him as his words registered. She'd begun the day prepared to reason with him, to accept the inevitable, and he was *threatening* her. He was threatening Seth. She made her voice as cold as she could, "Don't go there, Keenan."

He ducked his head. "It's not what I want, but I—"

"Leave," she interrupted him.

She grabbed his arm and led him to the door.

"We can talk later, but if you think for a minute that threats are going to help"—she broke off as her temper flared—"you really don't want to threaten me."

"I don't," he said softly, "but if I have to, I will."

She opened the door and shoved him out. She took several deep breaths, leaning on the now-closed door, and started, "Grams, I—"

"Run before he comes back. I can't protect you. Get your Seth, leave, go somewhere far away." Grams went to the bookshelf, brought down a dusty book, and opened it. It was hollowed out in the middle. Inside was a thick stack of bills. "It's running-away money. I've been saving it since Moira died. Take it."

"Grams, I—"

"No! You need to go while you can. She didn't have money when she ran; maybe if you do . . ." She went into Aislinn's room and pulled out a duffle bag, resolutely shoving clothes into it, ignoring everything else—including Aislinn's repeated attempts to talk to her.

CHAPTER 28

They are said to have aristocratical Rulers and Laws, but no discernible Religion.

> —*The Secret Commonwealth* by Robert Kirk
> and Andrew Lang (1893)

Keenan heard Elena's statements as clearly as if she were beside him, but he didn't stop. *What good would it do?* He couldn't go back inside.

He stepped onto the almost-barren walk outside their building and waited for Niall, who was sprawled on a bench across the street, to cross to him.

"I said not to follow me."

"I didn't follow you. I followed her"—Niall inclined his head toward Aislinn's building—"the queen. I thought it prudent after the Winter Girl's visit."

"Right." Keenan sighed. "I should've sent extra guards over there."

"You were distracted. Anyhow, it's what we do—look after

you. Might as well start looking after the queen." His words
were nonchalant, as if their queen had already said yes.

She hadn't. And as much as Keenan hoped she wouldn't
run, he wasn't certain.

As he'd waited there in the hallway—knowing his queen
lay with another, knowing that she'd die if she didn't accept
him, knowing that Donia would die when Aislinn did
accept him—he'd faced the ugly reality of the situation. He
had to do whatever necessary to win. There wasn't time to
wait. He couldn't force her, but he could use faery persua-
sion, offer her too much wine, threaten Seth . . . Aislinn
would accept him. There were no other choices.

"How did it go?" Niall asked as they started up the
street, the guards trailing them. "You seem better than last
night."

"It—" he started, but promptly stopped himself. "I don't
know. Moira was her mother."

"Ouch." Niall winced.

Keenan took a steadying breath. "But there are ways to
convince her—things I don't want to do."

Niall prompted, "The things Tavish spoke of?"

Even though Niall's tone was harsh, Keenan kept his
face blank. "It's business. I could bring her mortal to the
loft, let the girls have him, let her see him smitten and
senseless."

"It's not our way. Not the Summer Court." Niall made
a signal to the guards, and they shifted directions, slowly
steering him down another street.

"There will be no Summer Court if Beira kills Aislinn," Keenan said. He didn't like the options, but was the fate of all the summer fey and mortals worth the upset of one girl?

"True." Niall turned between two storefronts, cutting through a narrow alley. "I know Tavish believes it necessary to be expedient—regardless of the cost—but I've been with you as long as he has."

"You have," Keenan said slowly. He knew Niall was even more sensitive to questions of volition.

Niall's expression clouded, leaving him looking near sick. His voice was raw as he said, "Don't cross those lines, Keenan. Not if there's any way to avoid it. You've never been tolerant of that—if our king does it, why should any of the fey do otherwise?"

Niall stopped, putting his hand on Keenan's arm.

In the shadows of the alley before them, several thistle fey had cornered a wood-sprite, her back to a wall. She pleaded with them. They weren't touching her, but she was trapped—by Keenan's own guard. His rowan-men had blocked the opening to the alley, letting no one in or out.

Her skin was already striped with bleeding cuts where the dark fey's thistle-covered hands had touched her. Her tunic was all but shredded, exposing her bloody stomach.

"Is this scene for my benefit?" Keenan asked as he turned slowly to face Niall.

"It is." Niall lowered his voice, but the look on his face was brazen. He straightened his already-stiff shoulders. "I cannot sway you with the paternal influence as Tavish can, or with the Winter Girl's melancholy love."

"So, what, you stage an attack?" All the rancor Keenan had ever felt toward the atrocities of the dark fey seemed to flood him as he looked at his advisor—his friend—and then at the scene orchestrated before them.

"I had the guards find them and relocate them here. This"—Niall motioned to the three in the alley—"is what the Dark Court does. It's never been our way."

At Niall's signal, the guards between the dark faeries and sprite stepped back, leaving the sprite at their mercy.

The dark fey laughed as they caught the sprite.

The sprite's tunic was gone, leaving her topless. She shrieked and begged, "Please."

One of the fey pierced the sprite's arm, pinning her to the wall behind her, leaving her trapped and defenseless.

"We'll share," the dark faery called as he licked the sprite's bleeding wrist.

In an anguished voice, Niall asked, "Would you be able to do it? Watch them hurt the queen's mortal? Would you want your court doing that? Look at them"—he pointed at the dark fey, one of whom was licking his lips as the sprite tried to kick his legs out from under him—"is that what you'd turn our court into?"

Keenan couldn't look away from the weeping sprite, who was fighting desperately despite the odds, despite now being pinned to the wall by both arms. "It's not the same."

Using her legs, the sprite clutched a rowan-man

around his middle and pulled him in front of her like a shield. The guard looked positively ill as he disentangled himself from her.

"It's not?" Niall prompted in a tone that made no secret of his disgust. "You'd do *that* in our court?"

Keenan let go of his temper and swung at Niall, knocking him down. Blood trickled from Niall's lip where it had grated over his teeth.

None of the guards moved or looked away from the sprite.

Another of the dark faeries said, "Feels good, doesn't it?"

The other dark fey laughed.

Keenan didn't look away from Niall, who was crouched on the ground. "I will do what I must to stop Beira. And if I must . . . use something other than words with Seth or Aislinn, I will make sure that it's not violent."

Although he hated even thinking it, he couldn't let his distaste for it condemn them all. Aislinn might despise him, but he could *not* let her turn away. In time, she'd come to understand. If not, he'd do his best to make up for it.

"It doesn't matter. Not to her. You told me about what she said after the faire, how she worried"—Niall bowed his head, showing submission in his posture even though his words were defiant—"if you force her or allow the girls to use him, you will lose. There was a time when that would not be seen as a violation. Today, it is."

Temper barely contained, Keenan said to his guardsmen, "Free her. Get them out of here. Now."

Looking relieved, the guards—who far outnumbered the dark fey—quickly pulled the sprite free and dispatched the still-grinning dark faeries.

The sprite wept, clinging to one of the guards who'd shed his jacket and draped it around her.

"It's not the same," Keenan insisted. He wiped Niall's blood from his knuckles and held a hand out to him.

"With all due respect, my king, it is exactly the same, and you know it as well as I." Niall accepted Keenan's hand and rose. He inclined his head toward the bloodied sprite. "That one isn't weeping over the bruises on her skin. Beira wounds them far worse, and they stay silent. She weeps in fear of what could have been. She fought to prevent what they would've done to her."

Niall wasn't saying anything Keenan hadn't already thought, but there simply weren't any other options if Aislinn continued to refuse him. She needed to agree, and he didn't know how to persuade her to do so. She wasn't interested in him romantically; her dislike of the fey was a huge obstacle. Her entanglement with her mortal was another deterrent, and now the revelation about Moira seemed certain to eliminate any sliver of a chance he might have had.

After several of his guards gently escorted the sprite away, Keenan resumed walking. Quietly he asked, "If the choice is that or her death, *our death*, which would you have me pick?"

"Maybe you need to ask her." Niall motioned behind them.

Keenan turned, and there she was: Aislinn, his reluctant queen.

Niall bowed; the remaining guards bowed.

Keenan held out his hand, hoping.

She ignored it, shoving her hands into the pockets of the too-large leather jacket she had on. It wasn't hers, and he knew without asking that it belonged to her mortal.

She glared at him. "I thought we were to going to take a walk and talk about things. I had to ask one of your guards to help me find you."

Keenan blinked, baffled by her unpredictability. "I hadn't understood that you were—"

"Grams wouldn't talk. She gave me money to run away. I don't suppose I could get far"—she stepped close enough to him that his breath stirred the tendrils of hair around her face—"could I? Could I get away from you by running?"

"I doubt it," he said, half wishing he could answer as she wanted him to.

"It didn't work for my mother, did it?" she whispered as she stared up at him, an unfathomable expression in her eyes. "So talk. You seemed insistent enough, threatening me."

For the first time Keenan felt like stepping backward, away from her. He didn't. Earlier, in her home, he'd felt more assured. Now, with Niall's admonishments and the sprite's shrieks fresh in his mind, with Aislinn staring at him with shadowed eyes, he had to struggle to regain his balance.

She didn't move back, but she glanced at the guards who

stood—invisible still—around them. "Can they give us some space?"

"Indeed." Keenan motioned to the guards, glad to be dealing with a more familiar problem. He often found the guards' proximity stifling.

They moved away, expanding the perimeter of their protective circle.

One hand on her hip, Aislinn tilted her head and looked at Niall, who'd remained behind him. "You too, Uncle . . ."

After a broad smile, Niall stepped up and bowed deeply. "Niall, my lady, court advisor to our king these last nine centuries."

"Give us space, Niall," she said with that same edge in her voice, sounding quite comfortable issuing commands already.

"As you wish." Niall faded to invisible and joined the guards.

Once he was farther away, presumably unable to hear them, Aislinn narrowed her eyes and said, "Threatening me or Seth is really stupid."

"I—"

"No," she snapped, cutting him off before he could offer anything in his defense—not that he *had* anything in his defense that she would find acceptable. "Don't fuck with me. Don't go near my Grams or Seth. That's the first thing we need to get straight if we're going to talk at all."

"Oh?" He did step back then. Aside from Donia and Beira, no one took that sort of tone with him. He might be a bound king, but he was still a king.

"Yeah." She shoved him with both hands. "You need me to get your juice back from the Winter Queen, right?"

"I do," he agreed, dragging the words out slowly.

"So if something happens to me, you're out of luck? Is that about right?" Her chin tilted up.

"It is."

"If you think threats are going to make me cooperate, you're a fool. It won't." She nodded once, as if she were reaffirming her words. "I won't let you use me as an excuse to hurt anyone I love. Got it?"

"I do," he said after clearing his throat.

She walked away then, setting a fast pace.

The guards sped up to keep up with her furious stride, as did he.

After a few tense moments, he asked, "So, what do you, ah, propose? You are the Summer Queen."

"I am," she said softly. "I believe that, but the thing is— you need me far more than I need you."

"So what do you want?" he asked cautiously. He had never met a mortal—or fey, for that matter—so far outside his expectations.

She looked wistful for a moment. "Freedom. Not to even know faeries exist. To be mortal. But none of that is a choice."

He wanted to reach out to her, but he didn't. She was as unapproachable as when he'd first met her—not out of fear, but out of determination. "Tell me what you want that I can give you. I need you to rule alongside me, Aislinn."

She bit her lip again and then—so softly it was almost a whisper—she said, "I can do that. It's not what I want, but I don't see how I can turn away if it really is what I am."

"You're saying yes?" He gaped at her.

She stopped walking and caught his gaze—the fierce look back on her features. "But I will not live with you or be *with* you."

"You'll still need a room at the loft." He didn't say "when trouble arises," but there'd be time to address that later. Royalty could be murdered: his mother had proven that. "There will be times that meetings may run late or—"

"My own room. Not with you."

He nodded. He could afford to be patient.

"I will *not* stop going to school either," she added.

"We could arrange tutors—" he began.

"No. School, then college." She sounded determined, fierce.

"College. We shall find one that suits you then." He nodded. He might not like her insistence on independence—when he had first begun to search for her, women were more docile—but clinging to the mortal world wasn't unreasonable in her circumstances. It might even benefit their court.

She rewarded him with an almost friendly smile then, looking deceptively cooperative. "I can do this if it's a *job*, you know?"

"A job?" he repeated.

"A job." She had a strange tone in her voice then, like

she was musing on it as she said it.

He didn't say anything to fill in the silence that hung at the end of her words. *A job?* His consort viewed their union as a job?

"I don't know you. You don't know me." She gave him another strangely intimidating look. "I can work with you, but that's all I can be. I'm *with* Seth. That isn't going to change."

"So you're asking to keep the mortal?" He tried to keep his voice even, but it hurt. He knew she was implying it earlier, but to say it made it seem so much more real. His queen—his destined partner—was planning to be with another, with a mortal, not him.

She lifted her chin again. "No. I *am* keeping him. There's no asking involved."

He didn't argue, didn't point out how finite mortals were. He didn't tell her that he'd waited for her, *her alone,* for his whole life. He didn't remind her of how they'd laughed and danced at the faire. None of that mattered. Not now. All that mattered was that she was saying yes.

"Is that all?" he asked gently.

"For now." Her voice was thin then, no longer filled with temper or aggression. She seemed lost for a moment, and then, hesitantly, she asked, "So?"

He wanted to rejoice, to sweep her into his arms until she recanted her terms, to weep that she was saying no at the same time as she said yes. Instead he said, "So, my queen, we find Donia."

He pulled out his cell and punched in Donia's number. She was out—or ignoring him—so he left a message to call him.

After he disconnected, he sent guards to find her.

"I know where she lives," Aislinn murmured. "I can meet you there. You could call me and—"

"No. We'll wait together." Now that she was here beside him, Keenan was utterly unwilling to let her out of his sight until it was done. He wasn't sure he'd ever be willing to let her out of his sight. "Whether you see it as a job or not, you are my queen, the one I've waited for. I will be by your side."

She crossed her arms over her chest, hugging herself. "Remember how you asked about starting over"—she glanced nervously at him—"can we for real this time? Try to be friends, then? It's going to be a lot easier if we try to get along, right?" She held out her hand as if she were going to shake his hand.

"Friends," he said, taking her hand in his. The absurdity of it struck him then—his destined queen saw their reign as a job shared by friends. In all his dreams of finding his queen, of finally reaching this point, Keenan hadn't ever imagined it would be a strained attempt at friendship.

After she pulled her hand free, they stood awkwardly for a moment until he asked, "So where would you go if I weren't with you?"

"To Seth's." She blushed, lightly.

Keenan had expected as much; Aislinn seemed to turn to her mortal—*to Seth,* he corrected himself—more and more. Keenan gave her what he hoped was an encouraging smile and announced, "I would like to meet him." *I can do this.*

"Really?" She looked more suspicious than surprised. Her forehead creased in a small frown. "Why?"

He shrugged. "He is a part of our lives now."

"Yeah . . ."

"So I should meet him." He walked away so she couldn't see his face, pausing as he turned the corner to ask, "Shall we?"

CHAPTER 29

Their favourite camp and resting-place is under a hawthorn
tree . . . [which is] sacred to the fairies, and generally [stands]
in the centre of a fairy ring.
—*Ancient Legends, Mystic Charms, and Superstitions of
Ireland* by Lady Francesca Speranza Wilde (1887)

Aislinn stood motionless as Keenan walked on. Some of the
guards waited behind her; others shifted in front of Keenan,
like a moving fence around them.

"Introduce you to Seth," she tested the words on her
tongue. It made a certain amount of sense to introduce
them. At least that's what she tried to tell herself, hoping it
would loosen the tightness in her chest.

They walked like that—in tense silence—until they
were almost at the railroad yard.

"He's a good person, your Seth?"

"He is." She smiled to herself; she couldn't help it.

Several of the guards pulled back with pained expressions

as they stepped into the railroad lot.

Keenan had a strange, half-bemused smile as he murmured, "I've not spent much time around mortal males. The ones I've known haven't seemed very friendly when I've courted the other girls."

She choked on a laugh. "You think?"

"What?" Suspicion crept into his voice.

"Keenan, you're gorgeous. You've got this whole"—she gestured at his khakis and dark green pullover, casual on most people, stunning on him—"drop-dead amazing thing going for you. Most girls probably trip over themselves to talk to you."

"Most, but"—he paused to give her a wry smile—"not all."

She glanced at Seth's still-closed door before saying, "I still noticed how you looked."

"Of course. You're mortal." He shrugged as if her admission was to be expected.

And she supposed it probably was. Seeing him without his glamour was like looking at a perfect sunrise over the ocean, like seeing a meteor shower in the desert, and then having someone ask if you wanted to keep it for your very own.

She bit her cheek to stop from laughing at the idea of him trying to befriend Mitchell or Jimmy or almost any of their friends. They weren't anywhere near secure enough to go out in public with Keenan—even if he wore a glamour to look common. A half-swallowed laugh slipped out, and he frowned briefly at her.

"What?"

"Nothing," she said with only a trace of laughter. Then she had another thought. "Do the faeries treat you like that too?"

"I am the Summer King." He frowned again, looking confused.

Aislinn did laugh then, a full-out belly laugh.

"What?" he asked yet again.

Still trying to quell her laughter, Aislinn motioned to Niall.

Hesitantly he said, "My queen?"

"If you approach a faery, a girl, does she, umm, always reciprocate your interest?" Aislinn watched his face grow as confused as Keenan's had.

"I am the king's advisor. The Summer Girls have desires—" He glanced at Keenan, as if seeking approval. Keenan shrugged. "Our king has only so many hours to relax. The guards and Tavish and I do our best to keep the girls content."

Her laughter fled.

Turning from one faery to the other, she asked, "How many girls *are* there?"

Keenan lifted a hand in a waiting gesture. Then he looked at Niall and said, "No more than four score now?"

Niall nodded.

Keenan added, "They are far too numerous to care for without help."

Aislinn asked incredulously, "So no one says no?"

"Of course they do—not to Keenan—but to us." Niall gave her a look that said he clearly found her questions as baffling as Keenan had. "But then one of the others is there. They are *Summer Girls*, my queen. Summer is for the pleasures, the frivolity, the—"

"Got it," she interrupted. "So your court—"

"Our court," Keenan interjected.

"Right. *Our* court is rather affectionate?"

It was Keenan's turn to laugh. "They are. . . . But they also crave the dance, music, laughter. . . ." He grabbed her and spun her in a circle, letting his glamour drop for a moment so warm sun spilled over her. "We are not cold as the Winter Court or cruel as the Dark Court. We are not restrained as the High Court is, hiding away in their *otherworld.*"

Aislinn caught the guards smiling at them, looking happier as Keenan laughed. She felt happier too, and she wondered if it was because she, too, was one of the Summer Court now.

She shook off the languor and asked, "So the faeries that hurt people aren't ours?"

Keenan's smile faded as quickly as it had come.

"Many are not, but some still are. Once we are strong"—he paused and took her hand and stared at her so intently she had to fight not to run—"we can do more to stop them. The Summer Court is the most volatile of the courts, passionate. Without the guidance my father gave them, not all have limited their passions to honorable pursuits. We have much work to do."

"Oh," Aislinn said. The enormity of what she'd agreed to undertake suddenly settled on her, seeming impossibly daunting.

Keenan must have seen the worry in her expression, for he quickly added, "But we shall relax as well. The Summer Court is a place of dance and desire. To only work would be as untrue to our nature as it would be to allow the darker things to go unpunished."

"It's pretty huge, what I'm agreeing to do. Isn't it?" She clenched her hands in tight fists to keep them from shaking.

His voice was cautious as he agreed, "It is."

"What do I, I don't know, *do*?"

"You rouse the earth when the winter needs to loosen its grip; you dream the spring with me." He took her hands—unfolding her fingers so that her palms lay open atop his—and said, "Close your eyes."

She trembled, but she did as he asked. She felt his breath on her face as he spoke in soft whispers.

He said, "And they dreamed slender roots sinking into the soil and furred creatures stretching in their dens, dreamed fish racing the currents, field mice weaving through the grasses, and serpents basking on the rocks. Then the Summer King and Queen smiled at the new life they'd called to wake."

And she could see it—the world stretching like a giant beast too long asleep, shaking off the snow that had kept it dormant too long. She felt her body glowing, knew that she was glowing, and she didn't want to stop. She could see the white willow that she'd heard rustling in the breeze when she'd first seen Keenan; she could taste that fragile scent of spring flowers. Together they would stir the creatures, the earth itself. They would look on the waking world and rejoice.

As she opened her eyes to look at him, she realized that she was weeping. "It's so . . . huge. The things that need to start to live again . . . How will I? We? What if I fail?"

Keenan cupped her cheek in his hand briefly. "We won't."

"And the rest? The court stuff?" She wiped her cheeks, trying not to flinch as she saw that the tears were golden. Hurriedly she tucked her hands into her pockets and resumed walking. "I don't know how to rule anyone."

He shrugged when he strode up alongside her. "So you learn. I'll be there. I *do* know how to rule. But today we don't think about all that. That's the beauty of summer as well. There are balls to have and dancing to be done. If we rejoice, our court will, too. It is as much a duty as waking the earth."

"Right, sounds like an easy job. Wake the earth, rule the unruly, repair the broken stuff, and party." She swallowed with difficulty as they stepped into Seth's lot, anxious both at the enormity of the task and at the strangeness of telling Seth. "I guess anyone could handle that little list?"

"No, but the Summer Queen can," Keenan assured her; then he favored her with one last blinding smile before he turned his attention to the opening door and said, "Today, though, we begin with only the first step. I meet my queen's beloved and try to befriend a mortal, yes?"

"Yeah. That one is doable." She shook her head as if to shake away the stress, but then she looked up.

Seth stood waiting as patiently as he did any other day. The rest of her worries, her changes, the world itself faded. *How will Seth feel?*

She had a flash of worry that things would seem weird after last night, that he wouldn't still want her, that he'd be angry that she brought the faeries to his home. But he wasn't freaking out—about them or the faeries all around her. Aside from her and Keenan, they'd all stayed invisible, but she knew Seth could see them and that he was pretty aware of who it was that stood beside her.

Seth's expression was unreadable, but he held out a hand and said, "Hey."

Then the court, Keenan, Niall, the guards—it was all forgotten as she slipped into Seth's arms.

After watching Aislinn's and her mortal's faces, Keenan found it much easier to believe that his queen was making the only choice she could. He knew that look, had seen it in the eyes of several girls, had seen it in Donia's eyes.

"Come on." Seth motioned for him to follow. Then he stopped and looked at Aislinn. "If he . . ."

She paused. "Umm. Can you come in here?"

"I can." Keenan exchanged a brief look with Niall at Seth's obvious awareness of what he was and of the fey aversion to steel.

What else has she said to him? His curiosity piqued, he

added, "Cold iron doesn't harm a monarch."

Seth didn't miss a beat. He quirked his eyebrow and said, "Guess that means you're Keenan."

Aislinn winced. Niall and the guards froze. Keenan laughed. *Here's a brazen one.* "I am."

"Well, since the house won't make you sick . . ." Seth let his words fade away as he led Aislinn inside.

Keenan followed them into the dim interior. It was tiny, but well kept. His first thought was that Donia would find it appealing—if not for her inability to be around so much steel.

"You want anything?" Seth was in his small kitchen area, putting some sort of rice dish in his microwave. "Ash needs to eat."

"I'm fine." She blushed.

"Did you eat yet today?" Seth waited briefly, and when she didn't answer he turned back to his cupboards and began getting out dishes.

Keenan's positive opinion of Seth increased.

"I'm, umm, going to do it. The queen thing," Aislinn said in a shy voice. She sat down on one end of the sofa.

"Figured that when you brought him." Seth tossed a bottle of water to Aislinn and looked expectantly at Keenan.

He held a hand out and caught the water Seth tossed to him.

The microwave dinged. No one spoke for a moment while Seth gathered the food.

Then he asked, "So what's that mean for us?"

"Nothing, I don't think." Aislinn glanced at Keenan. "It was one of my terms for taking the job."

Keenan settled on one of the garish chairs and waited.

"School?" Seth handed her a bowl of food as he sat beside her. Some slight tension left him as Aislinn put her legs up and leaned back against him.

"That's good too," she said.

Seth was handling the situation with considerable aplomb, but Keenan didn't miss the mortal's possessive gestures—the casual touches that announced a physical connection to Aislinn.

Once he'd given Aislinn her meal, Seth turned to Keenan. "So now what happens?"

"Aislinn comes with me to see Donia and becomes a queen." Keenan kept his irritation at being questioned under control. They both wanted the same thing—Aislinn's well-being.

Seth looked truly ill at ease. "Will it hurt her?"

Aislinn seemed startled by the question, fork full of food held in midair.

"No," Keenan said. "And afterward, there's not much in your world or mine that can seriously hurt her."

"What about the other one, the Winter Queen?" Seth had entangled his hand in Aislinn's hair, stroking it absently while he spoke.

"She still can. Monarchs can wound or kill one another."

"Monarchs like you," Seth prompted. "*You* can hurt her."

"I will not." Keenan looked at Aislinn, curled up against Seth, seeming happy. It was what he wanted for her, happiness. There was little she could ask that he'd deny—even if that meant she would be in another's arms for now. "I gave her my vow."

They sat there then, in silence as Aislinn ate, until finally she asked, "Can Seth come with us?"

"No. No mortals, not at the test. It would not be safe for him," Keenan answered carefully, resisting the urge to cringe at the danger of a mortal there. Even without the Sight, the glare would be blinding when his power was unbound, when Aislinn's power slid into her.

Aislinn put her bowl aside and moved into Seth's lap.

Keenan didn't miss the tension around her eyes. He took a steadying breath and added, "Afterward, though, you could bring him to the Rath with us. He can join us to celebrate."

"What about seeing them . . . *us*"—she corrected herself before Keenan could—"giving him the Sight so it's easier."

"A monarch can authorize that." Keenan smiled at her attention to detail. She truly would make a wonderful queen.

"So if you—"

"Or *you*, Aislinn," he interjected.

"Right. If one of us approved it, it would be okay to find a way for him to see us?" she continued with a strange almost-fearful note in her voice.

"I already approve it. We'd just need to get the ingredients. I have a book at the loft." Keenan didn't miss their exchange. "Unless you've already found such a recipe?"

Neither answered. They didn't have to. He cursed softly, knowing exactly where they would've found such a recipe. Who else could have given them such a thing? He dropped that subject and said, "We'll need to work on you learning to hide your emotions better than that. Both of you. Now that Aislinn is summer fey, her emotions will be more *volatile*. It is the nature of our court."

At Seth's quirked brow, Keenan sighed. "You'll be around enough that it'd be useful for you, too. There are things you might do well to know if you're to be *with* my queen."

Aislinn said nothing, but Seth's expression tensed. He held Keenan's gaze for several heartbeats, and Keenan realized that the mortal was not unaware of their inevitable competition for Aislinn's attention.

Keenan's respect for Seth grew. The mortal loved Aislinn enough to stay beside her despite the odds against him. It was an admirable quality.

And as they spoke—not about the court or the future, but simply talking, trying to learn more about each other— Keenan found it surprisingly tolerable to sit with his queen and her lover.

He was still relieved, though, when Donia called to let him know that she was home, waiting for them, and to hurry. Beira's hags had been riding all over Huntsdale, wreaking havoc. Fey from the High Court had already begun to leave town, unwilling to stay while things were in upheaval.

Of course, they *won't stay.*

He sighed. It'd be nice to have at least one other court

that tried to stop trouble rather than start it or run from it.

When he hung up, Keenan told Aislinn and Seth of Donia's comments, and they made ready to depart.

Aislinn looked anxious at leaving Seth, despite his murmured assurances that he'd see her shortly.

Speaking softly, Keenan reminded him, "The hags cannot come in, but Beira can. Until we return, you must stay here. I would not want you at her mercy."

"Grams. Grams is alone," Aislinn whispered, her eyes widening. Then she was out the door, running.

Keenan paused only a heartbeat, glancing at Seth. "Stay here. We'll be back as soon as we can."

Seth nodded and shoved him toward the still-open door. "Keep her safe."

Outside, Niall was already sending guards after Aislinn.

"Leave someone to watch over him," Keenan instructed as he fled, following Aislinn, hoping that she worried for nothing, that Elena was safe.

When Aislinn got there, the door was ajar. She went into the living room. The TV was on, but she didn't see Grams. She stepped around the corner. "Grams?"

Behind her, the guards spilled into the room.

On the floor, eyes closed, lay Grams.

Aislinn scrambled over to her, felt for a pulse, for breath. Grams was alive.

"Is she . . ." Keenan pulled her to her feet and knelt beside Grams.

"She's hurt," Aislinn said. "You all come with us to the hospital. If anyone comes near her, you *will* stop them."

Grimly Keenan nodded. "Your queen has spoken."

The guards bowed. One stepped forward. "We will do our best, but if it's the Winter Queen herself . . ."

Aislinn heard the fear in his voice. "Is she that strong?"

"Only the Summer King—or the head of another court—could stand against her," Keenan said. "If I had my full strength, if *you* had your strength, we could. If we go to the hospital, we are not much defense to Elena. But after the ceremony, we can protect her."

One of the guards lifted Grams gently. He held her carefully aloft. The others filed out the door.

Aislinn swallowed, hating the idea of leaving Grams. "If we do this, and it's her that hurt Grams . . ."

"Even if it isn't her, it was at her command." Keenan scowled. "She has threatened you, Donia . . ."

"Well, let's go then." She looked at Grams, motionless in a faery's arms. Then she turned to Keenan. "Does it take long?"

"Not too long." He glanced at the guards. "Do whatever you need to do. We'll be at the hospital as soon as we can. Go."

As the guards raced toward the hospital, Aislinn took Keenan's hand, and they ran—faster than she'd known her body could move—toward Donia's and the test that would change everything.

CHAPTER 30

Never was there any one so beautiful as [he]. . . . The wolves did not ravage, the frost winds did not bite, and the Hidden Folk came out of the Faery Hills and made music and gladness everywhere.

—*Celtic Wonder Tales* by Ella Young (1910)

Donia knew they were coming, but it still made her gasp when they came toward her—holding hands and moving at the blinding speed that only the strongest fey could manage.

"Don?" He looked fevered in his excitement, face glowing, copper hair already radiating with the strange sunlight he carried inside.

She forced a smile and stepped into the yard. The last time she'd been through the ceremony, the test, she was the one holding his hand, hopeful that she'd be his partner, his queen.

All around the edge of the clearing were faeries—mostly Summer Court, but a few representatives of other courts.

That alone stood as a reminder of how very unusual this particular test would be.

Keenan came toward her. "Are you—"

Aislinn interrupted with a gentle hand on his arm. She shook her head.

He looked confused, but he stopped, staying farther away from Donia, not asking questions she didn't want to have to answer. Donia caught Aislinn's gaze and nodded; she couldn't deal with his kindness, not as she prepared to give him over to another girl.

Ash will be a good queen. Good for him, she reminded herself. Then she walked over to the not-yet-blooming hawthorn bush in the middle of her yard and laid the staff under it. Sasha moved to stand beside her, and she placed a hand on his head for support.

"Aislinn," Donia called from the center of the clearing.

The girl stepped forward, already glowing, only barely mortal now.

"If you are not the one, you will carry the winter's chill. You will tell the next of his"—Donia inclined her head toward Keenan—"mortal loves how unwise this is. You will tell her, and any that follow while you carry the cold, how very foolish it is to trust him. If you agree to do this, I am free of the cold, regardless of the results."

She paused to allow Aislinn a moment to consider her words, and then she asked, "Do you accept all of this?"

"I do." Aislinn came forward, her steps slow and deliberate as she crossed the openness between them.

Behind her Keenan waited, sunlight blazing from his skin, making Donia dizzy from looking at him. It'd been so long since she'd seen him glow so brightly, and she'd convinced herself that he wasn't truly as beautiful as he'd seemed in her memories.

She'd been wrong.

She forced herself to tear her gaze away from him. "Please," she prayed. "Please let Aislinn be the one."

Aislinn felt the pull, the insistence that she pick up the staff. She stepped forward.

"If you are not the one I've sought, you will carry Beira's cold." Keenan's voice wrapped around her like a summer storm racing through the trees. He eased closer. "Do you accept that risk?"

"Yes." Aislinn's voice was too low to be heard, so she said it louder, "Yes."

Keenan looked feral as he walked toward her, so radiant that she had to force herself to look at him. His feet sunk into the almost-boiling soil as he moved. "This is who I am. What I truly will be if you are, indeed, the Summer Queen."

He stopped a few steps from her and added, "This is what *you* will be if the cold does not take you."

She felt her muscles tense, but she did not back away from him.

Then Keenan, the King of Summer in all of his brightness, knelt before her and gave her yet another chance to turn away. "Is this what you freely choose, to risk winter's chill?"

The Summer Girls drifted into the clearing, watching. Beira's hags and a great number of other faeries, some more familiar than others, stood around them.

"Each mortal since Donia"—eyes wistful, he glanced briefly at Donia—"has chosen to stay in the sunlight. They would not risk becoming as she is."

Donia's corpse-white fingers tightened on Sasha's pelt as Keenan added, "You understand that if you are not the one, you'll carry the Winter Queen's chill until the next mortal risks this? And you'll warn her not to trust me?"

The rustling of trees roared around them, like a water-less storm, like voices crying out in a language she couldn't remember.

Donia reached out and squeezed Aislinn's hand.

"I do." Aislinn's voice was stronger then; she was sure this was right. Somewhere inside that knowledge waited; even if she hadn't had any of the other proof, in that moment she was certain she'd still have known this was right. She let go of Donia's hand and walked over to the hawthorn.

"If she refuses me, you will tell the next girl and the next"—Keenan followed her, radiating heat—"and not until one accepts will you be free of the cold."

"There won't be another girl." Aislinn grasped the staff, wrapped her fingers around it, and waited.

She watched them—the last girl who'd done this and the faery king who still loved her. She wished—for them and for herself—that it had been Donia, but it wasn't.

It's me.

The staff was gripped in her hand, but there was no cold to bring her to her knees. Instead that blinding glow was no longer coming only from Keenan: it flared from her own skin.

The Summer Girls laughed and twirled in a blur of vines and hair and skirts.

Donia—her white hair now a soft blond, her cheeks now flushed with health—said in a surprisingly musical voice, "You're truly her."

Aislinn looked at her hands, her arms, at the soft gold glow that covered her skin. "I am."

It felt like nothing she could've imagined before: the world made sense. She could *feel* the faeries all around her drinking in her happiness, reveling in the sense of security that she and Keenan gave them. It made her laugh aloud.

Then he grabbed her in his arms, swinging her in the air, laughing. "My Queen, my lovely, lovely Aislinn."

All around them, flowers sprang to life, the air warmed, and soft rain fell from the bright blue sky. The grass under Keenan's feet grew lush, as verdant as his eyes.

For several moments she let him twirl her in the air—until she saw a wounded rowan-man struggling to reach them.

"My queen," he croaked as he crawled over the grass, bleeding but still trying to reach her.

She paused, watching as her faeries—for they were truly hers now—carried him to her. Everyone paused. Keenan put a hand in the small of her back as he stepped up beside her.

"We tried," the rowan-man said, more blood coming to his lips with every word he spoke. "We tried as we would've if she'd come for you. The mortal boy . . ."

If it weren't for Keenan catching her, she'd have fallen. "Seth. Is he . . ." she couldn't finish the words.

The guard closed his eyes. His breathing was labored, and when he coughed, shards of ice spilled out of his mouth. He spat them onto the grass. "She took him. Beira took him."

Donia had slipped away, unable to bear watching Keenan with Aislinn. It was one thing to know he'd finally found his missing queen; it was another to feel the emotions that came with the knowledge. This was what needed to happen, what was best for everyone.

It still feels like a freshly reopened wound. She wasn't the one, had never been the one for him.

Aislinn is.

And Donia couldn't stay to watch them rejoice.

She wasn't far from her cottage when Beira's guard found her. *That didn't take long.*

She'd known Beira would be true to her word, known that her death wouldn't be far past Aislinn's ascension. Without the winter's chill to defend herself, she was almost as helpless as a mortal in their hands.

The guards weren't as rough as the dark fey, but not for lack of trying. When they tossed her at Beira's feet, the Winter Queen said nothing. Instead she kicked Donia in the face, flipping her backward with the force of her attack.

"Beira, how nice to see you," Donia said in a voice much weaker than she'd have liked.

Beira laughed. "I could almost like you, darling. A pity"—she lifted one blood-spattered hand, and manacles of ice formed around Donia's wrists—"you aren't reliable."

Donia had thought the weight of Beira's chill had ached before, but as she struggled against the freezing manacles, she realized she had no idea of how cold Beira's ice could truly be.

As Donia turned to answer the Winter Queen, a coughing-choking sound distracted her.

Crouched in the corner was Seth, trying to get to his feet, legs buried under several feet of snow. His chest was half exposed, his shirt in tatters from something's claws.

Beira bent down. Her icy breath brushed Donia's face; her frost gathered in Donia's hair. "You were to help me. Instead you were consorting with the enemy."

"I did the right thing. Keenan is—"

With an ugly noise, Beira clamped her hand over Donia's mouth. "You. Betrayed. Me."

"Don't make her angrier," Seth called weakly as he struggled free of the snowdrift. His jeans were in the same condition as his shirt. Blood trickled onto the snow around him. One of the bars in his eyebrow had been ripped out, and a thin line of blood ran down his face.

"Pretty, isn't he? He doesn't scream like the wood-sprites, but he's still entertaining. I'd almost forgotten how easily mortals break." Beira licked her lips as she watched Seth try to stay upright. He shivered violently, but he kept trying.

Donia said nothing.

"But *you*, well, I know how much more pain *you* can take." Beira cupped Donia's face, driving already-bloody fingernails into Donia's cheek and throat. "Shall I let the wolves have you when I'm done? They don't mind if their toys are already a little used up."

"No," Seth said in a strangled voice, proof that he'd already met the lupine fey.

Beira turned toward him and blew. Razor sharp spikes of ice jutted up from the floor where he was now trying to crawl. Several sliced into his legs.

"Persistent, isn't he?" Beira asked, laughing.

Donia didn't speak, didn't move. Instead she rolled her eyes.

For a heartbeat, Beira just stared at her. Then she smiled, as cold and cruel as the worst of the dark fey.

"Well. It *would* be more fun if you play. That's what you want, right? As if you can trick me, so you can run"—Beira slapped her, knocking Donia's head into the floor so hard that she felt nauseous—"but you won't get to run."

The manacles melted then, leaving frostbitten skin as the only proof they'd been there.

Donia scrambled over to Seth, ignoring the shards that drove into her feet, and helped him up. She couldn't actually beat Beira, but she was still a faery—strong enough to lift a mortal, strong enough to withstand more pain than him.

"The door's that way," he muttered as she half carried him forward.

"How darling!" Beira gushed. "The tragic lovers of the

damnable Summer Court working together. It's just so *sweet*."

For several minutes she watched them as they tried to cross the growing barrier of ice, cheering at each bit of progress and adding more obstacles as she cheered.

Donia didn't speak, saving her energy to try—unsuccessfully—to reach the door with Seth.

Finally Beira motioned the hags closer. "Did the rowan-man finally manage to crawl to my foolish son?"

When the hags nodded, Beira clapped. "Lovely. So they'll be here soon. What fun!"

Then she tilted her head inquiringly and asked Donia, "Do you think they'll be more upset if you're dead or still suffering?

"Decision, decisions," Beira murmured as she walked over the blades of ice, slowly and gracefully, as if she were entering the theater.

"Just to be sure, let's go for one of each, hmm?" Beira said as she pulled Donia up by her hair and kissed both cheeks. "I believe I already told you what would happen to you, dearie."

Seth slipped to the ground, reaching for Donia as he fell, but a wall of ice formed between them.

Then Beira sealed her lips to Donia's.

Donia struggled as the ice slid down her throat, choking her, filling her lungs. Then she saw Seth throw himself toward Beira. In his hand was a rusty iron cross. With surprising strength for a mortal—especially an injured one— he jammed it into Beira's neck.

Beira let go of Donia with a shriek and lashed out at Seth, slamming him into a wall.

"Do you think that little trinket will kill me?" Beira asked as she followed him in that too-fast-to-follow way. She dug her fingers into the skin of his stomach and—using his ribs as a handle—tugged him to his feet.

He screamed over and over, awful sounds that made Donia tremble. But she couldn't help him; she couldn't even lift her head from the floor.

Aislinn heard Seth's screams as she came through the door. When she saw Beira holding him by his stomach, she had to grab Keenan's arm for support.

Midway across the room, Donia was sprawled motionless on the floor, her lips glistening with shards of ice just like those the rowan-man had choked up. There wasn't time to stop to check on her, not with Beira driving her hand through Seth's skin like that.

Keenan was still moving, pulling Aislinn past everyone and everything, toward Beira and Seth.

Once they were beside her, Keenan grabbed the piece of metal that jutted out of Beira's neck and slashed it forward like a knife.

"I wondered if you'd ever get here." Beira dropped Seth onto the ground.

Seth's eyes rolled back as he blacked out. He was still breathing, though, his chest rising and falling unsteadily.

Even with blood dripping down her neck, Beira seemed

undaunted. She reached up and tugged the metal free. After a cursory glance at it, she dropped it on the floor in disgust. Blood rolled away in the puddles from the melting ice.

"It doesn't have to be like this." Keenan's voice was low, pained. "We can work it out—like it should've been before. If you'll agree . . ."

Beira laughed, eddies of frigid air swirling from her lips. "Do you know that's *exactly* the sort of thing your father said before I killed him?"

She lifted her hand and gestured. A thick wall of ice formed between Aislinn and Keenan—leaving Seth with Aislinn, and Keenan alone on the other side of the wall with Beira.

"Aislinn," Keenan called as he put his hand on the ice.

She followed his lead and put hers on the other side of the wall, mimicking his position. Between them the ice hissed and popped as their touch slowly melted it.

Beira just watched for a moment. Her face was a distorted mask, more horrible through the thick ice. Her voice, however, was perfectly clear as she asked Keenan, "How long do you think it will be until there's another Summer King?"

"There won't be another Summer King," Keenan snarled at her, reaching out to grip her arm.

"Ah, ah, ah, sweetling." She put her hand on his chest and pushed him away from the ice wall separating him from Aislinn.

The ice on Keenan's chest melted as soon as it formed, leaving him soaking wet and steaming. He was stumbling, though, unable to stand steadily on the sheet of ice that crept over the floor.

Seth moaned and briefly opened his eyes.

Several of the hags walked into the room, and without even glancing at them, Beira said, "Kill the Winter Girl, and the mortal."

They moved toward Donia.

Keenan turned toward them.

While he was distracted, Beira grabbed his face and blew ice over his eyes. The thick white flakes clumped his eyelashes together. It was melting almost as quickly as it formed, but in the interim Keenan couldn't see.

With a glance at Aislinn, Beira lifted her arm. A long, thin blade of ice grew from her outstretched hand. She winked at Aislinn and drove it into Keenan's chest.

He slumped forward, still blind.

Furious, Aislinn pounded both fists on the ice wall, and it melted under her touch as quickly as it had formed under Beira's.

Aislinn grabbed both of Beira's arms to stop her from stabbing Keenan again.

Then—thinking *hot*—Aislinn blew into Keenan's face.

Not only did her breath warm Keenan, but her skin grew hotter until Beira's arms were smoking, steam pouring off of her until the room was cloudy with it.

Keenan blinked several times; then he grabbed Beira's face in his hands. "You're right, *Mother*. It will never work with both of us still breathing."

With Aislinn still holding Beira's arms, Keenan leaned closer, until his lips were almost touching Beira's mouth. Then he just breathed. Sunlight poured onto her like some viscous fluid. She struggled to turn her head and couldn't. She was held in place by Keenan's glowing hands, as she choked on sunlight. The heat burned through Beira's throat, and steam hissed from the wound in her neck.

When finally she was limp in their hands, Keenan stepped away, and Aislinn lowered Beira's body to the floor.

He stroked a finger over Aislinn's cheek and murmured, "You are far worthier than I could've asked."

Keenan stepped over his mother's empty shell. He'd once hoped that they'd not come to this place, that they'd find a way to coexist. They hadn't, but he didn't regret it.

The hags stood quietly, murmuring among themselves. They'd disobeyed Beira, but she wasn't there to discipline them.

Her face pale with shock and worry, Aislinn crouched on the soaking floor trying to rouse Seth.

One of the hags held out a length of cloth, and Aislinn mutely bound Seth's bleeding ribs. He didn't look good, but the rowan-men had arrived and already summoned healers—both fey and mortal.

Keenan went over to Donia's still motionless body. Healers wouldn't help her.

He cradled her in his arms and wept.

Donia opened her eyes to find Keenan holding her. For the first time in far too long, she was in his arms.

She had to cough before she could speak. "Beira dead?"

He smiled then, looking like every dream she'd denied having. "She is."

"Seth?" It hurt to talk, her throat raw from the jagged pieces of ice she'd swallowed and thrown back up.

"Injured, but not dead." He stroked her face, gently, as if she were something delicate and precious. Tears ran down his cheeks and dripped onto her face, melting the ice that still clung to her. "I thought I'd lost you. I thought we were too late."

"Doesn't matter. You have your queen." Despite her words, she pressed her face closer into his hand, feeling more at peace than she had in decades.

"It's not like that with us." He blew on her face, melting the last traces of Beira's ice that had clumped in her hair.

"She's keeping Seth, calls this a job"—he laughed then, a small sound, but a laugh nonetheless—"ruling beside me, but not mine. When you get well—"

One of the hags knelt beside them, interrupting him.

"My queen," she rasped. "Your staff."

The hag held out the Winter Queen's staff, the repository of Winter's weight.

Keenan's eyes widened. "No."

The hag smiled her nearly toothless smile and reiterated, "*My* queen. Not yours, Summer King. This one"—she gestured silently—"carries the winter's chill. It grows."

Keenan snarled at the hags, looking far from human. "You knew."

"Beira's time had passed." The hags exchanged calm looks. "She knew the terms Irial'd set, should've known what would happen if she interfered: her choice, her failure."

The same one spoke again, "Donia will be a strong queen. We waited until one survived winter's kiss. She"— the hag looked at Donia with something like awe in her eyes—"is ours now."

They all bowed, looking graceful despite their haggard bodies, and said, "We serve the Winter Queen. It is the order of things."

Donia struggled to sit up. She lifted a hand, her fingertips brushing Keenan's face. To spend eternity with Keenan—this was a fantasy she'd kept silent for decades.

He held her gaze. "No, Don . . . There's another way. The healers will be here and . . ."

"This doesn't need healing. The Winter Court is mine. I *feel* it; the winter fey, I feel them."

"The hags can do something . . . I don't care what. Stay with me, Don. Please." He held her tighter, scowling up at the hags and the lupine fey that had come into the room. Behind them, several of the hawthorn people waited.

Healers from both the Winter Court and Summer Court stepped forward. Some were tending to Seth under Aislinn's careful watch.

Briefly Donia glanced at Aislinn, and the Summer Queen stood. She, at least, understood the inevitability of what needed to happen.

"Keenan." Donia reached up to him and pulled his face closer to her. "The chill is already in me. If I fight it, it'll take longer to grow, but it won't change."

Aside from the overwhelming urge to wipe away the horror in Keenan's eyes, Donia wasn't upset. She'd expected to die today. Ruling was far from a bad trade-off.

Before it was too late, she wrapped her arms around Keenan and let herself glory in the sort of kiss they hadn't been able to share in far too long.

When she pulled away, Keenan wept, his tears like warm rain hissing as they fell on her face.

Then Aislinn pulled Keenan away and held on to him as the hags helped Donia over to Beira's body.

Black clouds gathered and ripped open, drenching them all, as Keenan's emotions grew more volatile.

Grasping the staff, Donia pressed her mouth to Beira's still body and inhaled. The rest of the Winter Queen's cold flowed into her, rolling through her like an icy wave, churning until it suddenly stopped and lay quiet—a fathomless frozen pool surrounded by ice-laden trees and unmarred white fields.

The words came to her from the white world, sliding through her lips like a winter wind, "I am the Winter Queen. As those before me, I will carry the wind and ice."

And she was healed, stronger than she'd ever been. Unlike Beira, Donia did not trail icy shards in her path as she went over to Keenan.

His sun-kissed tears shimmered as they fell into the puddles on the floor.

She reached up to pull him to her, careful to keep her chill contained, thrilled that she could do so now. Then she whispered, "I love you. I have always loved you. This doesn't change that."

Eyes wide, he stared at her, but he didn't speak. He didn't repeat the words.

Then Donia lifted Beira in her arms, and with the hags trailing behind her, went to the door. Pausing on the threshold, she caught Aislinn's gaze and said, "We will speak soon."

After a quick glance at the still-speechless Keenan, Aislinn nodded.

Then—eager to be out of their brightness—Donia wrapped her fingers around the staff and walked away from the Summer King and Queen.

EPILOGUE

FIRST SNOW

Clutching the silk-smooth wood of the Winter Queen's staff—*my staff*—Donia walked out of her cottage and into the shadow of the barren trees.

Outside, her fey waited; Keenan's guards were gone—all but Evan, who'd stayed on as the head of her new guard. There were grumblings over that one—a summer fey heading the new Winter Queen's guard—but it wasn't anyone's right to challenge her choices.

Not anymore.

She wound her way toward the riverside, trailed by six of the guards Evan had chosen from among the winter fey as the most trustworthy. They didn't speak. The winter fey weren't a chattering lot, not like the insipid Summer Girls.

As if she had always done so, Donia tapped the staff as she walked the earth, sending freezing fingers into the soil, the first taste of the winter that would soon follow. Beside her, Sasha loped.

Silently Donia stepped onto the now-frozen surface of
the river. Looking up at the steel bridge that crossed the
river—no longer poisonous, not to the Winter Queen—she
tilted her face to the gray sky and opened her mouth.
Winds shrieked from her lips; icicles gathered on the metal
of the bridge.

On the bank of the river, Aislinn stood, wrapped in a
long cloak. She was already changed, looking more like
what she now was every time Donia saw her. The Summer
Queen lifted a hand in greeting. "Keenan would be here if
he could . . . He was worried about how you were feeling
about all of this." She gestured at the ice.

"I'm fine." Donia slid across the frozen water, graceful as
she'd never been as the Winter Girl. "It's familiar, but not."

She didn't add that she was still lonely: that wasn't something to share with Keenan's queen.

They stood quietly, snowflakes hissing as they landed on
Aislinn's cheeks. She pulled a fur-trimmed hood up, hiding
her newly gold-streaked hair. "He's not all bad, you know?"

"I do." Donia held out her hand, catching snowflakes
like a handful of white stars. "I couldn't tell *you* that,
though, could I?"

Aislinn shivered. "We're learning to work together. Most
of the time." She rubbed her arms, finally wearing out
under the cold. "Sorry. I can still go out, but I guess I can't
stay too long near both you and the ice."

"Another time perhaps." Donia turned away.

But then Aislinn said the last thing that Donia could

imagine the Summer Queen, could imagine anyone, saying: "He loves you, you know."

Silently Donia stared at her, the faery who shared the throne with Keenan.

"I don't know. . . ." Donia stopped herself, trying to quell the confusion inside. Maybe he did, but if so, why hadn't he answered her when she told him that she still loved him? *That* was a conversation she wasn't ready to have with Aislinn.

Donia had no true understanding of how much Keenan had changed when Aislinn freed him, how connected they were, how much she truly knew of him; most days, she didn't want to know. Their court was not her concern, not now.

She had enough trouble sorting out her own court. They might not be a loquacious group, but they still grumbled— over her former mortality, over her insistence that order be restored, over her curtailing their cavorting with the dark fey.

That's a trouble I'm not eager to face. The king of the Dark Court was pushing already, testing the boundaries, tempting her fey. Irial had been too long aligned with Beira to back away gracefully. Donia shook her head. Snow fell around her face, an almost-electric touch as the flakes landed on her skin. *Focus on the good.* There would be time enough to deal with Irial, with Keenan, with her fey.

Tonight was hers.

As quietly as the snow falling around her, Donia turned back to the frozen night and skated across the river, spilling her handful of snow like glitter on the ice.

SOLSTICE

Aislinn and Seth stood in the common room of Seth's train with Keenan while he struggled to recover from the brief excursion in the cold.

"Go on." Seth nudged her toward Keenan. "I need to get a few things."

Aislinn sat beside the Summer King, strangely comfortable. "Keenan?"

He opened his eyes. "I'm fine, Aislinn. Give me a moment."

She took his hand in hers and concentrated, letting the warmth of summer roll through her. It had become surprisingly easy already, as if it had always been in her. She felt it, a tiny sun blazing inside her, and she leaned over and blew gently in his face. Warm wind poured over him.

She kissed both his cheeks. She didn't know why, any more than she understood why she'd done it that night in the alley. It simply seemed *right*. That was the first thing she had understood about her changes—listening to her instincts.

Keenan stared at her. "I didn't ask—"

"Shhh." She brushed his copper hair off his forehead and pressed one more kiss there. "Friends help each other."

Keenan felt almost fine when Seth came back into the room.

Seth dropped a lighter and a corkscrew on the table.

"There's candles on the shelf. Some food I got from Niall. Some of your summer wine, and a bottle of winter wine."

"Winter wine? Why?"

Seth laughed. "Niall said you owe him for getting that." Despite a daunting look from Aislinn, he winked and added, "It's all good."

Then Aislinn stood up and slipped her arm around Seth's waist. "I'll keep my cell on. Tavish knows I'm on tap if there are any problems."

"You're both leaving?" Keenan sat up. He trusted his queen, but this was growing stranger and stranger. "I'm to be trapped here then?"

Aislinn and Seth exchanged another curious look. Then Seth pulled his jacket on.

"I'm out." He grinned at Keenan, not with the lingering tension that the mortal seemed to be wrestling with since Aislinn's ascension, but with genuine amusement. "See you in a few days."

After Aislinn shut the door behind him, she smiled gently at Keenan. "Happy Solstice. It's safe. We even had Tavish check on it for us."

She hugged him briefly, and then she slipped away, leaving him alone and confused.

Trapped. She trapped me. He paced to the window and watched his queen leave with her mortal lover. *Now what do I do?*

Donia let herself in with the key Seth had given her. She heard Keenan pacing, heavy footsteps as he moved angrily, like a caged thing. It didn't frighten her, that temper, that dangerous energy. For the first time, they'd meet with equal strength, equal power, equal passion.

I hope.

She slipped off her boots, folded her wrap, and uncorked two of the bottles of wine. She'd just poured the first glass when he came out to the front room.

"Don?"

"Umm?" She held out the glass. When he didn't take it, she set it down on the counter.

"What are you . . ." He seemed unusually nervous, watching her warily. "Are you looking for Aislinn?"

"No." She poured a second glass, out of her bottle. She'd need to remember to send a token to Niall for thinking to procure it.

"I've seen Ash." She held up the house key, dangled the tiny skull key ring where he could see it. It felt good to have the control, the power.

I could get used to this.

Ruling the Winter Court had come easily; she could be just, fair, to her fey. But having power over Keenan—that was a dangerous thing. She wanted him to sway to her wishes as she'd done so long to his. She licked her lips and was rewarded by a flash of darkness in those summer eyes.

He moved closer, hesitantly, but the look in his eyes was hopeful. "Why are you here?"

"For you." She sipped her drink, casually, calm as she'd never been able to be around him.

He stepped closer again. "For me?"

She set down her glass and reached back to the tie that held her skirt together.

His breath caught in his throat. Sunlight flared from his skin, glorious and brilliant. "For me."

Snowflakes swirled around her as she reached out for his hand. "Yes."

And he smiled, that impossible earthshaking smile that had haunted her fantasies for longer than he should ever know, than he would ever know.

Summer and Winter must clash. We'll never be able to . . . but to try. She wrapped her hand around his wrist and pulled him closer.

Every bit of her body burned as if she were nothing more than an ice carving, ready to melt from the touch of the sun. Her ice rose to meet that sun, wrapping them both in a snow squall.

I love you. She didn't say it, not this time. She stood as his equal now; she wasn't going to risk tipping that balance in the hopes that he'd say the words that would quell the murmur of restless confusion inside.

I still love you, have always loved you. She wouldn't say it, but she thought it over and over as the flowers blossomed in his eyes, as the flare of sunlight made her tremble.

"Mine. You're finally mine," he whispered. Then his lips came down on hers.

She wanted to laugh for joy, weep for the sizzle of ice and heat as they fell into the snowbank at their feet.

This is far better than negotiating the terms of our peace.

It would sway his wishes when they did negotiate, she knew it. *It's not why I'm here.* But in the whispering part of her mind, she admitted that it was reason enough to be there, that she would be a fool not to take advantage of it.

"I thought I'd never have . . ." Keenan was murmuring soft words, sounding lost. "My Donia, finally all mine."

The snow melted, steamed away like vapor, as they touched.

"Shh," she covered his lips with hers, unable to agree to his foolish words.

Aislinn stepped carefully over the icy ground. The guards she'd had follow them were waiting alongside Seth. They were still unfamiliar faces, on loan from Donia for the winter months while the summer fey were trapped inside.

"No one disturbs them." She let her gaze drift over the guards, looking at each individually.

They waited, as quiet as winter nights.

She smiled as she added, "For any reason. If there's any problem, call me."

Aislinn nodded and held out a hand to Seth. "Come on. Let's go introduce you to Grams. If she can accept this"— she gestured around them at the faeries and at herself—"she can accept you."

He quirked his eyebrow. "You sure? Niall said I could bunk there."

"Trust me." She grabbed his hand.

He looked at his ripped jeans and battered jacket. "Maybe we could stop by the loft at least. I could change. . . ."

"No." Aislinn linked her fingers with his. "I showed her the other college apps you picked up for us. She thought we could go over them."

His eyes lit up, and he pulled her closer. "I like the philo program at State best. They have a good poli-sci program for you too."

She laughed. "We can relocate if we want. Keenan and Grams are both petitioning for that."

Behind and in front of them, the winter guards spread out. None of the summer fey could come out in the blowing white drifts. Only the winter fey and dark fey played in the still night, solemn even in their revelry as she passed them—though more than a few snowballs sizzled into steam as the less easily intimidated fey saw her.

Even after almost three months, they weren't any less terrifying, not really, but Aislinn felt safe for the first time in her life. *It's not anywhere near perfect, but it can be.*

Using Seth's hand for leverage, she pulled him closer. "Let's go home."

They walked through the snowy streets, her skin glowing enough to keep them both warm. The rest—her fears, the court's demands, Keenan's worries—it would all wait.

When the Summer Queen rejoiced, her fey would too.

And so she rejoiced, letting that feeling spread out to her fey, feeling it echo back from Keenan, seeing it reflected in Seth's eyes.

It's not perfect, but it will be.